They're Demons

Cameron Dawkins

ISBN: 978-0-9957639-4-4

DEDICATION

To my Mum, who never let the bedbugs bite.
My two little angels, noses eyes eyes dinosaur.

CONTENTS

ACKNOWLEDGMENTS

Ben Costigan , genuinely the best photographer out there.

Sara Oakden, for going above and beyond with editing this.

Steve Viner for his incredible artwork.

BRAIN MATTER

Jack came tumbling through the door, shoulder leading, the rest of his body hastily following. A splintered piece of timber spun and skidded away. Ignoring it, he scanned the roof. The wind battered against his ears, white noise filled his mind and he tried his best to think over the top of it.

It hadn't been that gusty on the ground, but now he was standing on gritted roof felt about fifty floors up. He shielded his eyes from the midday sun that displayed its brilliance directly overhead, then spotted what he was looking for.

'Mr. Shilling,' he called, using the back of his throat to keep his voice deep and authoritative – not loud enough to startle him, but stern enough to let the man know that Jack was still the law enforcer, even up there, high in the sky.

'Just step back over this side of the railings for me, and we can talk. Talking's good, it's easy and it won't hurt anywhere near as much as going the other way. Just step back over this side for me, please.' He approached slowly, arms low, hands spread wide, like a hunter sneaking up on prey.

The man on the edge didn't turn around, he didn't even so much as acknowledge Jack's presence at all. He looked down; he might as well have been watching fish in a pond.

His loose-fitting brown suit flailed violently in the wind and the sound of sirens just about carried their way up and over the ledge to the detective, but the man was in his own place, one where none of that had reached yet.

'Don't worry about them, Mr. Shilling.'

'Chris,' the man replied calmly, not turning his head at all, 'call me Chris.'

'Chris, ok, Chris don't worry about them—' Jack started to say but got cut short by the other man.

'I'm not. Nothing to worry about anymore.'

Jack was unsure how to reply, but he could feel how ominous the man's statement had been. 'Good, right, let's just have it me and you for now. Nothing needs to happen, just talking.' Jack was at the metal barrier separating him from the lip of oblivion where Chris stood with ease.

He lowered himself down and sat on the floor a few feet away, not close enough to grab him, but not close enough to startle him to fall either.

'It's ok, Chris, just us for now. Just us.' Jack took a heaving breath – the flights of stairs had caught up with him now and adrenaline could only do so much for his unkept muscles.

'I know why you did it, it's fine, plenty of people would have done the same. They call it a crime of passion. You heard of that before? It's when emotions take over and you lose yourself for a bit, you know, you lose your own mind. Not your fault if you lose your mind, Chris.'

The man standing on the precipice scoffed, 'Passion? Is that what you think it was?'

Jack patted his chest and coughed some of the phlegm out of his throat. 'Yes, crime of passion, you couldn't control it.'

'And you would have done the same, would you?'

Jack thought about it. Images of the other man's wife with her sewing scissors sticking out of her throat blighted his vision. Her white dressing gown had been a deep crimson, the ideal material for soaking up the huge loss of blood.

'Yes,' he lied. He would say anything to get this guy back on the safe side of the barrier – he was close to telling him that he may not even go to prison if he came down quietly with no fuss.

Chris laughed again defiantly. 'Even if it was your own brother?'

Jack now pictured the other victim he had seen earlier that day, skull fragment stuck to the fire poker and clots of blood scattered up the living room wall. There hadn't been enough of a face left to go on, but the wallet they found had told them all that they had needed to know, and it didn't need a detective to work it out.

'Even if it was my own brother,' Jack lied again.

'Fucking liar.' Chris turned to face to the detective for the first time. 'He had everything, you know. I lived in his shadow for too long. A lifetime too long. Looks like I won in the end, doesn't it?'

Jack stood up, leant over the railing just long enough to make him feel dizzy, and then looked back at the man in the brown suit.

'To be honest, it doesn't look much like winning from here.'

Chris laughed mirthlessly. 'And what do you know about me, huh? This is the only way out for me now.'

What do I know about you? Jack asked himself. He looked around at the door that he had come through. The piece of wood that had been exactly the right size to jam it shut now lay in two pieces.

'You brought that with you,' Jack mumbled, 'and you entered the building only a couple of seconds before me, but beat me here easily. Because you knew exactly where you were going, didn't you?'

Jack spoke softly, barely audible to the other man.

'What?' Chris shouted at the detective, the first sign of irritation setting in.

'You've been up here before, haven't you, Chris? You've been planning this for weeks?'

The man, who had now positioned his feet so that they were hanging over the edge, stared at the detective.

'You think I planned all of this?'

Jack's head tilted as he read the man in front of him. 'No, not all of it. Not your wife and brother. Those were just unfortunate, you cracked, lashed out. But this, this moment right now. How many times have you stood on that edge, now, Chris? Once? Twice? No, it's more than that, isn't it? Enough to work out what you would need to jam the door shut with. Enough times to know that it would take you a long while to take that final step. You had to plan it to give yourself time didn't you, Chris, because you don't really want to do this, do you? Do you, Chris?'

The man looked at the door where he had strategically placed the length of baton. 'I've been up here every week for the last few months. Wanted to jump every time.' His voice had become solemn and hollow; all emotion had seeped away just as quickly as it had risen.

'Every time I think I'm ready, I see her face. My beautiful daughter's face. I want to see that smile forever. I want to die with that in my mind.'

Jack knew how that felt, at least. 'She'll hate you, you know? You took her mother and now you're going to take her father.'

'She's better off without me.' The man's eyes flooded and dribble cascaded from his trembling lips as again he began to feel. Jack could see that the man's brain was in survival mode, switching emotions off and on, desperately trying to find a way of getting through this moment. But he could also see that it was failing to do so.

'That may be,' Jack said, edging forward.

'Tell her I love her, tell her I'm sorry.'

Jack moved ever so slightly closer. 'I can't do that. It would be a lie.'

The man looked accusingly at the detective, spite in his eyes.

'If you loved her, you would come down from there and be what little father you can be to her. It's easy to die for someone, it's hard to live for them. Show her how much you love her by your actions now. Show her you're not going to abandon her.'

To Jack's surprise, the man smiled.

'It's too hard.'

With that, the man let go of the railing, looked up to the sky, his face grinning with acceptance and his body gently, and with the ease of a breath, fell back.

Jack moved as quickly as he was able, grabbing the brown suit as it began to disappear. His knuckles locked tightly on the thick material. His grip was strong but his hips behind the railing failed. All at once, Jack's waist, thighs and knees were brought over the top of the metal bar. He let go of the clothing and scrabbled his arms against squared concrete. His fingers caught the lip and his body crashed into the side of the building, knocking the wind from his lungs.

Everything was silent. Panic operated Jack's body independently of his brain. A sickening, damp thud cut through into his psyche. The body of Chris hitting the floor, hundreds of feet below, was the stark reminder of how much he wanted to live, forcing his arms to reach up and over the edge to find a purchase. His flat, hard-soled shoes scraped against the shiny cobbles, begging for even an ounce of grip, whatever they would give. The sharp angled edges dug into the crook of his arms, pushing on the elbow joint and nearly forcing it out of position.

Jack finally, after what felt like a lifetime, brought his torso up onto the edge of the building. He swung a faithful leg up and rolled down onto the secure rooftop, the gravel giving a comforting sting to his landing.

'Fuuuuuuck!' he shouted at the passing clouds. He was partly annoyed that he had not been able to save Chris, but mainly at the fact that he had been scared like never before and was angry at the world for doing it.

He lay quietly for what felt like hours, but he knew was more like seconds, until Officer Nitin Kapoor stood above him. Panting for breath, he hunched over with hands on knees, his head obscuring the sun, giving himself a crimson outline.

'Bloody hell, sarge, you ok? We thought you were a goner then for a second.' He reached out a hand to his superior and helped him up to his feet.

Jack didn't speak. Instead, he turned around and peered back over the edge of the hotel to see the mess below. Even from this height, he could recognise the light pink and yellowy coloured brain matter ejected from the man's head.

Nitin stood back – Jack's near-death experience had obviously had an impact on the other police officer, whose respect for superior was ambitiously high. It wasn't that Jack was brave to look over the edge, it was that he wasn't too bothered about falling. It had only been his primal basic instinct that had clung to the building, none of Jack's conscious thought had been involved.

Nitin checked his watch. 'You know you're due in court in twenty-five minutes, don't you, sarge?'

Jack pulled away from the barrier. 'What?' he asked, his mind still racing slightly.

'Court, sarge. The Peters case. I'm on stand tomorrow. You're due there at two-thirty.'

Jack's brain was pulled back to reality with a similar thud to the one he had just managed to avoid.

'Ah, yes. I was hoping that would just not happen.'

Nitin followed Jack as they headed towards the exit of the rooftop.

'You want a lift, sarge?'

Jack waved a hand vaguely over his shoulder. 'No, it's just as quick to walk and if I'm lucky I'll get knocked over by a bus on the way there.'

'I'll probably survive that too, knowing my luck', he thought to himself as he began to take the stairs.

Jack walked through the doors and into the large atrium of the courthouse. The cavernous space threw sound around for fun, footsteps pronouncing themselves clearly. Most clear of all were those of Jack's commanding officer, Detective Chief Superintendent McQuade. She waited as Jack was brought through the metal detector and given a quick once-over by a security guard with a handheld device. He collected his phone and wallet from the table.

'Glad you could join us,' she said sarcastically. She pulled a blue tie from her pocket and began turning up Jack's collar.

'Peters is pleading diminished responsibility, trying to get a manslaughter verdict.' She tossed the tie over his head and started the various loops and tucks.

'No tricks or anything, please, Jack. Rumour has it they are going after you for the way he was arrested. Keep your wits about you and just answer *yes sir, no sir, three bags full, sir.* Ok?'

She pulled the knot up to his throat, giving him a no-nonsense stare.

Jack grimaced and pulled the knot away from his throat a touch. 'Yes, ma'am.'

Sitting down in the dock, he wondered why on this particular occasion his tie felt more like a noose. More eyes were leering in on him than usual. In the courtroom itself, there was a section for the public, but on this occasion it had been cordoned off for relatives and friends – everyone else had been shunted upstairs to the overhead viewing gallery. Most cases involved a barrister for the defence, one for the opposition, a judge, a clerk to assist the judge and a court officer to call people to the stand and assist anyone needing help in the courtroom. That would be the usual status quo, but not in a case as popular as this. There were at least three lawyers on either side and, tension being as ripe as it was, they had brought in several more bar officers and at least two more clerks. All dressed in black and pushing paper around, they looked like some strange administration-based cult having a get-together. Six police officers had placed themselves strategically around the friends and family of the victims – it was fairly common to see grief overspill into violence.

Jack watched as the judge sat down, sipped from a cup some of her hot beverage, and then restarted proceedings.

The detective didn't know the barrister questioning him, but he knew his type. Young, hungry and with something to prove. Jack was one of the only people on the force that didn't mind this type of questioning. It was quite entertaining for him, watching highly educated defence layers trying to goad him into playing games, the ones where you're meant to trip yourself up or contradict something you have sworn on previously. It wasn't because Jack enjoyed playing by these rules, but rather because he played by his own, answering monosyllabically when he could and by picking a story and sticking to it – if that story happened to be the truth, all the better.

The lawyer strutted the room, more for effect than necessity.

Jack gave his usual, '*Yes sir, no sir, you are correct, sir*' answers and the whole thing was proceeding as painlessly as possible. This was up until the man in the wig asked for some precise detail.

'So, detective, if you look at this statement here, you see the time there? Could you read that aloud for me, please?'

Jack took the piece of paper. 'Yes, it states the warrant for a mobile phone trace of Mr Peters was released at six thirty-six p.m.'

The man running the defence smiled and took back the evidence. 'Well done, detective, that wasn't so difficult, now, was it? But what *is* difficult to understand is why you were able to pinpoint my client's location precisely ten minutes previous to this warrant being issued. Could you explain this discrepancy to me, please, Detective O'Connor?'

Jack smiled sweetly back at the man. 'Yes, as I have confirmed in both of my statements, it was by a process of elimination, luck, and more luck.'

The barrister took a deep breath. 'Please explain how you came to eliminate the entirety of the city of Bristol bar this one road.'

Jack edged to the front of his chair and looked directly into his opponent's eyes. 'A mass murderer escalating as quickly as our suspect would have been looking for a heavily populated part of the city to find a victim. While he may have started as an opportunist, he was now operating under a greater thirst for blood. That time of night on a Friday, the most likely places to find vulnerable people would be somewhere with alcohol. An inebriated victim would be much easier to overpower, which leads me to conclude that Park Street would be a lucrative hunting ground.'

Jack's unblinking stare forced the other man to turn away. 'Almost word for word with your first statement, Detective O'Connor, bravo. But I, however, have a conclusion of my own. You traced Mr Peters via his phone without the warrant in place. Therefore, illegally accessing the personal data of my client.'

Another man in a wig stood up. 'Objection, Your Honour, the accused has already put forward a plea of diminished responsibility. The circumstances to his arrest are now all but circumstantial.'

The woman who had spent most of the proceedings sitting quietly up above the rest of them in contemplation nodded. 'Sustained. I think now would be the time to concentrate on your client's defence of the murder conviction currently being campaigned for by your learned friend. Detective O'Connor, you are free to leave, I believe the defence is done with you.'

'Well, that went well,' McQuade said sarcastically as she and Jack walked back to the station. Jack took the tie off and offered it back to his commander.

'Keep it. You could even try wearing it if you were feeling daring. Only Officer Kapoor to stand now. As long as he follows your story with the warrant, that should be the end of it. They're only trying to show a discrepancy in the arrest so they can knock a year or two off. Waste of time if you ask me. Always trying to show us in a bad light. That'll be the press, pushing them for headlines. Got everyone in their pockets, the papers. Are you even listening to me, Detective?' McQuade asked Jack as they started walking down corridors in the labyrinth that was the police building.

'No, ma'am.'

McQuade held the door to her office open. 'Smart arse. In,' she said, standing back to allow Jack to enter. 'You seem in shock, Jack. I mean, I'm not surprised.' She picked up her mobile phone from her desk and began accessing something on it. 'I was sent a rather interesting picture earlier.' She turned the phone around for Jack to examine.

'If you look closely,' she continued, 'that looks a lot like you, hanging from the side of the Marriot Hotel. Now, I told myself, that's impossible, he isn't working on that case, no, my lead detective has been put on the missing child case as an extra. And the only reason he is on that case at all is because he has refused to take any leave. This picture, however, was sent to me by a member of the press – a kind heads up of tomorrow's front page.'

Jack's heart sank. He hated causing his superior grief – especially when it involved the papers. He somehow, however, had managed to gain a particular prowess at doing so.

The detective unconsciously rubbed at his stubble,

thinking about taking an unsporting low blow at his boss.

'Have you considered my request, ma'am? Me being in another country could be more convenient for you.'

McQuade narrowed her eyes. 'Oh, nice try, Jack, but I'm not biting. Have I considered your ridiculous request to take yourself and my best pathologist on a jolly to Italy to investigate an unsuspicious death of a priest? Is that seriously what you're asking me?' She laughed sarcastically. 'Of course I bloody haven't.'

She recognised the detective's frustration. Placing her phone down and taking a seat, she moved a small picture frame holding a photo of her father on her desk and straightened it next to the computer screen.

'Jack, what in hell's name makes you believe I have the authority – let alone the *manpower* – to sanction something like this?'

Jack sat opposite her, hands together, almost pleadingly. 'Only Aubrie and me, that's all I need. You must know someone who can?'

'I struggle to communicate and get cooperation across the Seven with Welsh departments let alone halfway across Europe, and it involves the Vatican, of all places.' She sighed. 'Jack, if you want to investigate this, you'll need to find a way off your own back. And I'm sorry, but Aubrie is flat out at the moment, we can't afford to spare her.'

Jack leaned back and looked up at the ceiling, searching for inspiration that wasn't there.

'They won't let me within a hundred miles of the Vatican if they know what I want to investigate.'

'Then force their hand,' the superintendent said, sitting up straight.

The detective looked at her, confused.

McQuade rolled her eyes. 'Really? And you're my best detective. This case I asked you to help on, the missing child.'

Jack scoffed with resentment, 'We got the man, he's in a cell just down there,' Jack pointed at the door. 'You knew it was him before I even started on it.'

'Yes, I did, what I was hoping for from you was some sodding evidence.' She opened the top drawer beneath her desk, pulled out a file and slammed it on the desk. She opened it up and flicked through the pages before turning it to the detective.

She slammed a finger down on a list. 'Look. All of the other suspected victims. Two from Pembrokeshire, two from Cumbria and one from Northumberland. All the same M.O., all the same age, sex, all missing in similar circumstances.'

'Yes, I know, and all from schools where our suspect has either worked or lived near,' Jack said.

'Precisely, and all from these schools.' She pointed at a small handwritten list, compiled of school names. 'Notice anything about them?'

Jack took a closer look. 'They're all Catholic schools.'

McQuade raised her eyebrows. 'If it's the one thing the church doesn't need at the moment, it is a paedophile serial killer being associated with them. Especially after that bishop business last month. For once, you may be able to use your bad reputation with the press to your advantage.'

McQuade's face softened. 'Look, we have a family missing their little boy. Find him, even if he's dead. Let's give this family some peace and then I can try to open up some lines of communication with the Italian police. If that fails, you can use the fact that the Catholic schools failed to vet their staff sufficiently as leverage to try to get you in there. Now, we've had our Mr Pearce in a cell for thirty-two hours. I've asked for an extension but it has been denied as we have nothing but circumstantial. That leaves you with four hours to crack this, get me something that'll stick. Christ, if you find the boy alive, you'll be a modern-day hero. You'll probably be able to investigate anything and anywhere you want – petty theft in the Maldives if you fancied it.'

THAT'S MR TO YOU

Jack walked into the busy police station. The tables down the left-hand side were all working on the missing child case, all looking very busy and fraught.

Jack spotted a young officer looking down at a desk. He didn't need to use his BPD to empathise with him, he could clearly tell that the younger officer was trying to stay inconspicuous. Jack didn't mind, it was intimidating working under these pressures, every other officer wanting to be the big shot who cracks it and solves the case. Oh, sure, on the surface it's all about the teamwork, but deep down, all of them are vying for some glory. Jack often wondered if his bitter conclusion of people had started the day his wife and child had been murdered or if it had been there all along and just needed a window to escape from.

'You,' Jack shouted at the other officer over the melee, 'what's your name?'

'Timmins, sir,' the man stuttered in response. To the man's credit, the detective had startled himself with the authority his voice had commanded. He didn't know he had it in him.

'Missing boy case?' Jack asked, receiving a reticent nod in return. 'Good, grab your coat and info file and follow me.'

The young man struggled to put his coat on, held the cardboard file and kept up with Jack as he led them out of the station and into the car park.

'Well?' Jack said as they stood in front of a line of vehicles, 'which one's yours?'

'Er, none of them, sir.' The man sounded apologetic; Jack could feel him willing the universe to appear a car for them magically.

Jack turned to look at the man, only feeling half as appalled as he actually looked. 'Not even your own car?'

The officer looked embarrassed. 'I cycle to work, sir, you see I only live …'

But Jack didn't listen; he had spotted an officer getting out of a patrol car and quickly walked over to it before it was too late.

Jack recognised the driver, he had worked with her a couple of times, many years ago now, so there was precious little chance of him remembering her name.

'We just need to borrow this,' he gestured at the car and held out his hand for the keys.

'Just bring her back in one piece, won't you?' the female officer said in a tone that sounded as if she remembered what working with Jack was like very well.

Jack threw the keys to the young man that he had stolen from the incident room. 'Don't worry, he's driving.'

'I am?' the young man stammered as the keys bounced out of his hands and rolled under the car. He placed the paperwork on the bonnet and climbed under the vehicle. A gust of wind attempted to steal the sheets away but Jack caught them and picked them up so as to examine on their journey.

'God help me but yes, you are,' Jack said, opening the car door and sliding himself in.

Southmead had a bit of a bad reputation still, even if it did now have one of the best hospitals in the country on its borders – it being one of the best in the country had been professionals' take on the facility and not the detective's. Once Jack had found out that the lighting system high up in its atrium made up of three different coloured LED formations had actually been a clock, he had decided that perhaps a hospital was not the place for style over substance.

The police had made conscious efforts in those more stubbornly stained areas to clean up, but when money was tight it only made for more desperate people and the uncomfortable truth was that desperate people committed crimes to survive.

'This is the house?' Jack asked as they pulled up. It never did cease to amaze him how ordinary potential crime scenes were in reality. It was just your typical three bedroom semi-detached, pebble-dashed, run of the mill house.

'Could this really be the scene of a murder or kidnap? It looks like my gran's old house, for Christ sake.'

'Apparently, sir. It's been swept through – even had dogs in there. Not a sausage from what I heard.'

Jack eyed the building suspiciously. 'Nothing, hey? Come on, looks like no one is in. Let's go looking for those sausages.'

Jack knocked at the door just in case a relative was there – they usually did swarm around and contaminate crime scenes pretty quickly – but no one answered.

'Look, sarge, the garage door is open, must have been left like that from the last search.'

The young man gripped the bottom of the door and lifted, it slid up and back on rollers with ease.

'Better check nothing's been nicked, I suppose,' Jack said, entering the cold, dark room.

Jack could see that it had once been tidy, but everything had been moved or dislodged slightly. Jack looked at a couple of boxes on the shelf, recognising a bike inner tube and some felt nails, usually used on shed roofs. There were tools all scattered across the metal racking-type units, but there was not even one blood-stained hammer to be seen.

He looked around at the floor; he wasn't sure what he expected to see, a trap door, maybe? He leant on the arms of a pallet truck, feeling deflated.

'Felt nails,' Jack said aloud, unsure himself of where the thought had formulated.

The other officer looked blankly at him.

'There're felt nails, does that mean there's a shed?' Jack didn't wait for a response, instead he left the garage and made his way around the side of the house. The view from the garden wasn't half bad for that sort of location. The lawn ran slightly downhill and was lined with low hedging with skirts of bedded flowers.

Jack spotted what he was looking for: a shed, situated just off from the concrete path that ran from one end to the other. The lock hung on the latch, broken severely in half where the bolt cutters had been used. He had never envied someone who had to have their property searched – a gentle approach the police did not use.

Opening the door, Jack found more of the same: a once tidy shed, just looking a little disturbed. He bit his top lip, looking around the quite small wooden room, thinking hard and feeling harder. His senses tingled, the blood flowed a little warmer through the palms of his hands and he could feel that small knot in his stomach that told him he was close. He moved paint tins around on the back shelf, hoping to find just a small piece of evidence.

'Anything, sarge?' the other man said, arriving at the door.

Jack took another hard look at all the tubs of emulsion, 'I don't know.' Jack stepped out of the shed. 'I think I need to talk to this guy. There's something going on.' Jack looked back at the main building, it wasn't large, but he could think of a couple of places to hide a body, but all of them would have been checked and rechecked by officers. And none of them were out of range of the dogs' noses. 'Come on, back to the station, we're running out of time.'

Jack had phoned through on their way back as they navigated the streets, most busy with slow moving cars. He had wanted the man ready for interrogation; there was little patience left in him now to be faffing around with paperwork.

Like most cases, the accused looked little more than the neighbour next door. A fairly short man with a small, round tummy hidden beneath a cardigan sat with a calm exterior, hands forming a steeple on the table. His red nose and cheeks suggested someone who liked a drink or plenty.

'If his white beard had been a little bit longer, he could have made a fair Father Christmas impersonator,' Jack thought as he sat opposite him.

'You know why you're here, Mr Pearce, and you know what I'm going to be asking you?'

The older man smiled. 'I do, would it not be prudent to wait for my attorney?'

Jack mimicked the smile. 'Probably. As you're guilty, I should imagine you will need all the help that you can get.'

The battle of the grins continued as Pearce's grew larger. 'The accusations that you have found no evidence of and will be releasing me for within,' he looked up at the clock, 'just under four hours? That's what you are going to ask me about, is it not, detective?'

Jack went to open the file in front of him, but halfway through lifting the top flap open, he stopped, paused and then dropped it.

His mantra popped into his head.

'Empathy; the ability to understand and share the feelings of another.'

It was one of the greatest strengths of his borderline personality disorder; to be able to understand people so completely it would sometimes become difficult to know where Jack ended and they began.

He looked deep in through the accused's glasses and into his eyes.

'Young men, always young men, isn't it? Not old enough to understand, innocent enough to manipulate. Not interested in a challenge, are you? No, it's that innocence that turns you on, isn't it? Does that get you hard, Robert Pearce? Do you touch yourself at the thought of them being scared, not understanding what's happening to them?'

Jack watched as the other man's already red face deepened in richness, blue blood vessels coming to the surface as he held himself back.

Jack smiled. 'What's wrong? Have I touched a nerve, Pearce?'

Even Jack was surprised when the man's hand clenched into a fist and came down hard onto the table. It echoed loudly in the small room; it took all of Jack to keep his body from twitching with shock.

'It's *Mr* Pearce to you, boy!' the man shouted, his chest heaving beneath the knitwear with furious deep breaths.

Jack tilted his head, considering the man. When Jack was in his zone, each word could be a betrayal, revealing a mountain of truth from what could be mistaken for a grain of sand.

'And in that entire sentence the word that seemed to stick was Mr, *now why might that have been?'*

'You don't have a clue about who I am, what I am capable of, don't pretend like you have even the slightest inkling of what you are talking about,' Mr Pearce said, steadying himself.

'Is that right, *Mr* Pearce?' Jack pronounced the man's title with venom. 'I couldn't possibly understand the inner workings of a paedophile. I'm not going to even open this file and let's see how close I can get, shall we? Now, I know that you were a teacher, but I want to talk about the *real* Mr Pearce. Daddy.' Jack examined the restless creature opposite him. 'Now, what would he have done as a career, do we think? Ah, I've got it, he was a teacher.'

The older man looked away. 'No, he wasn't just a

teacher, he was a *head*teacher.'

His arms folded, telling Jack that he was on the money.

'See, there we go, now we're getting somewhere. He was *your* headteacher, wasn't he? They were strict back in those days, weren't they? How strict was he on you, Pearcy? The cane met your backside plenty of times, I bet. And at home— nah, it would have been the belt at home. I wonder what sort of behaviour would earn you the belt. Disobedience, maybe?'

Jack saw the man's jaw clench tightly as he desperately avoided glancing in the detective's direction.

'Not doing what you were told. And what was it that he told you to do? Get on your knees, Robert, be a good boy for Daddy, Robert, you don't want to make Daddy angry, do you, Robert?'

Jack wasn't surprised by the man's actions this time when he saw a small tear run from his eye and collect in the wrinkles making up the bags below.

'But where was mummy? She wasn't there, was she, Robert?' Still the man stayed as blank as he could, trying against his might not to react. 'Oh, wait, she *was* there. She was always there, and she knew. She knew your dirty little secret, didn't she? What a disgusting little boy she had. That's it, Pearcy, cry like a little boy, like all those little boys you've abused over the years.'

The man stood up and grabbed the table to upend it, but Jack was too quick, pushing it back down as he matched the man for height and strength.

The older man pointed at Jack, right in his face. 'I said it's *Mr* Pearce to you, boy.'

Jack slapped the man's hand away. 'I'm not *boy* to you, I'm *detective*, and I'm the one who is going to find something concrete to put you away.'

And that's when Jack saw it, a little flicker of suspicion race across Robert Pearce's face.

The door opened and in came a lawyer followed by

Officer Timmins.

'Sorry, sarge, he insisted.'

Jack waved a hand. 'Doesn't matter, we're done in here. Come with me, Timmins.' Jack didn't even give the accused a second look as they both walked from the room, but not before Pearce shouted, reeling Jack's temper back inside.

'Time's nearly up, detective, not long now until I will be walking out of here.'

Jack stormed across the room, his sudden presence over the now seated man having the desired effect of causing him unease. He roughly pulled up the man's sleeve, there on his left wrist was what Jack wanted, a watch. He loosened the leather strap, making sure to catch Pearce's skin in it.

Jack threw it to the ground and stamped his heel through the glass face. The detective then walked over to the clock on the wall above the door and took it down. He threw this plastic timepiece to the floor with force behind it, smashing it to pieces.

This time, there was no quick-witted retort from the accused. Instead, silence followed Jack from the room as he walked down the corridor.

The detective stopped and scratched at his short, thinning hair. 'He flinched. I said concrete and he flinched. What does that mean, Timmins? *Concrete.*'

The young officer pulled his hat on and watched Jack pace a corridor. He cleared his throat. 'Maybe he's buried him in concrete, there was a big garage floor, could have dug up part of it, buried the body, and then covered it over.'

Jack stopped, he could feel the already narrow corridor closing in on him. All of a sudden he felt hot, unbearably hot. Frustrated at his clothing, he tore his jacket and tie off. The hubbub from all the offices slowly started to increase in volume, the noise boring into his head with impacting ease. Jack buried his eyes in his hands. 'I can't think, I need air, I need space. I can't think, I can't fucking think.'

Timmins took a hesitant step closer. 'The car's out the front still, sarge, shall I drive you somewhere?'

Jack looked up, his frustration was tearing up inside him, too hot, too noisy, too much of everything. 'Take me home— no, take me to Clifton, I need somewhere to think for a minute.'

BY SMELL

Jack leaned his head against the cool glass of the car window, pressing as much of himself against it as he could as his anger threatened to consume him. The other policeman hadn't spoken except for asking where exactly it was that Jack wanted to be driven to. If Jack still had the ability to become embarrassed, these would have usually been the situations that would have induced it. Right now, though, he couldn't care less who saw him going into one of his rages. He knew it wasn't normal but he had decided a long time ago that normal just didn't suit him anymore.

Jack jumped out of the car, just managing to stay upright as he barely waited for it to stop.

'I'll wait here, sarge, shall I?' the young officer called nervously, not receiving a reply.

Jack walked up to the house and thrust his keys into the hole with more force than necessary, causing more aggravation than anything else as it took several attempts to turn the lock and actually bruised his hands. He pushed the door so it hit the inner wall and closed itself behind. He leaned back against the still vibrating wood and slid down to the floor. The house smelled clean, homely almost, and he could tell that something had been recently cooking in the kitchen by the welcoming aroma. This was the first time since the murder of his wife and daughter that he had managed to cross the threshold without feeling physically sick – in fact, he actually felt like he was safe. He placed his hands flat on the tiled floor, the welcoming frigid embrace moving slowly up into wrists and then up further.

'Jack?' the voice of Carla came down the stairs. She was a young girl, now sixteen, who Jack had saved from her abusive father a few weeks before. She was the sister of a boy called Daniel, a young man that Jack had accidentally acquired as a friend and who had been brutally murdered by one of Jack's own officers – the one he had been giving evidence against. Jack had taken this particular murder almost as personally as that of his own daughter and his guilt this time was, in his mind, fully justified. The boy had been murdered out of spite, nothing more than as a message to him and nothing less than the bleak reality of death. Carla now lived in Jack's old house as way of a pathetic apology to her for not saving her brother. Jack had been more than happy in his boat for the last few years and the one time he had left the house unoccupied for a few weeks, squatters had moved in and used the internal doors as kindling.

Carla came running down the stairs, clearly startled from the way that Jack had made his grand entrance. The detective righted himself and straightened his creased shirt the best he could with as little energy as possible.

'Sorry, I thought you would be at college,' he said, giving a weak smile and walking straight past her through to the kitchen.

'No, day off today, teacher is off sick.' Her voice was unsure and hesitant. 'Everything ok, Jack? Has something happened?' she asked, following him – albeit at a safe distance.

'No, no, just work stressing me out, needed somewhere to come and think for a bit. Thought I would check in, make sure there are no bills that need paying or whatever.'

'Do you want me to go, to leave you alone for a bit?' Carla asked, taking one step towards the door.

Jack looked around at her, for the first time realising that he had made her feel uncomfortable. 'Oh God, sorry, I shouldn't have come here while I'm like this. No, let's put the kettle on and make a cup of tea. Tell me what's been happening with you. Could do with some good news and just some idle chit-chat for once.'

Carla smiled, her confidence clearly restored, and she skipped to the kettle, filling it with water and flicking on its little light switch.

'Well, now you come to mention bills. There was this PPI letter addressed to your wife,' she said softly, obviously treading the conversation gently, 'was going to bin it, but then thought that if there was money to claim back, it might help with the cost of me being here.'

Jack remained thoughtful while the kettle clicked to signify it had boiled. Jack put two tea bags in mugs and slid them down the counter to her playfully.

'Don't you worry about the cost. In fact, if you need more money for food or school stuff, I've told you to let me know. Yeah, just bin anything like that. It's not like I'm going to read it. What about your dad? Have you been to visit him?' He hadn't meant to change the subject deliberately, it had just become second nature.

Carla rolled her eyes. 'Yes, and get this, he asked me to bring him some drugs in. He said some coke or, what was it now? Spice, that's is. Like I even know where to get that crap, let alone how to sneak it in to prison. I only went because it was my birthday, thought he might want to see me. What a joke. So glad he's banged up. And he had a black eye.' She smiled gleefully.

Jake sighed. 'So someone gave him a taste of his own medicine for once by the sounds of it. So you're still happy being here, then?'

Carla smiled at him, positively lighting the room. 'Yes,

Jack, it's the happiest I've ever been. Thank you.'

Jack laughed. 'Stop thanking me, you deserve it – you deserve better. Like I said, anything you need, you had better let me know.'

Carla got the milk from the fridge but stopped to hug Jack before pouring it.

'Oh, yeah, there was one more thing – your neighbours,' Carla said, spooning in sugar.

'Which ones?' Jack asked.

'The rude ones.' Carla handed him his cup of tea, holding it by the top.

'Oh yeah, the web designers. Both look like they only eat celery and humus.'

Carla laughed. 'Yeah, that's the ones. Well, they came over with a bill. Apparently you share a septic tank with them and they got it emptied, so you have to pay half the cost. I said to him, how come you pay half, while I live here on my own, and they've got four people in there? They thought I hadn't noticed that his brother and sister in law had been there for over two weeks now. Do you know what he said?'

Jack shook his head and sipped his tea gently.

'He said, if you don't like it, you'll have to take it up with him yourself, he won't negotiate with a squatter. A *squatter* he called me.'

Jack almost spat his tea out with a chuckle at how appalled the girl had become and by knowing that if she wanted to, she could have probably upended that neighbour quite comfortably.

'I'll have a word, see if I can drum some manners into …'

Jack trailed off, transfixed at a blank bit of kitchen wall. He placed his tea down with no conscious thought, the cup somehow managing to cling to the edge of the kitchen worktop.

'I have to go, I think I've had an idea,' he told the girl, who looked baffled.

'Ok, glad I could help,' she called sarcastically after him.

'Sarge, everything ok?' Timmins asked as Jack pointed to him, telling him to lose the cigarette and start the car with a mere finger gesture.

'Get us back to Pearce's house now.'

The flashing lights and siren got them across Bristol in just over ten minutes, aided by Jack swearing at the top of his voice at anything too slow to get out of the way.

Jack checked his watch, one hour to go until they had to release the bastard, one hour to get something, *anything*, to at least keep him locked up.

The police car skidded up to the house, mounting the curb with a thud. The men approached the house, Timmins placing his hat onto his head and Jack heading straight for the back gate.

A man came running from the front door, 'What the hell do you think you're doing? You can't just barge in like this, you've already searched my father in-law's house from top to bottom and you didn't find anything.'

Jack ignored him and continued walking, up until the other man made a mistake. He held out his arm across Jack's chest as an attempt to prevent him from walking into the garden. Jack grabbed his thumb and twisted it inwards, forcing the man's hand to tuck in under his own armpit, tendons overstretching perfectly to manipulate the man's whole body.

This wasn't even one of the holds taught during training, this was just a little something that he had learnt on the street and it worked efficiently. The man yelped and then fell silent as Jack's other hand grabbed his throat.

'Stop me when I'm walking again, and I will have you banged up for obstruction. Nod if you understand.'

The man's eyes tightened as Jack applied pressure, but he managed a small nod.

'Good,' Jack said, relinquishing his grip and continuing

his fast pace around the side of the house.

Timmins had to jog to keep up. 'Sarge, what is it?'

The detective walked up and behind the shed. 'Look, tracks.'

And there in the grass were remnants of two parallel lines, made by wheels, running about twenty feet down the garden.

'That pallet truck in the garage, a bit heavy duty for DIY, isn't it?' Jack said, circling the shed some more, his body language somewhere between excitement and anticipation, his muscles trying to remain fluid, but rigidity setting in with each step.

'But the dogs, sarge, they searched all up here, they would have found something, surely?'

Jack took a look at the house; they now had three bystanders: the son in law, the daughter and another friend of the family.

'Get some blankets,' he shouted down to them. They didn't move. 'Now!' Jack's scream did the trick and the daughter disappeared into the house, albeit reluctantly.

'Yes, Timmins, the dogs. If you were hiding someone and knew dogs would be looking for them, how would you hide them. By sight?' Jack asked, pushing at the side of the shed, testing the strength of the structure.

'No, sarge, by smell,' the young officer replied, slowly formulating things in his mind, trying desperately to catch up with Jack's freight train of thought.

Jack opened the door. 'How about with paint and chemicals?'

'Would that be enough?' The officer took his hat off and threw it down to the ground as he took more of an interest into the small wooden building.

'No, but combine that with—' He interrupted himself to give the other man directions, 'Here, grab that bottom corner and lift.' The two officers lifted with all of their might, forcing the shed to fall on to its back, the roof caving in somewhat and the sound of falling paint tins taking time to clatter to the floor.

'Combine it with human shit.'

Both policemen looked down at the ground where the small outbuilding had stood. There in front of them were three large, thin concrete slabs. Two with vents at both ends and the middle with a large iron hoop protruding.

'Concrete, sarge.'

Jack inhaled and felt sick with a new smell hitting the back of his throat. 'Yep, concrete.'

The daughter of the house owner came walking up the path quietly behind them, holding blankets. She gasped at what she saw, the realisation of what they had just found and what might yet be left to find finally settling in.

Timmins stepped forward to grab the metal ring but Jack pulled on his arm to stop him – he didn't want the young officer to rush into something his heart wasn't ready for.

'Just before we do this, it's quite likely there's a dead body down there, just prepare yourself.'

The woman behind them began to cry, whimpering and spilling gentle tears onto the woolen material in her arms.

The officer nodded and handed Jack a small torch before straddling the septic tank, pulling up hard from the knees and lifting the centre section out.

With one heave, the piece lifted and Timmins managed to swing just enough to one side for a person to squeeze in. Jack got on his stomach and lowered his top half into the hole. The smell was overwhelming this time, to the point of the detective gagging on his empty stomach, and the space seemed to absorb the light from the small hand torch. Jack twisted himself to look the other way and the light found something white sticking up from the black sludge. Pushing his arm further in, he recognised two pale legs with weak child's arms tightly wrapped around them.

A young boy sat waist deep in human waste, colourless like a deep sea creature and not moving.

DEALS WITH THE DEVIL

Jack sat on the stairs, head leaning heavily on the handrail, just watching as teams of people walked up and down the narrow hallway. Some in boiler suits, others in uniform and some in plain clothes, but all quiet and dogged in their work. All except Jack who, after the rage of earlier and effort of forcing his brain to work everything out, was now exhausted and empty. He wasn't part of the world in these moments, just an observer and not a very good one as he was seeing without translating any more information.

Officer Timmins couldn't help but smile, but Jack didn't mind, with all the slaps on the back and congratulations, what else was a young man supposed to do? He heard one of his colleagues tell him that a newspaper had already been in touch, wanting to interview him. Jack was happy for him; he really was, but with a note of weary on the side. Doesn't take much notoriety to turn you into a target – something he knew only too well.

'Jack, you with us?'

McQuade was standing in front of him, a half-smile greeting him, although it looked somewhat uncomfortable on her face.

'Yes, sorry, just thinking,' he replied, standing to meet

her.

'Well, you solved it, time to stop thinking and start celebrating.' McQuade couldn't help but sound like she was giving him orders.

'I'm not so sure,' Jack replied, sounding obviously deflated. 'Come and look at this.'

Jack led his commanding officer up the stairs to the spare bedroom, the third and smallest in the house.

They both entered and Jack shut the door behind them, looking out deliberately to ensure no one was watching them. He didn't want to sew bad blood in front of the others quite so early on in the case.

'Look,' he said, pointing at the door handle. It was an innocent looking round plastic one, probably an original from when the house had been built.

'No lock, no chain, no way of keeping someone locked in. I've checked all of the rooms, they're all the same. And the windows all open right up. Not much of a prison for keeping children in.'

McQuade turned and looked at the window. 'Right, so you're saying easy for a prison escape in that case. So what? We know he was putting them in the septic tank.'

Jack shook his head. 'No, that's not it. What's the point in that, steal a kid, put them straight in the ground. Why would he do that? Why would all these kids be abducted and then just put in a hole to rot? It doesn't make sense. It goes against every single motive in the book and out of it.'

McQuade's eyes narrowed as she tried to think. 'So what would make sense, then, Jack?'

Jack's hands went up to his nose in prayer formation, rubbing between his eyes as a divergence of ideas formulated. They crashed together, trying to create one single perfect solution.

'I think the kid was never meant to be here. I think Pearce was the groomer and then someone else was meant to come and take him, but we got on to him too quickly. They panicked and agreed to put him straight in the pit.'

McQuade shook her head. 'But Aubrie has found remains of more children in there already. And that's within five minutes of sifting. If he was just there to deliver the kids, why would others be in there?'

Jack bit his top lip. 'I don't know, maybe he's also a disposal man. He has minimal contact, probably gets paid a great sum for his services. Maybe he book ends these sort of …' he waved his hands, searching for a word, '*transactions*. He's there for collections and returns, maybe.'

The commanding officer's phone rang. She pulled it out and took one look at the screen. 'Shit, it's the nursing home again.' She hung up and put the phone away.

'Your dad? He's got Alzheimer's, hasn't he? Is he ok?' Jack asked. He was a little surprised that she had just canceled the call like that.

'Yeah, well, no, they think he's developed Alzheimer's now, it was just brain damage before. He had an accident. They're phoning me all the time, at the moment he's gone quite bad. Saying some crazy shit about priests and God. I think he hates the church as much as you.'

Jack started to protest the comment – it wasn't the church he hated, just the pedophiles in it. But McQuade brought them back on focus.

'If you're right, there will be money somewhere; we have tech support already picking through his computer, we'll find it.'

Jack went to walk past his commander, back down the stairs, but she stopped him. 'Also, Jack, if you're right, he's a small player in a much bigger game, and unless we find any evidence of who else he might be playing with, we're on our own …' She paused.

Jack rolled his eyes. 'You'll have to offer him a fucking deal.'

McQuade shrugged her shoulders. 'Sometimes you have to make deals with the devil, Jack, if it means catching the bigger fish. If this really is what you think it is, if he really is just some sort of delivery man, we might have to offer him a deal.'

'Yeah, but when you make deals with the devil, you normally end up paying with a life.'

FLORENCE

Jack had to decline offers of lifts from three different people before he finally got away from the house. He needed some air, some room to think, his mind was as claustrophobic as that box room and felt as though it could shrink down to the size of the septic tank if people didn't stop talking at him.

That part of the city still had the old wide roads, houses placed at a respectful distance apart. Snooping neighbors really did have to linger at windows there for a time to spot anything interesting going on, unlike the rest of the city where people lived almost literally on top of each other.

It was a long walk back down Muller Road, but a Burger King was waiting at the bottom – some greasy food and full fat Coke would probably do him good at the moment – his liquid diet had a way of catching up with him, or perhaps it slowed him right down.

A black van started to mirror his pace, sitting just out of his peripheral vision but not far enough to be inconspicuous. Jack had never received anti-surveillance training, he had never considered himself worthy enough to be followed, but had certainly started making a habit of it of late.

'For Christ's sake, what have I done now?' Jack thought as he slowly turned round to greet his stalkers. He gave them a small sarcastic wave before shouting, 'Taxi!'

The van stopped and the side panel door slid open enthusiastically and with completely unnecessary force.

'Hello, Jack, going our way?'

Jack sat in the back of a plush, custom finished Mercedes minivan. Leather seats, shag carpets and LED lighting told him he was in somewhere with too much money and not enough class and the fact that Casper Collingwood, MI5 agent sat opposite him meant it had been funded by taxpayers.

'Could we just go through the drive-through, I'm starving,' Jack said over the top of Casper's head, addressing the driver.

'Just shut up, Jack. You've been summoned, so just be a good little police officer and sit there quietly,' Casper replied, checking something on his phone.

'*Detective*,' Jack said quietly, looking around his ride. He pushed a panel that flipped open, revealing two cup holders.

'Ha, look at that. Think of everything, don't they? You could put your protein shake in there, hey, Casper,' Jack taunted.

The MI5 agent sent a scornful look at another secret service man who sat beside Jack and had laughed at the quip.

A few minutes later – and to Jack's surprise – they pulled up at the police station. Not wanting to seem on the back foot, the detective didn't question anything but instead confidently followed the two men in through the old wooden doors.

He didn't even betray how uneasy he actually felt inside as they walked through the various corridors, it was apparent that the building was empty. Collingwood kept giving him a sideways glance, egging Jack on to ask what the hell was going on.

'No, I'm not biting,' the detective told himself. *'But what the hell is going on?'*

'In here,' Casper told Jack sternly, holding open the door to McQuade's office. The other MI5 agent waited outside the room as Collingwood closed them in.

McQuade's office was sparse, all the usual paraphernalia was gone, replaced with cardboard boxes piled on top of one another. Only the desk remained in its usual place, behind which another man sat.

Jack walked over to the empty chair on his side of the table. The other man pointed for him to sit and, without realising it, Jack obeyed.

'Oh great,' Jack thought as he now became aware of who he was about to meet. He didn't know the man exactly, but he knew the type – the type who could get people to sit with a point, the type who were so powerful and used to being powerful that it only made sense for people to do what they said.

Jack took a deep intake of air, readying to speak when the man lifted a finger again to stop him.

'Jesus Christ, I might as well be a dog to this guy, put a lead on me and make me beg for treats, why don't you?'

Jack was amused by this behaviour for now and watched. The man wore a strange pinstriped suit. It was clearly too large, but cut in the old fashioned double-breasted style, like the gangsters of the nineteen twenties seemed to choose. But what Jack felt was a little too peculiar was that the man had a small metal briefcase open on the desk. While that would normally be rather innocuous in most occasions, this time what made Jack feel uneasy was that the man had just removed a boiled egg from the case.

The other man, not even noticing that it was his peeling off the egg that was stalling proceedings, slowly picked the shell from the hard white. He next pulled a small silver salt shaker from the case, dusted the egg with it, and then took a bite.

Jack took a quick, sideways look at Casper, who was doing a very good job of not showing any discomfort at the situation, but the detective could just see a tightening in his posture.

A few bites later and the egg was gone. A napkin appeared from the metallic case next and the man cleaned himself up and placed away the salt shaker.

The man took a deep breath and finally looked up at the police officer.

'You know McQuade doesn't like her things being touched?' Jack broke the silence. He kicked himself after – he had lost this mental game of chicken spectacularly.

The other man looked around at the boxes, scratched at his chin nonchalantly and smiled gently.

'She no longer needs this office, Detective O'Connor,' the man finally spoke. It was slow and felt tired to listen to, but still, Jack could gauge a sense of purpose in it.

'Why, what have you done?' Jack asked, showing a slither of anger.

'Fucking hell, Jack, wise up,' Casper said, walking around to the other side of the desk to stand with the man in the strange suit.

'The station has moved around the corner; it was this department's moving day today. *Your* department. Have you even seen your new office yet?'

'I've been busy doing real work,' Jack replied tartly.

Casper Collingwood laughed. 'Of course you have, hanging off buildings is what I heard.'

'What do you want, *Casper?*' Jack emphasised the name, making it sound as ridiculous as he could.

Casper laughed again. 'I don't want anything to do with you, Jack, I'm only here because I know you and what I know is that you're a pissing liability.'

The other man, who was far quieter than the other two, began peeling another boiled egg, nonplussed by their bickering.

'So why am I here?' Jack asked, looking from one man to the next.

A moment of silence passed before the seated man spoke, 'Do you know the origin of the Easter egg, Detective O'Connor?'

The man looked at him now, clearly wanting a coherent answer to his ridiculous question.

'The egg represents the rebirth of Christ, doesn't it? You know, in the cave and that?' Jack replied, furrowing his brow with confusion.

The older man took a bite. 'That is what is commonly believed today, but it is not true. The word Easter actually comes from the Babylon word *Astarte*. The Babylonians, as I'm sure you know, were of a Pagan religion.'

Jack nodded, he wasn't going to let on that he didn't have a clue what the other man was talking about.

'Now, the egg in this religion actually represents fertility. You celebrate the time of year that you would like to make the women in your village fertile.' The man took another bite. 'You see, nine months later it was essential that your village had babies abundantly. Now, Astarte was the mother, and Nimrod the father, of a child called Tammuz, the god of the sun. And with the sun god came fire, and with that fire came sacrifice. Exactly nine months after the celebration of Easter, would you believe it, but there is Christmas. Now, the people of the village would sacrifice their babies to Tammuz in these fires to ensure that the sun would continue to shine fortunately upon them.' The man finished the last of the egg in three large bites. 'Now here's the real kicker,' he said, showing the contents of his mouth unashamedly. 'Tammuz's father, Nimrod, actually had many names, the most commonly known one was Satan. The devil himself, no less.' He wiped his hands on a napkin that he handed to Casper, who took it diligently. 'So when you see all these folk running around with Easter eggs, and hot-cross buns, it makes me smile, all of them without realising it are actually unequivocally Satanists. It's the irony in it that I really like.'

Jack was confused but kept his face as impassive as possible. He never did like poker much, but he had to admit he had the face for it.

'I hear you want to fuck around with the church, Detective O'Connor; you want to get in their faces and make a load of trouble for British intelligence. Is this correct?' the older man said, far more intently than he had been speaking before. His voice now had composure and purpose.

'A man was murdered—' Jack started to reply but got cut off.

'I'm agent Charles, a general director of MI5, and you, Detective O'Connor, have the potential to be a pain in my arse. And no, a man died, he was not murdered. There was no evidence, no motive and no suspicious circumstances. Now, as you can probably guess, the man in question is linked to an ongoing investigation, hence my appearance here today. The only reason I am indeed speaking with you now is to ensure that a common detective doesn't become a fly in our much more important ointment. As you can tell, my knowledge of the Catholic Church is one of depth, and I know exactly what an English detective questioning their policy could do to current relations.'

'I don't want to cause trouble, but it is my belief that Father Lopez was killed over something he found out. Now wouldn't the church be just as interested in finding out the truth if I'm right?'

The older MI5 agent looked at the other and laughed, giving the younger cause to copy, albeit less convincingly.

'If you're correct, it would most likely be the church behind it. Your naivety worries me, detective. Which is why I will be keeping a very close eye on you during this investigation.'

Jack realised what the man was implying.

'I'm going to the Vatican? I'm going to investigate it?'

The older man laughed once more, even harder this time. 'I would definitely not be letting you go to the Vatican whether I had the authority to or not. No, you can go to Florence and visit the small parish just outside the city where Father Lopez was working. You can visit his home and his office, and that is it.'

The man reached into a leather holdall type bag that Jack hadn't noticed until then and pulled some paperwork from it. Placing it on the desk, he slid it precisely across.

'These are your flight tickets. You leave in two hours and you have exactly forty-eight hours to investigate. Any longer than that, you risk damaging more than you realise. You requested that a pathologist accompany you, but the body will be cremated today, so that would be fruitless. Just don't annoy too many people – our relations are delicate and worth much more than one man's life and I am not talking about Father Lopez's, Jack, if you understand my meaning.'

FLICK FLICK

Jack stood in a hallway that smelt of antibacterial cleaning fluids and was warmer than was comfortable his usual day clothes. Nurses came and went up the corridor, scanning the ward doors and unlocking them with their key fobs. He had an hour to kill before he needed to be at Bristol airport and this was the only place he could think to come.

A nurse tapped him on the shoulder. 'Are you looking for someone?' she asked, clutching a file in her arms.

'Yes, a Cameron Dayley,' Jack replied a little nervously – he hadn't been told so, but that didn't mean that the boy hadn't died in the last couple of hours.

The nurse smiled. 'I thought so. You're a police officer, aren't you? Were you the one that found him?'

Jack smiled weakly, hoping not to receive any praise. 'Well, I was one of the officers on the scene, yes.'

The nurse's grin grew. 'Just taking his file back through now, would you like to follow me?'

She led Jack into the heart of the ward. The rooms seemed to peel away in all directions except one. One room jumped out at Jack; it was this specific room that had given him some difficulty with crossing the threshold initially: the room where his daughter had been when she had to have emergency surgery on her appendix, removing it before it had burst.

*

'It won't hurt, will it, Daddy?' she had asked Jack while he sat on the side of the bed.

Jack laughed a fake laugh to settle her. 'Not for you, no. The only thing that will be hurting is the poor surgeon's feet – they stand up doing surgeries all day long. You, darling, all you need to do is fall asleep and wake up. You see that thing in your hand?'

Felicity gently held her left hand up. 'This?'

Jack cupped her hand. 'Yeah, you see how the tube goes into your body? Well, that is where the doctor puts his medicine to help you go to sleep, and then before you know it, you'll wake up.'

The little girl writhed with the pain deep in her gut, her face screwed tightly, punishing Jack too. All he wanted was to take this from her, give it to himself if he could.

A tear ran down Jack's face, he wiped it away before she had a chance to notice. 'And when you wake up, all this silly pain will be gone. And then when I know you're ok, Mummy here,' he pointed over his shoulder. Jessica stepped closer and ran her fingers over his shoulder and down his chest and put her hand on top of theirs.

'She will sit here with you while I go and get you a Happy Meal. Now how does that sound?'

Felicity managed a smile. 'And ice-cream?' she asked, pulling another strained face under the pain.

Jack leant in close. 'Nope, two ice-creams, for being so brave. But don't tell the doctor. I might be a policeman, but they will still tell me off.'

A woman dressed all in scrubs came in, followed by a porter. 'Right, little one, the surgeon is all ready for you now.'

Felicity turned to Jack. 'I won't tell them about the ice-cream.' And she mimed zipping her mouth.

Jack turned over her hand, so the palm faced the ceiling. 'I'll see you in just a few minutes, my little Flick Flick,' he said, flicking the palm of her hand twice, something he did every night he was able to before she went to sleep.

*

The present-day Jack watched the doors from the outside now just as intently as he watched from the inside then. He still remembered the relief of seeing her being brought back through, the half-smile on her face that he had known was for the ice-cream more than him. Not that he had minded.

'He's just in here,' the nurse said, pointing through a window.

Jack looked above the door and noticed that this particular part of the ward had ICU written in bold letters.

The nurse left Jack outside the room and entered to join the two people beside the bed who were currently speaking to a doctor. The mother cried on her husband's shoulder, who now shook the doctor's hand and comforted his grieving wife.

'Poor bastards. I couldn't wish that upon anyone. Well, at least they got their son back I guess,' Jack thought before looking down at the boy, whose skin was still pale and barely managed to cover the bones attempting to protrude from beneath. *'What's left of the poor bugger?'*

On leaving the room, the doctor spotted the detective. 'Ah, you are the policeman who found this young chap, are you not?'

The man was of Indian descent and sounded like it too. His strong accent only aiding him to sound more comforting and wise. A ridiculous stereotype, Jack knew, but he also knew how these little things had a big impact on worried parents and patients.

'How did you know?' Jack asked, a little surprised at the man's accurate guess.

The doctor took out his phone, spent a moment flicking through pages on it and then held it up. 'You have just made the news, detective, look.'

Jack saw an old photo of himself, looking at least twenty years younger, above the headline, *Bristol's unlikely hero again.*

'You have got to be kidding me, I let that Timmins guy take all the praise, why can't they just leave me out of it?' Jack had asked accidentally aloud, not really expecting a reply.

'Well, if he survives, I wouldn't be surprised if they make a movie out of it,' the doctor replied, holstering his phone back onto his belt.

'*If?*' Jack asked, his momentary anger instantly diminished.

'He is a very poorly boy, how he survived so long is anyone's guess. He is currently suffering from hyperthermia, pneumonia due to the fluid and fumes in his longs, septic shock from his sores being left in feces. His immune system has had a catastrophic failure. The next forty-eight hours are crucial, I am afraid to say.'

Jack nodded that he understood and stared in at the helpless boy, his hand being clutched tightly by his mother. She looked as though the tighter she held on to him, the less chance there was of him fading away.

'If only that worked'.

Jack removed the tickets from his pocket and looked at them.

The next forty-eight hours are crucial. You don't say?'

Jack looked from the flight number to the victim in the bed.

'Is this really a happy coincidence? I find a little boy who was moments away from death and then all of a sudden I'm allowed to investigate whatever the hell I want, in another country.'

Jack shook his head. '*There can't be a link between this*

paedophile and Father Lopez and Felicity and Jessica's murders, there just can't be.'

Jack's wandering mind may have been why he hadn't noticed the father of the child cross the room and open the door right in front of him.

By the time that Jack had realised the man was approaching, it was too late to formulate an appropriate reaction to meeting him. But this wasn't a problem, the man had an agenda of his own and he was ready to attack with it.

'Look at my boy, he's nearly dead because you took too fucking long searching form him! All you had to do was your job. If you don't make sure this scum gets what's coming to him, I'll do it myself, do you understand me? You lot of fucking incompetent.' The man stood close to Jack, trying with all his might to intimidate the detective with his body's pose.

It wasn't the father's fault, how was he to know you can't scare a man who has lost everything he could ever care about? It was having nothing to live for that gave Jack the freedom to act however he damn well pleased in nearly all situations. If Jack's BPD had a switch, this disgruntled parent had just found it and inadvertently turned it too high.

Jack knew that the hardest part of his Borderline Personality Disorder for others to comprehend was often the rage. Not the amount of it, or its ferocity, but how quickly it could emerge. Normal people living within normal perimeters had a natural ebb and flow to their emotions. BPD, however, could come in tidal waves and with no warning. And just like real tidal waves, it could destroy pretty much anything in its path. It was exhausting and nearly all the time out of order and unhelpful, but very occasionally it could be just the thing the situation called for.

Jack grabbed the man, who was at least six inches taller than himself, by the shoulders and shoved him back against a plastered wall. It gave under the pressure, leaving it looking like a crushed meringue.

'You take things into your own hands and I'll make sure you go down as well,' Jack said quietly, somehow remaining respectful enough not to disturb the other patients on the ward.

The man struggled a little, but Jack had anticipated it, his BPD now firing on all synapses, predicting everything and reacting accordingly. The detective grabbed the other man's head and slammed it back against the wall, which gave for a second time under the blow.

Jack felt the doctor's hand in the crook of his arm, but he shook it off easily.

'Detective, please,' the doctor begged, 'let him go, please.'

But Jack ignored the reasonable request. 'Now you fucking listen to me, that boy in there doesn't need you wasting any energy on anything other than being a father. You want to shout, you want to punish someone, now, I get that, but what you don't get is—' Jack shoved him back a third time, this one was less hard as it was more for effect and the wind had already left the man's sails and his lungs. '—it's not about you anymore. It's about what that boy needs and nothing else. In that pit where I found him were the bodies of other children. Now, their parents weren't given the opportunity to even see their little ones again, let alone care for them.'

Jack let the man go; he wanted to keep talking at him, tell him how he didn't even deserve to have his son back, how he should have delivered his daughter instead. The scales had tipped as if an ocean had been dropped on one side – a dark ocean full of fear and jealousy.

Jack stumbled back away from Cameron's father, his back hitting the window of the ICU room hard. The doctor grabbed him by the arm again, this time not in restraint but as support, helping him to remain on what now felt like tired legs.

Jack's eyes stared widely. He wanted to smash this man's head in, he wanted to kill him in exchange for his daughter's life. He wished the boy had died too.

That would fucking teach him. Why should he get his child back, why shouldn't he feel the pain I feel?'

And that's where the true nature of his Borderline Personality Disorder would stem from – a child's belligerence at the world not being fair, a belief that the entirety of the universe was against him and it was not just fair. It was always him and no one else had to suffer like he did, no one else was always handed the end of the stick covered in shit, no, it was always him. The world was systematically stacking the odds against him, making sure that his hand was always the losing one and giving up was the only option in a life that was fated to be fixed.

Jack pulled himself back into the room. He saw the man he had pinned moments before standing still, in shock. The detective's eyes darted around, not sure where to look. He caught sight of the doctor's eyes staring transfixed at him and then the plane ticket on the floor – he must have dropped it without realising.

Jack picked up the paper and tucked it away in his pocket. 'I'm sorry.'

The man nodded and ran a hand over the back of his head before inspecting it cautiously for blood.

The rage was real, and Jack needed help, he could feel that demon of him, the one that lay dormant most of the time, stirring from within its nest. It could smell blood and it wanted to feed on something— no, on some*one*.

'Doctor?' Jack said tentatively.

It had taken him ten minutes to convince the doctor that he needed the diazepam urgently, because an articulate person who doesn't seem in a great deal of pain on the outside never really does appear to be in crisis, but the doctor was not a negligent one. He could tell that Jack was suffering and that the detective knew exactly what he was talking about when it came to dosage and side effects. Jack even braved saying that he definitely wasn't addicted to the stuff, which he knew was risky as that's exactly what an addict would say.

With ten milligrams in his system, Detective O'Connor finally managed to corral the BPD away into a dark corner of his mind. He got a taxi to swing by the houseboat only to pick up his passport and a handful of medication before delivering him to Bristol airport. The fee had made him swear out loud, but it wasn't like he had a choice anyway – his Ford Capri had been in the garage for five days as hunting for spares had been trickier than either Jack or the mechanic had anticipated. It was his own fault, Jack conceded, because he told the man that he had only wanted genuine production parts, no reproductions whatsoever. It hadn't even been a conscious thought, it left Jack's mouth before he had even realised what he was saying, so he figured he must have developed feelings towards the old girl subconsciously because, up until this point, he hadn't given a flying toss what was original and what wasn't.

The medication turned the departure lounge into quite a serene experience for Jack, so much so he had almost forgotten to contact a friend, one who he knew was already in Italy.

A quick phone call and Father Vincenzo Camaldo had agreed to help Jack by being his translator – it was, after all, he who had contacted the dead priest in the first place and Jack knew how guilt could confuse the mind. Jack had asked Father Camaldo about some pictures with ancient forms of Aramaic text in them, which was linked to the case of his wife and daughter's death. Father Camaldo had been more than happy to help, contacting an old friend in Italy hoping for a translation or some information that could finally give Jack a concrete lead. Within days of receiving this request, Father Lopez was dead, by all accounts no foul play involved – a common heart attack – but the timing was too convenient for the detective. Something just wasn't sitting quite flush.

Jack hoped that his intentions were noble and that he had only decided to investigate the death of Father Lopez as an act of friendship, but the fact that within days of receiving Jack's photos the man was dead kept intriguing his mind back to his own devastation, actually giving him a macabre sense of hope.

What if this was a link to who killed Felicity and Jessica? What if he actually found some cause to why they were taken from me?'

These thoughts excited and frightened him. If it was some strange Catholic occult thing, well, there would be no way of bringing someone to justice, and if it wasn't a link, well, then he was back to square one, back to chasing his own tail, trying with all his might not to give up on a world that had given up on him or give in to a handful of too many pills.

The flight was busy and hot – the two things that without those drugs would definitely have seen the beast in Jack awaken again. But the diazepam had been strong, sending him into what he liked to call his walking dead status. It was a strange sensation, one that he had always found hard to describe. He had never smoked cannabis before, but the way that people looked while doing so seemed to epitomise how the medication made him feel. It numbed him, sound became less harsh, movements became slow and clumsy, but in a comforting, enveloped way.

RATS

He felt childlike, not in the usual way, where his BPD used to take away that adult confidence, but physically. He was small and puny, and weaker even still than his stature would suggest. It was so dark, pitch black, and cold. The air was cold on his skin; he tried to cover himself with the little fabric he had, pulling his top down over his knees.

If only there had been the headroom to stand up, to move, or walk, he might be able to warm up. No, if he just concentrated on being quiet, if he wrapped his arms around his torso where his heart and lungs were, they'll move him on soon. They had said this was only a pit stop; they told me not to get comfortable, probably thinking they were funny. Just stay alive a bit longer. The next place can't be so cold, nowhere can be this cold.'

He rocked, breathing hard, keeping his mind busy with thinking about the easiest way to keep his body from shutting down. It wasn't easy; he wanted to give in, he wanted to sleep and slip away. The rats crawling over his feet didn't bother him anymore, the idea of them biting him had been the main concern once upon a time, but not for some years now. He had been in a few places where the rats had freedom to come and go, not once had they tried to nibble on him like in movies or nightmares. They would push under him, burrowing into his warmth or scavenging for crumbs he might be unwittingly concealing.

'Just rock and stay warm, they'll move me soon.'

He wasn't sure why his location had been changed with such haste, but there was a frantic air amongst his keepers. They had barely remembered to bag his head. It had been a while since his face had felt the full scope of sunlight, but that single moment had rekindled something that had died a long time ago, the minutest thought of escape.

SHOWER STOPPED RUNNING

'Sir, the captain has initiated the seatbelt sign.'

Jack woke with a start. He had been dreaming that he was a captive in a cave. He rubbed his eyes and pulled himself up, taking a couple of moments to realise where he was. The lights of the cabin were on and their illumination was hard on the retinas.

The small airport was clean and quiet. It looked painfully similar to Bristol's, only it wasn't rammed with people. Jack hated spaces that weren't built properly for the capacity they were trying to accommodate, but this place was not that. No one dithered in his way, the toilet had more than enough cubicles and not once did he have to apologise for his small suitcase being a trip hazard. He exited the airport and lifted his head up into the brilliant sunshine. For a second it brought his strange dream from the plane back and a surge of hope for escape ran through him.

'This job is getting to me,' he thought as he searched the road for a taxi. But instead of the friendly face of an Italian taxi driver, he was met by the smarmy one of Agent Casper Collingwood.

'Don't get too used to the weather, less than two days

and I'll be making sure you're on a flight back home. The car's over there, get in.' The smartly dressed man thumbed towards a conspicuous black Mercedes, the type that only government agents actually drove.

'Nice ride. Oh, grab my bags for me, will you?' Jack said to the agent and pointed at two red suitcases, neither belonging to him.

Jack bet on the plump lady that the suitcases belonged to being one that you wouldn't like to mess with, and he was right.

As he opened the black car door, he turned to see Casper being hit with quite a substantial handbag.

Jack smiled smugly as the flustered agent climbed into the driver's seat.

'You're not funny, Jack, you being here is not a jolly,' the agent said, checking the mirror to examine if his slick hair was still in place.

Jack laughed. 'Ok, sorry, I couldn't resist. If you weren't mollycoddling me, it wouldn't have happened. What's with the shadowing anyway?'

Agent Collingwood began driving. 'Like my superior said, we already have vested interests that this may interfere with, so like it or not, I'm your handler.' He handed Jack more plane tickets. 'This is your outgoing flight, I'm here to make sure you are first in line, waiting to board.'

Jack looked at the time on it; true to his word, Agent Charles had given him exactly forty-eight hours.

'Now, you do not contact anyone at the Vatican, you do not question the police, you do not stray from Florence, and you most certainly do not go to the Italian press stating that there has been a murder. Am I understood?'

Jack looked out through the window, the architecture was bleak, again reminding him of home. Large, derelict buildings skirted with dark grey roads looked out of place here, though. Probably owing to their backdrop being vast green and beautiful mountains. It wasn't what he had imagined, it felt like two worlds colliding, the dark shadow of the human race contrasted against the beauty of true nature.

'Understood,' he replied calmly, he didn't want an argument. Surprising himself, he wanted to enjoy the journey. It was short, but Jack was surprised at how quickly the scenery changed. He wasn't used to the way the slums seemed to immediately give way to the beautiful, almost cinematographic city centre of Florence. The car juddered over narrow cobbled streets, the tall buildings now eclipsing most of the beautiful blue sky.

'This is your hotel, now get out and don't cause any trouble, please, Jack. I mean it.'

Jack shut the door on the agent and turned to see his lodgings. It was nice, not bad considering he thought he would have to be sorting out his own place to stay. Jack had just walked into the lobby when his phone vibrated in his jacket pocket.

He hadn't even realised that it would work outside of England and the number on it was odd, definitely not like any he had received calls from before. He answered hesitantly.

'Hello?'

'Hello, Detective O'Connor,' a man replied, speaking very good English but with a tuneful Italian accent laid over the top.

'Speaking,' Jack replied, stopping in the middle of the small lobby.

'Ah, Detective O'Connor, I am the concierge here at Portrait Firenze, I would just like to let you know that your room is available for you to check in.'

Jack looked over to counter labeled concierge. 'Ok, great, I have just walked in.'

The man on the phone went quiet. 'Really? I cannot see you, are you inside the building?'

Jack looked around, there was only a woman sitting

behind the reception desk to be seen.

'Yes, I'm stood about four feet from the door. Where are you?'

'I am looking at the door, sir, and I cannot see you. Are you sure that you are in the correct hotel?'

'Hang on.' Jack held the phone to his chest and walked outside to look up at the small plastic sign. 'No, this says Il Albergo.'

The man came back quickly, 'Ah yes, easy mistake. We are located a few hundred yards south. If you follow the road down, or I can send someone to fetch you if you have much luggage?'

Jack felt uneasy, he was sure Casper wouldn't have gotten the wrong hotel unless this was a payback prank for the airport.

'No, that's fine. I'll be there shortly, I guess.'

The man had been correct – it was only a few hundred yards down the road – but what Jack had not been expecting was the oversized foyer with a real marble floor and attentive staff.

'You do travel light, detective. Come this way and I will show you to your suite,' the man said, taking Jack's small red suitcase from him.

Jack didn't say anything; it appeared he didn't have to – he'd rolled into the type of establishment where you didn't have to do anything for yourself at all. He passed dry cleaning being delivered to a room, doors that had names rather than numbers and even a guest walking a poodle.

Jack was uncomfortable, not because of the five-star surroundings, but because he knew that there was no way anyone would have paid for this for him – especially not the secret service. They would have stuck him in a hostel if they could.

'Please enjoy the mini bar, free of charge, and the spa is on the lower ground level. The telephone has connection straight to the front desk, and room service is twenty-four hours. Is there anything else I can help you with?' the concierge said happily, his smile looking more real than any other Jack had seen on any hotel staffs' faces.

Jack, who was still on the back foot, managed to correct himself enough to start searching his pocket for money as a tip. It would have to be English pounds, but surely that was better than nothing.

'Don't worry, it is my pleasure, detective,' the concierge told him quickly before handing Jack his key card, bowing slightly and leaving the detective at his door.

Jack slid the plastic in, waited for the green light, and opened the door with his toes.

The large suite was cavernous, making the bed look a usual proportion until Jack approached it and realised it must have been at least six foot wide. A separate room with an ornate table in the middle and writing desk at one window led to a balcony and also the bathroom.

It was then that Jack noticed a slight echoed sound that shouldn't be there – the running of water through what sounded like a very expensive power shower.

'I knew this room wasn't meant to be for me.'

Even though he suspected it to be an honest mix up of rooms, his natural 'You're not getting the jump on me,' reactions kicked in, causing him to grab the nearest object for a weapon.

The shower stopped running and he gripped his makeshift baton tighter.

Steam billowed out from the space under the door, the ornate gold handle turned and the door opened. There was so much steam a swell of backdraft obscured the identity of the hotel guest.

'What are you going to do with that? Whip me to death? Actually, saying that, would be a rather nice way to go.'

BELL

Jack's heartrate took a sudden and welcome fall, like a marble off of a table, with a hard thump at the end.

'Tanya, what the—! Seriously, you, I mean—' Jack's brain wasn't even trying to formulate a sentence, it just wanted to berate her for the sake of it.

Tanya walked into the room wearing a white robe, her small frame barely keeping it from dragging along the polished marble. She dried her hair and walked past the stunned detective as if he had been there the entire time.

'Pull yourself together, like I was going to let you go on a holiday without me?'

Jack looked at his hand, a little shocked to see that he had by the throat what appeared to be a swan.

There was a matching one on the bed – it was an intricately folded towel. Tanya pushed it aside before jumping on and deliberately pulled the gown up to reveal as much leg as possible. 'Have you seen the size of this bed? Imagine how many we could fit in it.' She rolled around a little, playfully kicking her legs in the air.

Tanya was the deadliest person that Jack had ever come across, arguably his best friend, and most definitely the biggest pain in his neck. By the age of twenty-one she had killed more people than Jack could imagine and as hard as he tried, he just couldn't get any evidence on her. He had wondered hundreds of times whether he would have tried harder had all of her victims not been paedophiles. But he also had the advantage of knowing that even if they hadn't been complete scum, he probably would never have found enough evidence anyway. She was a genius with an IQ that could barely be registered and the temperament of a lioness. Jack knew that he intrigued her when everyone else was convinced she was nothing more than an innocent victim – he alone had worked out the truth. And so the strange, unorthodox friendship was born, whether Jack wanted it or not. It took a while to realise it, but it was easier to roll with Tanya's punches rather than fight them. In her own messed up way, she was always looking out for him, making life a little bit less simple, but always falling down on the side of good when needed. He would never admit it, but he always felt that little bit safer when she was around.

Jack managed to string some coherent words together, 'Seriously? How the fuck did you even know I was here?'

Tanya smiled. 'But you weren't here, you were down the road at that hovel. I paid for this room for you. I thought, after all that happened, you deserved an upgrade. Come on, don't tell me you don't like it.' She flashed her large eyes at him, blinking her eyelash extensions.

The detective looked around. He had to admit it was nice. Then he noticed a felt-covered chaise lounge.

'Ok, fine, it's an amazing room, only I'm sleeping on that,' he pointed at the couch, 'and I haven't got time to argue.'

Jack headed to the door.

'Wait, I'm coming,' Tanya said, jumping up from the bed.

Jack checked his watch; he couldn't think of a decent enough excuse to leave her behind. 'Fine, ten minutes, down in the lobby.'

The taxi journey away from the city was just as fractured, the hills full with rows upon rows of trees and vines, punctured with high rises adorned in graffiti and kids playing in their small groups in worn out clothes. Leaving the city's limits, the road widened and stretched its legs in front of them, heading towards hills far in the distance.

The car pulled into a small village courtyard. All the surrounding buildings looked to have been built centered around the church. It was small but picturesque with white walls and a single bell tower. A couple of children chased a dog, almost tripping up a man who approached the car. He shouted something in Italian at the two playing and Jack could tell it had been playful as the boys laughed and continued with their game.

'Detective O'Connor, my friend, it is good to see you. How was your journey? Wait, Miss Red is with you too. How splendid. Please, come in, let us escape the midday sun.'

The priest Father Vincenzo Camaldo who Jack had somehow acquired as a friend greeted him with his usual kiss on each cheek and, just as before, the detective returned them uncomfortably. Tanya, however, looked just as at home as ever with the European custom. Jack often wondered how he managed to find himself in the company of some unexpected characters and wondered even more often why on earth they wanted to be friends with him.

Tanya was so at ease that she even spoke in Italian to him.

'Come stai, Signor?'

'Bene, grazie, e tu?' the father replied, giving her a second hug.

'Yes, yes, aren't we all clever speaking Italian,' Jack said sarcastically, even though he believed it to be true.

The priest smiled his large smile. 'Maybe we should speak in English – I have even picked up some real

Bristolian in my time. Isn't that right, my mucker?'

The localism sounded spectacular to the detective in the broad Italian accent and he couldn't help but laugh.

'Ok, ok, you can speak some Italian, just don't leave me out of the loop. Is this where Father Lopez worked?' Jack asked as they entered the small church.

It had been well-loved, all of the pews looking original but kept better than most household furniture. The small, colorless windows lit the room well, showing why it was better that it hadn't been made from stained glass. The cool room echoed just as churches should and the air was actually cold on the skin compared to that of the open landscape outside.

Jack rubbed his forearms and his detective mode kicked in; he started soaking in everything around him, letting his senses absorb.

'This indeed was the church of his parish. His time was spent between here and a shared church office on the edge of Florence. I have not managed to arrange access so far, but I'm sure it wouldn't be a problem to attend this afternoon. They are aware how pressed for time we are.'

Jack nodded as he walked around the sides of the building. It really was beautiful, he could quite easily spend his working day in here if he brought a jumper with him and if they provided something else to read other than the New Testament.

Suddenly, a tremendous noise rang out through the building. All three of them darted their eyes around for a second, Jack a moment longer than the other two, even once the realisation of it being a bell had set in. It had been sensory overload on his ears and when he was deprived of one sense, Jack often overcompensated with the others. He was overly paranoid, and he knew that, but what he also knew was that it was exactly this anxiety that had saved his life several times.

MUST NOT GO

'It is ok, detective, it will only be a local in mourning, ringing the bell for Father Lopez. It was, after all, his funeral today.'

The priest led them through to a room in the back where the long ropes hung, hidden away in the bell tower.

A young woman, early twenties at most, Jack concluded, pulled down on a long rope, the bottom half covered in worn red material. Her eyes fixed on it, following it as it rushed up smoothly between her hands, the action as solemn as the sound.

'Hello? Hello?' Jack called to her, his voice easily drowned out by the echoes pushing down on them and bouncing around the tall space.

'Hell—' he started to try again but was cut off by Tanya taking matters into her own hands.

She had raised her hands to her lips, placed her fingers on either side of her mouth and whistled louder than a steam train, almost matching the bell for ferocity.

The woman was startled, her hands slipping from the rope.

Jack recognised some terror on her face and to his surprise, it looked as if it was at the sight of Father

Camaldo rather than the startling noise.

'Hi, I'm police, is it ok to speak?' Jack asked, unsure of how the average villager would react to English.

The woman looked at the priest momentarily and then back at Jack. Her large brown eyes appeared to be searching for something.

'An exit, probably,' Jack thought.

'It's ok, you're not in trouble. Were you ringing the bell for Father Lopez?'

The woman looked at the man of the church again for a slightly longer period before answering,

'Yes, for respect. He was a friend.'

Jack nodded and kept his palms and arms open like he was taught in his crisis prevention training. This was called a non-threatening stance, which Jack had realised only really worked on non-guilty people. The real criminals didn't give a toss how you stood – they were going to either run from you or stab you anyway.

The woman again looked to the man on Jack's left, almost as if waiting for his permission to speak.

'Hey, over here,' the detective said gently. 'It's ok, talk to me. Father Camaldo here was a friend of Father Lopez, too. We're all friends here, I'm just trying to find out what happened to him. Understand? Understand what I'm telling you?'

These words did the trick – as Jack had suspected, he now had her full attention.

'You know he was killed?' she asked, a small glimmer of hope shining through her now.

Jack smiled, it had been a lucky guess that she might be on their side, as it were, but it was easy to take pot shots when you didn't have anything to lose. 'I don't know he was killed, but that's what I am here to find out.'

The young woman's demeanour stiffened again. She was now examining the detective just as he would a corpse, wondering if it was as harmless as it seemed or if it was going to turn on her like a zombie.

'Why would an English policeman be here? You don't care what happens here.'

Jack dropped his hands — no point trying to do anything by the book here, she was clearly too worldly for any of that nonsense anyway. It was easy to spot people who had been educated by the streets, just difficult to convince them to trust you. Because why the hell should they? No one ever did anything for them without wanting something in return.

'I was telling you the truth when I said Father Camaldo here was a friend of your priest. And I'm here as a friend, too. I'm a detective back in England — mostly murder cases. I thought I might be able to do some good here. But I will need the help of people who knew him.'

'Come on, BPD, do your stuff, let's work our way in.'

The young woman seemed to consider this, then turned her attention to Tanya. 'You are friend, too?'

Tanya smiled, walked over to the girl and held out a hand. 'I'm Tanya. We're just here to help. Shall we sit down and talk and we can ask you some questions? I think Father Vincenzo was about to make some coffee for us all.'

The girl shook her head. 'No, not coffee, Father Lopez said caffeine was not good for you. He would only drink red wine while speaking with the people here.'

'Good work, Tan.' Jack felt at ease now. A woman's touch normally did work better than a man's in nearly every circumstance.

'Course he did,' Jack said under his breath.

The priest clapped his hands together. 'I believe I have seen one of his favourites in his office. Why don't you three take a seat somewhere and I will fetch it. We can drink in his honour.'

The girl led them back through to the main body of the church. Jack noticed her small frame, it was very similar to that of Tanya's and her height only beat the redhead by an inch or two, but even Tanya's long hair couldn't compete with that of the waist length of the other woman. It wasn't just long but slightly unkempt, not dirty, but not cut symmetrically either. Jack was used to the city women, the ones who waxed their eyebrows off only to then draw them back on again. Every strand meticulously placed and extended, probably with someone else's hair like this girl's. Maybe he was spending too much time in Bristol, perhaps this was what real people looked like, maybe he was too quick to judge, holding people up against the wrong standards.

Father Camaldo returned and, to Jack's surprise, he clasped, along with the bottle of red wine, four pristine wine glasses.

The priest poured them all a generous helping and held his glass up. 'To a good man, who shall be missed.' His voice sounded warm and forgiving, as if he was telling the heavens, *it's ok, you can have him now.*

The detective took a sip, ready to fake a smile at the sharp, bitter taste, but again he was pleasantly fooled. The wine was actually something he could tolerate, or maybe even enjoy. Serve it with a meal full of meat and maybe he would turn connoisseur.

'So, what's your name?' Tanya asked the other girl.

'My name is,' she sipped from her glass, 'Sophia Florenzi.'

She didn't look at any of them; her guard was such that Jack wondered if that even was her real name. He had felt similar energies before on people. The first that sprung to mind were prostitutes. They were always too nervous to give up any information because of what their pimps might do to them, always fearful of some sort of repercussion. Sophia didn't feel exactly the same, but similar enough for the detective to feel concerned for her and not about her.

'So, how did you know Father Lopez?' Jack asked, matching her for mouthfuls of wine.

'I owe my life to Father Lopez, he was an angel to me,

he saved me and brought me here. He found me foster parents who love me. I have a home, a job and a life because of him,' she answered flatly, saying it like it was a simple matter of facts and keeping emotion somewhat out of sight.

Father Camaldo placed down his drink and took the girl's hands, cupping them in his own. 'This is a hard time for you, my child. Keep your faith, it will help you through.'

The girl pulled away. She wasn't angry, but Jack could tell that her faith wasn't as strong as she wanted it to be.

'Do you know of anyone who would want to hurt him? Did he have any enemies? We've been told that he died of a heart attack, does that seem likely?' Jack asked, now gaining the girl's full attention, the eagerness in his voice rubbing off on her.

She laughed. 'He ran two marathons last month for charity. What do you think, detective? Does that sound like a weak-hearted man to you? As for enemies, I can think of only one. The Church.'

Jack looked at his friends, hoping that it might make sense to them. He downed his drink – he thought he might be needing it. He wiped a small drop from the corner of his mouth, his hand had been too eager for his mouth.

'What do you mean? He was a priest. He worked for the Church.'

Sophia rolled her eyes. 'He was a priest, yes, but the Vatican, that is a different story. He taught me how all of its people were power mad. How much money went into those walls and never came back out. It is as corrupt as the Italian government, maybe more.' She too downed her drink. Her eyes flicked towards the bottle fleetingly, but she clearly thought better of it and tucked her glass under the pew on the floor.

The detective looked at his Catholic companion for confirmation. His eyebrows raised in amusement at her statement.

'This is true of some people, certainly. Father Lopez and I were always good friends because we were the same – both outsiders. We did not, how would you say in English? Conform?'

Jack nodded to confirm that his friend had indeed used the correct word in English, the most perfect word, probably.

The detective rubbed the stubble on his chin. 'Are you saying that you think the Church killed him?'

Sophia nodded and stared, her eyes fixed on a wooden cross up high on the wall. Her hair hid most of her face, it was thick and had endless layers. She tucked it over her ear and Jack saw emotion for the first time. A single perfect tear ran over the olive skin on her cheek, but she quickly ruined it with a wipe of her hand.

The detective sat back on his chair and pushed his fingers into his closed eyes to massage them awake some more, the alcohol wasn't helping with his tiredness.

'Maybe it is a cover-up. Maybe they didn't want him to find out what was in those pictures I sent him. It had the insignia of the pope on it; there must be records of what they were doing investigating it, somewhere, surely.'

The young Italian woman became agitated, sitting close to the edge of her seat. 'It was you? You sent him those pictures? He mentioned them, told me the investigation had been deleted.'

Jack nodded, but he felt uneasy. Who was this girl? Why would a priest confide in someone such important information unless he trusted them completely? She was hard, like dry bark, protecting her core, protecting whatever she was keeping inside. Maybe the priest knew what this young woman was working so hard to keep safe inside.

'He did say something else, something that might help.' She looked uneasy; she was battling with betraying the trust of her deceased friend. 'He thought it might be connected to something else he was investigating.' She hurriedly added to the end of the sentence, 'But he never told what that was. He didn't like telling too much, he thought it might be dangerous. I guess he was correct.'

She lowered her head, hands gripping the church bench, arms straight and tight, she looked like she wanted to run away.

Jack contemplated her words. 'An investigation stretching from England to Italy. I guess that's feasible. He never told you what this could have been about?'

The girl shook her head and took a large intake of air.

'We'll need to try to access his computer and files,' Tanya said, addressing it at Jack before turning to Sophia. 'Did he keep any of that here?'

Sophia shook her head. 'I don't think so, I believe he had an office where he would do all of his work.'

Jack chewed the inside of his cheek *Well, there certainly is something going on here, what it is, I can't even begin to guess at this point. What the hell have Felicity and Jessica got to do with this place, if they even do?'*

Jack continued to just ruminate for a moment, aware that the others were waiting for him to decide what to do, but he wasn't in the mood to be rushing into anything.

'Right, well, let's search around here, see what we can find, and then make our way to this office.'

'Here, this is my number,' Tanya said to the other woman, handing her a card. 'If you think of anything or just want to talk, you can call anytime.'

Father Camaldo raised a hand, like a schoolboy in class. 'Just one question, if you wouldn't mind. Why did you not attend the funeral this morning?'

Sophia regained some of the anger and fight that they had seen previously. 'Because we were ordered not to. A cardinal came here and told us that we must not go. You must understand, the people here are not brave, this is a quiet village and that is how they would like to keep it. Nobody here wants any trouble.'

THEY'RE DEMONS

'Now that is interesting,' Jack said.

THE EDUCATION OF THE VIRGIN

It was obvious to Jack that Father Lopez had lived a simple life in this village, his bedroom was bare except for the odd painting and small wardrobe. Thin sheets lay on a hard bed with a single pillow, no luxury items like cushions or throws, not much sign of the hidden wealth that Sophia had described the Vatican hoarded.

'The man couldn't have spent less on himself if he tried,' the detective said to himself as he looked around, feeling less hopeful of finding anything by the second.

Jack did see one interesting thing, a carved wooden wall-hanging plaque, shaped like the traditional church window, with two symmetrical doors closed on its front. He opened them. It was deeper than it had looked previously, with a wooden figure standing inside. It was delicately painted and was clearly very old, all of the images desperately trying to shine through a layer of thick, built up grime. He closed it back up and continued searching.

A painting beside the door caught his eyes. He recognised it immediately. It was a copy of a painting he had once seen in the Bristol museum. He even remembered its name – in truth, he only remembered the painting because of its name.

*

Jessica had been heavily pregnant and Jack had managed to wrangle a day off work. They had spent the morning in Clifton village when Jessica had decided that the Bristol museum would be the best source of entertainment. Jack had tried to convince her that the walk alone would take too much energy, describing it as a mile long waddle, but as always, she had known best. Jack had never been able to use his BPD to manipulate her like he had others.

There was a Banksy exhibition and, being the type of woman she was, she knew one of the various managers there, meaning a well-justified queue jump. The lower levels, given over to the street artist, were busy, each person vying for that perfect angle from which to take a picture. Jack's natural instincts were to go and hide in the toilets, but he stuck it out for as long as he could. His eyes had become a hard stare, looking at everyone around him as a possible threat to his mental health now. It was exactly the sort of situation that could aggravate him. It wasn't because he didn't like people – or art, for that matter – it was just this hustle and bustle, everyone becoming selfishly fixated on their own agenda that was stressful to him.

'Go upstairs and find a nice quiet spot to relax,' Jessica had whispered in his ear.

Jack returned a weak smile. 'I'm fine.'

'There's only a couple more that I want to see and I'll meet you up there.' She kissed him on the neck and pushed him away. 'Go on, before it gets too much.'

Jack had fallen in love with her all over again at that moment. She had recognised him so truly, picked up on his anxiety and showed compassion. She didn't care that what was going on in his head was making it difficult, in that moment she had only cared about him. He knew his needs seemed foolish or even childish to rational people, but still, they were his needs. At this time in his life, he hadn't quite managed to square this with himself, he had not received a diagnosis yet, so sometimes he would kick himself for not being normal. He didn't quite have a handle on what *was* normal, exactly, but there were always signs that he wasn't it.

The cold stone bench meant that Jack sat facing a large oil painting, its gold plaque below reading, 'The education of the virgin.'

Jack thought it was basically an old man telling an incredibly young girl where the penis has to go. The bearded depiction held one index finger up while the little girl recoiled in what looked to Jack as fear – something the artist had captured very well indeed.

Jessica had finished with the street art and found him on the upper level; she sat next to him on the bench.

'Look at that,' he had said to her, giving a judgmental nod towards the canvas. 'A bit sick, isn't it?'

Jessica laughed. 'It's art, it's meant to provoke strong emotions.' She rubbed her bump and took an interest in the imagery.

'But she's a little girl, what, about eleven or twelve looking?'

'And at what age are you going to educate this little virgin?' She raised her eyebrows and pointed to her large stomach.

Jack stared at her, stone-faced. 'I'm not going to, that's your job and she'll be twenty-five at least before she even thinks about having sex.'

Jessica rested her head on Jack's shoulder. 'If you say so, dear, how old were you again when you lost your virginity?'

Jack spat, 'Too fucking young.'

*

This memory had never come back to Jack before. It

had been such a perfect day, yet it had slipped between the bars and disappeared.

'They always do, the ones where nothing goes wrong were just to be expected,' he thought, tracing a finger along the back of the small girl on the picture. It was just a print, so was smooth, but Jack thought about how this would have felt on the original. How much small detail would be revealed with a gentle touch, how much effort and care would have been put into its creation?

But, as he had allowed himself a happy memory, a disgusting one would come to violate it. The black and white, the light must be followed by the dark. His mind slowly moved back through time, but not as far as before. This vision always started the same, he had visited it many times before, an anxious pool gathering in the pit of his stomach. This was yet another nice treat brought on by his borderline personality disorder, the recurring and recycling of negative thoughts. As if reliving them in his head was going to bring a different outcome somehow.

*

'Not now, Jack, you can see I'm busy,' Jessica responded to him nibbling her neck.

He had tried again. 'Come on, the little monster is having a nap. It's been weeks.'

Jessica hit *Save* on her computer and shrugged him away from her. 'I'm busy, ok? This story is huge and I need to focus. I'm doing this for us since what happened. And don't be ridiculous, it hasn't been weeks.'

Jack stood up, hurt and defensive. 'What, since I got passed over promotion you mean? I told you I wasn't ready, that my mental health—' But he didn't get a chance to finish his sentence, Jessica had taken to skeptical laughs at even the mention of mental health.

Jack took one step backward from her, a single tear gathering in his eye. He did his best to stop it from dropping. He didn't say anything.

Jessica opened a new file on the computer and realised that she had been too harsh, but was still unable to look at him. 'This is the biggest story of my career; if I can get this right, we'll be made up for life. You won't need to worry about promotions or providing for us.' Her voice was gentle, she tried to make it playful. 'And it hasn't been weeks. Remember when we stayed in the hotel, after the spa?'

Jack gritted his teeth, nodding. 'Yes, I remember, Jess, it was for my birthday, three months ago.'

She stopped typing, her eyes still resolutely on the work in front of her, refusing to engage with him. 'I'm really busy, Jack. I'll come to bed later, but right now I'm too busy.'

*

Jack wasn't sure if she had refused to look at him that day or whether he was deliberately misremembering the incident to protect himself from the way she most likely looked at him – like a failure, like a man who couldn't even beat depression, barely a man at all. Somewhere deep inside him, he knew this wasn't her opinion of him, but he was projecting his own self-hatred. But when something is hidden that far down, it becomes difficult to see it for what it is.

'Anything?' Tanya's voiced jerked him back into reality, breaking the connection to the past.

The detective took a heavy breath. 'Nothing. If there's anything, it'll be at his office. No doubt that's been gone through by friends of ours at the Church.'

'So, what now?' she asked, taking an interest in the picture that Jack was still looking at.

'We'll have to hope that they missed something.'

GIVING UP

The sun hit Jack's eyes hard as they left the church. A couple more of the town folk had obviously heard about their presence and stood conspicuously around, staring at them. The detective saw Sophia sitting casually on a moped. He'd had one similar one as a kid, but where the panels on his had been blue, Sophia's were simply missing.

She licked across the paper that made up a hand-rolled cigarette and put it to her mouth. Jack approached, squinting and shielding the sun from his eyes, looking incredibly touristy.

'Is there anything else you can tell us? Anything at all, no matter how small, it could really help.'

She flicked open an old-fashioned petrol lighter, burned the tip of her cigarette and took a long drag. Her eyes closed as she enjoyed the deep penetrating smoke before blowing it slowly up into the air. She looked at the burning embers and then threw it to the floor, killing it under her boot.

'Like why you didn't find anything?'

Jack looked at the floor with the extinguished cigarette. 'Yeah, that would be a start.' He pointed at the floor. 'Was that even worth it?'

Sophia smiled. 'I'm giving up, so only one …' She waved her hand to her mouth, showing she didn't know the correct translation.

'Drag?' Jack helped.

'Yes, one drag, I enjoy it every time and then throw away.'

Jack gave a conceding tip of the head, then noticed the metallic instrument in her hand. 'Nice lighter. I used to have a couple when I was younger.'

'You smoke?'

Jack's smile was a clear one of reminiscence. 'When I was young and foolish. I thought it made me look cool. Used to be able to flick it open and light it on my leg in one go.' Jack pointed at the lighter. 'May I?'

Sophia threw him the lighter quickly with no response, a test to see how serious he was. The detective swiftly brushed it down his hip, lifting the lid and stoking the flint in one fluid motion.

The flame jumped into life.

'Hey, look, I've still got it.'

'You didn't find anything because people came before you. They took boxes of things.' Sophia had been less impressed by his trick.

The detective watched the flame. 'Were they from the Church?'

Sophia shrugged. 'Maybe. They were in suits; they didn't speak to anyone. After one hour they had what they wanted and were gone. They looked like you.'

Jack looked at her, confused. 'Like police, you mean?'

Sophia laughed. 'No, English.'

Jack's fingers held the cold metal tight; his fingers ran over something unusual as he thought. It was only slight, but it was there – a heavily fatigued engraving. He flicked it shut and took a closer look. There were markings, making up a symbol. It took a few moments as some lines were worn through but he soon realised why it was jarring to him.

'This symbol here.' Jack turned the lighter to the young woman. 'Do you know what that is? Have you seen this before?'

Jack had been trained many times on body language and no matter how hard Sophia tried to hide it, Jack could see the tension in her.

'Yes, around the church, maybe,' she replied, her eyes avoiding Jack's.

Jack tossed the lighter back to her. 'You know what the symbol is, don't you?'

Sophia caught the metal instrument but she held her hand tightly around it, clearly not wanting to look at it.

'Yes, I do.'

Jack didn't offer any relief from the awkward silence, he watched and waited.

'It was a gift from Father Lopez. From a life he left behind.' She looked over Jack's shoulder.

None of his detective training had taught him how to recognise when someone was not going to give up any more information, no, that had taken years of painstaking experience.

Father Camaldo joined them. 'We have a meeting in Florence in half an hour, detective, I think we must leave now, we do not wish to be late.'

Jack nodded. 'See you again, maybe?' he said to Sophia, more to gauge her reaction than get a valid response.

'If you are lucky.' She threw the lighter back to him. His arms still had some natural reflexes left in them and his hand took it out of mid-air. He looked down at the etched insignia in his hand.

Sophia smiled as she started to remove her helmet from the handlebars.

'Don't you want this?' the detective asked her.

Sophia stamped on the kick start, the engine choking itself into life.

'I'm giving up. We all must start somewhere, don't you think?'

'*Good girl*' Jack thought to himself, '*don't show them where it hurts.*'

LIKE BACTERIA

A chrome bowl slid along the floor, filling the air with sharp scratching noises that echoed off the hard stone walls. It only came to a halt as it collided with his knees. It might have hurt had there not been skin calluses there now. The constant rubbing on cold, hard floors had left thick layers more like that of an animal hide.

The thin beam of light from the open doorway illuminated something pretending to be food in front of him.

'That's dog food.' He was feeling confident enough to turn the meal away as it had only been two days since he had eaten. That was nothing anymore – anything up to a week was easily manageable. Seventeen days had been the longest. His capturers had tried to convince him it had been forty-two days in total, but they hadn't noticed the scratch marks on a windowsill that he had made with a sharp stone he had picked from the mortar. Even the simple task of making a notch on wood had, however, become difficult. Waiting for the sun to come up had started as his only task, but had soon become a chore after day eight. His body had started to shut down after day five, but add on a couple more days and it was the brain that had started to function defectively. Hallucinations of his father had become a common occurrence, even a relief at times. Hearing a voice of comfort, having the company of someone who he knew would try to keep him safe, even if it had been nothing but his childish imagination. This cruel punishment had been his capturers' proof, evidence that he was not human, that there was evil inside keeping him alive now. After day eleven, he had found the trick of pushing a fist into his abdomen. The pressure of something in his gut could almost trick his brain – or at least his body – into thinking he had eaten. He started sleeping on his own clenched hand, the bruising on his stomach was a small price to pay for the pressure he needed in his intestine. The first day back on food, they had given him bread. It was too heavy, the first five attempts at taking a mouthful had made him sick. Instead, he hid the food and soaked it in his daily ration of water. It had taken three days to eat one slice of bread, but the sweet starch was heavenly, like all his previous birthday sweets had come at once.

Some of those early days of being locked away would come back in vivid, colourful memories, the words they used still trying to break him down even further.

'You are a demon, you harbour evil inside you, therefore, you are locked up. We cannot risk the innocent by having you live in the world. You need to let us destroy this evil inside you, banish it from you. You are less than human, and we will continue until you have been saved. You will go to the fires of hell and your soul will spend an eternity in damnation.'

He had been so young back then, so innocent, but even still, there was a fight inside of him, an instinct for survival. They had burned his skin with flames and acid, cut his skin to use the blood in ceremonies, but all he had to do was survive.

His hair was long and matted now, with patches of scalp scratched down to an open wound. They hadn't given him water to wash in months now. He longed for the hot water that they had forced him to stand and wash in, in front of an audience before. This had been a one-off and, at the time, he had never been so scared. A room of at least twenty people, all in masks and hoods, watched in silence as he and two other children were bathed by nuns. Three copper tubs had been sat in the middle of the small stone room. It had felt like a cellar, only it had religious images on banners, hung from the ceiling and adorning the walls. After the cleaning of their bodies, the other children, who had been girls, were led away, taking portions of the congregation with them.

The imagery in his mind became blurry from this point, masks swimming in and out of view, bobbing around above naked adult bodies. This must have been the elixir that they had given him – a drink said to bring him closer to God, to free him of evil. The drink may have taken away some of the pain of that night, but the open wounds he was left with the following days were intense. He could feel that his back had been torn apart and kept finding blood down the backs of his legs. He had been chastised for stains on the tattered sheet in his bed and was lashed, freshly opening the wounds each time. What he wouldn't give for a bed now, he would take a lashing for a bed comfortably.

But it changed, his capturers morphed at the same rate of his body. He had hair now where he hadn't before and he no longer had that look of innocence.

He hit the food away. 'It's dog food, I'm not eating it.'

A man who had been most of his way from the room turned suddenly and walked towards his kneeling body.

'You are an animal, you are not even at the same level as a dog, you are more like bacteria, you don't deserve this food, let alone anything else. But, as for the moment, we intend on keeping you alive.'

The other man, dressed all in black, silhouetted by the half-open door, reached down and picked the bowl up. He grabbed his captive by the hair, wrenching it back so that his head faced the ceiling and poured the bowl into his mouth. He tightened his lips together, the juice running over his face and up his nose, forcing him to snort some of it back and choking. Still, the man's hand would not relinquish its grip and tightened so much so that it was difficult to even turn away now. Eventually, his face moved from the direct spill of the food, the fingers released his matted hair and he coughed, coughed until blood came up while the other man stood laughing.

'What's going on?' a new voice asked, stepping into the doorway, his profile coming into relief.

'Wouldn't eat, so I made it,' the first man replied.

The second adult spoke in a harsh Welsh accent, 'Stop fucking about. We have to move them in the morning; I don't want to be in a car with them covered in shit. If they don't want to eat, fine. Come on, we have a meeting to attend.'

The door shut, leaving him in darkness again. He picked up the bowl and threw it at the exit. He wasn't going to cry, not anymore, instead he turned on to his back, his thin t-shirt giving some protection from the flagstone floor and kicked at the brick wall. If he kept fighting, eventually there would be a way to escape. His trainers, thinning and oversized, pounded the masonry, hoping that there would be some give.

ALMONDS

Jack could hear the pounding, hear the rubber soles on stone, could hear the grunts of energy, could feel the shock of muscles trying to hit their way through something impenetrable. Slam after slam of hope and fury. When his eyes shot open and his fist wildly flew forward, it connected with the car seat in front of him.

His heart thumped in his chest like a sea wave against a cliff edge; not erratic or panicked but rhythmic and determined. The detective's eyes flashed around, taking in his surroundings and processing his situation.

'Jack? Are you ok? You were sleeping and mumbling.'

Jack looked vaguely at Tanya, whose seat he had just hit.

'I was trapped, they were feeding me dog food.'

Tanya laughed. 'Yeah, you said something about dog food. I thought I misheard.'

Jack shook his head. 'They're moving me soon.' He shook his head again, trying to encourage his thoughts to line in to place. 'No, not me, *him*. A young lad.' He rubbed his head. 'Fuck, that felt so real.'

Tanya narrowed her eyes. 'Have you been taking your meds?'

'*Yes*,' Jack replied. He surprised himself at the venom in his response – he was offended. It had felt real and it was an insult to think otherwise, but he couldn't explain why.

He looked back out the window. The narrow streets of Florence were more beautiful than any he had seen before.

'*Bristol should be ashamed of itself,*' he thought as they weaved through the buildings to their destination. A stab of questionable lack of enthusiasm hit him. He was losing his drive with this case. Not that it was a case, no, it was a jolly by all accounts. What was he doing here, chasing ghosts, when back in his home country children were being kidnaped, raped, used as slaves, and here he was, looking for a killer that probably didn't exist?

'*No, Jack, don't do this,*' he spoke clearly and flatly to himself. He knew what was happening, it was his BPD interfering. The truth was, he hadn't taken his medication and it was starting to feel that way. It was sometimes described in old medical papers as being fickle, which is slowly being debunked, but still at times could be seen as accurate. Jack could feel it happening now, the tide of boredom excusing his current situation as being on the wrong trajectory. But in reality, it was the pace at which he wanted things to happen that became boring, which turned into questioning if it was correct. The passion he felt for things, if it wasn't quenched, would turn to look for other targets to aim at. It had taken him many years, but now he knew it needed refocusing, needed to be empowered and harnessed.

'*There's something going on here, Jack, and you know it. And it could be linked to Felicity and Jessica – you might find their killer. Come on, Jack, you can do this.*'

The car stopped outside one of the more modern, yet still beautiful buildings, where a priest, dressed in full garb, greeted them. He stood smiling, hands together in a way that only priests can hold them. He had strawberry blonde hair and a pale complexion, making him stand out even more so in this climate.

He gave Tanya and Father Camaldo a kiss on each cheek, but Jack had a firm handshake ready.

'Detective.' The man gave a respectful nod. 'My name is Father Moon, I will escort you around.'

To Jack's surprise, the short man was English, possibly even a Bristol or West Country accent in there.

'By escort us, you mean show us around, yes? We're not on a school trip here, I don't need anyone to hold my hand.'

The priest laughed at Jack's response. 'Yes, of course, detective. I am only here to assist.'

Jack looked up at the building. 'And where is *here*, exactly?'

Father Moon walked towards the sleek glass doors and held one open. 'Why don't I show you?'

The small party of people walked into a surprisingly cavernous area, straight, sharp-edged walls holding many paintings. It looked incredibly modern, probably emphasized by the age of the surrounding buildings being the furthest thing from contemporary.

'Oh, it's a gallery,' Jack said, walking over to an imposing portrait.

Father Moon stood beside him. 'In part. They also restore newly discovered classical paintings and investigate missing antiquities. Follow me and I'll show you.' He gestured towards a locked doorway.

Jack hadn't realised the amount of security here. It had been so unassuming on the outside, but now he was standing, watching Father Moon place his hand on a scanner to enter another room.

'Wow, that's impressive,' Tanya said, taking a closer look at the recognition plate.

'Well, they have millions of pounds' worth of artefacts in here, not to mention priceless information. It would be a private collector's dream. So there is no expense spared when it comes to security,' the priest sounded proud, like a parent speaking of their child. 'This is one of my posts; I oversee several sites.'

'And it's not like the Church can't afford all of this.'

Father Camaldo gave a stunted snigger at Jack's dig. The detective spoke on, glossing over his friend's laugh to what was essentially his employer, 'So, you knew Father Lopez well, then?'

Father Moon's proud smile evaporated. 'Yes. Yes, I did. He was a very good man. He was incredibly busy, but still had time for the people. I am very proud to call him a friend.'

Jack couldn't put his finger on it, but he couldn't like Father Moon, he could feel a slight sense of unwarranted arrogance. People who had earned their arrogance weren't exactly pleasurable to be around, but there was reasoning behind their exaggerated self-opinion, at least.

'You *were* very proud?' the detective said harshly.

'Indeed. His office was just up here.'

They all followed Father Moon up some stairs to a more recognisable and conventional layout of corridor and doors.

The door to Father Lopez's office was unlocked, his name in gold letters still stuck crisply in place.

The workroom was substantial and segregated by a large arch. The two halves were starkly different, the rear obviously devoted to artwork. But not as Jack expected, it was more like an artist's studio.

Jack quickly decided to save that area till last, if there was going to be any evidence, he assumed it would be at his workstation.

But it was immediately apparent that something was missing.

'Where's his computer?' Jack said angrily, his patience waning with all the pretence.

Father Moon wasn't helping with the detective's mood, his voice was close to patronising, something that Jack would not tolerate, 'Well, of course, we could not leave it here. It would have had sensitive information on it. It would have been taken to our main IT department and stripped. Detective, if any information ended up in the wrongs hands—'

Jack interrupted him, 'Yes, fine. Is there any way I can access the information that would have been taken from it?'

The priest's face told him all he needed to know; Jack wouldn't give him a chance to speak again.

'That's what I thought. It's always cloak and dagger with you lot. Thank you for showing us up here, now if you wouldn't mind, please can my colleagues and I have a look around, by ourselves?'

The priest looked incredibly uncomfortable, but Jack could see that his brain searched and failed for an excuse to remain in the room.

'Yes, certainly. I will wait downstairs for you.'

'You're in a good mood,' Tanya Joked, watching Jack as he poked around the remaining paperwork on the desk.

'I don't trust him. There's going to be nothing here. This is all old newspapers, paperwork on paintings, they've cleared everything of any use. Even the drawers are unlocked and empty,' he said, opening one on the desk and instantly slamming it shut.

'This would not be unusual, detective,' Father Camaldo said, a lack of conviction to his voice. 'They would usually clear any important information, etc. out before letting anyone in – even the local police.'

Jack kicked the desk with the bottom of his shoe, forcing it to slide on the tiled floor a few feet.

'What are you doing, Father? You're an intelligent man, you are caring, you want to help people, yet you're part of an organisation that hides behind walls and separates itself from normal society, thinking it's better than the rest of us. I don't understand it; I don't understand *you*.'

Father Camaldo looked shocked at Jack's frankness – not offended but wounded.

Jack's shoulders and chest began to rise and fall heavily with anger pinned behind frustration. He felt like a wild animal being forced to do tricks, for everyone else's pleasure. He didn't want an answer from the other man, no, what Jack wanted was to grab him and slap some sense into him, beat the bullshit from his mind. Being in this environment was causing him to lose all respect he had for the man.

'It's all bollocks, Father, look.' Jack pointed at a golden cross on the wall. 'Look at the colour of that cross. Your saviour was nailed to wood and look how he gets represented now, in gold.' Jack took the image from the wall and looked at it closely. 'It's hallmarked, it's actual gold.' He threw it down with despair. 'All that glitters is not gold, unless you work for the Church.'

Father Camaldo didn't approach the angered detective and Jack knew why. He was embarrassed, ashamed of what Jack thought he represented, but also regretting dragging the detective here.

Jack rubbed his head and paced around, walking to the back where the makeshift art studio was laid out. Sheets were taped to the floor and a couple of benches set up, holding a variety of paints and brushes. Even the pallet was left in place, different coloured oils built up like layers of sediment.

He leant on one of the workbenches and began breathing heavily, slowly calming his body and, as such, his mind. It was getting hard to focus, hard to look for evidence, hard to even care. A small part of him knew he should apologise for his outburst, but a larger part was determined not to let that happen.

He looked up. There was a portrait, like that of downstairs, but with much more dynamic colours and thick brush strokes.

'Is this Father Lopez?' Jack asked the priest he had just shouted at, his voice much gentler than before.

'Yes, and look.' He approached the detective and the

artwork. 'He has signed it here. It must have been a self-portrait.

The priest in the image was mainly head with some shoulders in view and his hands up in front of his mouth. He was holding white rosary beads to his lips. They stood out vibrantly against the dark outer patches.

'*Explains the mirror,*' Jack thought as he looked next to the painting at his own tired reflection.

'He was a talented painter,' Jack said, a hint of *why didn't he just do that instead* to his voice.

'Yes, indeed, I assume that is why he was placed here – for his love of art. He never kept any of his own artwork. He would always give it away to poor families,' Father Camaldo said, a fondness for his friend apparent in the way he spoke. He saw Jack's confusion.

'He said that they needed something beautiful in their lives, and art was beauty. Also, he would tell them that when they had no money left, that they could sell it for whatever they could. He truly was a good man, detective.'

Jack couldn't deny that; the more that he found out about the man, the more he realised he was on the same side as Father Camaldo, his previous words playing guiltily over in his mind.

On the desk was a carved wooden box. It was small and unassuming and, unlike the rest of the room, it actually looked old.

Jack opened its top and looked inside. It held the rosary beads from the picture and a couple of other ornamental pieces. Jack took a heavy breath and tipped the box from side to side to gauge if the contents were worth examining further, quickly deciding they weren't. Until something caught his attention – not from looking in the box, but by a burning sensation in his nostrils.

'Wow, that stinks.' He took a delicate sniff. 'Smells kind of musty and ...' He took one more breath, slightly heavier, this one burning his eyes. 'Like a weird almond smell.'

'What did you say?' Tanya asked from across the room, her voice sounding urgent. She raced across towards them, grabbing a bag from an empty wastepaper bin.

Her urgency gave Jack's brain the excitement it needed to fire up, work on most cylinders – those that still had life in them.

'*Almonds*,' he repeated, slamming the lid closed on the box and throwing it to Tanya. She opened the bag and caught it directly in it then spun it and tied the top with a tight knot.

PINOCCHIO

Father Moon looked relieved to see them – it was clear that every second he had waited had been agony.

'Did you find anything?' he asked, his eyes wide and welcoming.

Jack responded quickly and in autopilot. 'No, nothing. We are going to head back to our hotel. Sorry to have bothered you.'

'It is no bother. I needed to see Father Camaldo anyway. Father Lopez left this for you. He didn't bequeath any of his belongings, but in his will, it did insist that you received this letter.'

The man handed over a thick envelope. An old-fashioned wax seal had once enclosed it on the rear of the paper, but had been clearly broken.

'Given permission to read the letter, were you?' Tanya Red said sharply.

Father Camaldo took the letter and thanked the other man. 'It is ok,' he reassured Tanya, but she shook her head.

'No, it isn't, it was a dead man's last and only wish and they desecrated it by opening it and reading it. I thought you were supposed to show respect for each other, respect for the dead.' Tanya took a step towards the paler priest, but Jack reached a hand across to stop her.

The detective noticed a new look in the smaller priest's eyes, a fire to them, a heat that hadn't been there before.

'It was Father Lopez that didn't show respect, that seal had the papal symbol on it. He had no right to use it and as a matter of trying to protect our holiness, it was our duty to examine it. In reality, we were well within our rights to keep it and not pass it on as he requested at all.' He bowed to the older priest and walked away, giving Tanya a sideways glance.

Jack laughed. 'Just making friends wherever we go.'

They walked out of the building, the detective, deliberately keeping his voice low and his lip movements minimal, as he could see the priest still watching them while on the phone from inside the building.

'So how do we test for cyanide?'

Tanya stood on her tiptoes next to him and kissed his cheek gently, then whispered, 'This is why you brought me. Leave it to me; I just need to pick up a few bits.' She turned to Father Camaldo. 'Father, would you like to accompany me on a short shopping trip?'

He smiled. 'My dear, it would be my pleasure.'

The two walked away, Tanya linking arms with him. Jack laughed at what onlookers would think.

'Meet me at the hotel in an hour – the one that you booked,' he shouted after them.

Jack looked back into the building. 'Who are you phoning? And what are you planning?' the detective spoke quietly, his comfort zone feeling just as far away as his little canal boat in Bristol. He was trying hard not to miss it.

His thoughts were interrupted by an Italian man. 'You buy a rose, you have a wife?'

Jack turned to look at him. 'No, thank you. I don't have any money.'

The man persisted, 'No special lady? How about a special man, come on, ten euros to you for two? Two beautiful roses, you can have two beautiful women.'

Jack pushed the roses away from him; the man had confidently thrust them beneath his nose.

'Look, I don't have any euros on me, only pounds.' Jack stopped and looked at the man for the first time in the face. He was young and well-built and clearly not a street seller. 'Wait, how did you know to speak to me in English?'

The man's eyes flicked down, forcing Jack's to follow, where they found a gun.

'Typical stupid English,' the man said.

Jack didn't have time to react, the distraction in front of him had done its job and the detective hadn't seen it coming. His knees lost rigidity, his gut felt sick and his body felt as though it was falling through thick water. Adrenaline had tried to save him but it was too late, it was the last thing he tasted before his body hit the ground.

Faces came swimming into view, his hearing still stifled with confusion as if his own head was listening in through a wall. He could feel blood running down his face and his underarms felt sore where his entire weight was being carried on them.

'Fuck, he's coming round.'

'So hit him again. Here, use this.'

Jack saw something small and black pass in front of his eyes. His first thought was that it was a small shoe, but he had just about enough sense, in reality, to establish that it was more likely something heavy and hard.

'Please, please,' the detective begged, trying to pull one of his feet beneath him, he desperately tried to bear his own weight. One of the men pushed him to the floor, his back landing against a wall, again causing his vision to go blurry. Through the haze, he watched as a man straddled him and brought the hard-black object down on his temple.

All was gone again.

Sharp pains blanketed his body, taking his breath. He gasped, frantically trying to swallow air.

'Wakey-wakey, detective,' a voice in the distance taunted him.

Bright lights irritated his corneas and then they faded again.

He was in the room with the dog food. There were three men now, grabbing him, pulling him to the floor, he kicked and screamed and a high pitched noise came out – a child's yell for help, not his own voice.

He pushed one of them with some force. The man fell back against the open door, but regained his posture like a boxer off the ropes and, like a fighter, flew forward with a fist, landing it on his jaw. He didn't want to be moved, not again, each time it was getting harder to survive. This could be his last fight, he didn't know how much further he could be pushed.

Another punch hit him, this time in the back of the head, but his capturers wouldn't let him fall. They carried his weak, small frame easily now, colliding his elbow against the doorframe, sending shooting pain up his arm and into his shoulder blade.

'I said fucking *wake up*,' the voice was bringing Jack back into reality. He recognised it, but again his eyes struggled to focus on his surroundings.

After several seconds of effort, he focused on a face, a gleeful, expectant face.

'Surprise.'

It was Father Moon. He had gotten out of his religious clothing but still stood head to toe in black. Jeans, turtleneck jumper, army boots and leather gloves. His posture was straight and his wiry frame now looked sleek and muscular.

'Predictable,' Jack said, grimacing as his own speech hurt his head.

The priest's face dropped. 'That may be, but nevertheless, you are there and I am here. I am in control and you are, well, you look like a puppet at the moment. I guess that makes me the puppet master.'

Jack screamed in agony; the feeling was coming back to his body, his muscles now realising that he was suspended by his arms, which were straight behind his back. He quickly pried his legs from beneath him and stood up, relinquishing the torture on his upper arm muscles. Jack looked up and examined the room.

The priest was obviously feeling brave as he stood alone.

'See, this is what I mean.' He pulled at a rope that had been wound around a hook on the wall. It was connected to the detective's hands on a pulley and pulled them upwards, towards the ceiling. The strain was back on his tendons in his shoulders, the joints being overextended. Jack's head dropped and he tiptoed, trying desperately not to pull on his arms. It was hard, he was still only just breathing and the shock from being covered in cold water had not yet worn off.

'Great, isn't it? I learnt this trick while I was in the States. I worked alongside some Pentecostal vicars. Now those guys really are nuts. This is what they would do to the young nuns. It would break down their spirit, make them more amenable. They would tie them up, just as you are now, and leave them. Leave them in a room with only their own thoughts of how they had disappointed their own God. Honestly, these guys could get away with anything. They would tell the young nuns that having sex with them wasn't losing their virginity, no, because they were more than men, they were instruments of the Lord Almighty, so, in fact, they were privileged to have them inside them, to have the greatness of God rape them right in their tight little cunts. They had some balls those guys, I tell you. Now, I've always wanted to try this, but never quite had the excuse. So I suppose I should be thanking you.' Father Moon approached the detective and punched him in the jaw. It had barely healed from when a drug lord had interrogated him and Jack felt the telling sign of a break in it. It wasn't the pain in the jaw that told him, but the stabbing deep in his ear, where the tendons had been drastically pulled out of position.

'Now, I've heard that you have survived a pretty horrific interrogation recently, from Polish gangsters, no less, so I have decided to make this one more interesting – wouldn't want them to get samey for you. Now all I want to know is what you know, and who else knows it. You aren't here dragging up Father Lopez from his grave for no reason, now, are you? So, it's very simple, two questions, the easier you answer, the less painful your death will be. Do we have a deal?' He crouched down in front of Jack, giving him an arrogant grin.

Jack smiled back, matching his confidence, and then spat in his face.

'Go fuck yourself.'

The priest stood up and yanked the rope above the detective's head. He yelped in pain.

'Dance for me, Pinocchio,' he said, laughing gleefully. Jack's face screwed in pain, he couldn't hide it, as much as he tried, he hadn't felt torture like this. He could barely think, let alone bluff.

'Different, isn't it? Now, you act like a good boy, I must go and see to something and when I return, I will have lots of toys for us to play with.' The priest kissed his hand and slapped it on the back of Jack's bowed head. Even this put more tension on his arms, sending razor blades into the sockets.

The faint sound of a door closing registered in Jack's head. He was barely conscious. He felt like resting, like closing his eyes and never waking up again, sending all this reality away for good.

LITTLE TOE

The room went black. His eyes weren't closed, though. He was confused and the air was dank and barely breathable. He cried now, now they couldn't see, he cried. Over the years, he had often wanted to die because it would release him from an inevitably more severe pain, but then he got strong, he let them do what they wanted and showed no emotion. Now was different, he was sure they were taking him to be killed, to take him away never to return – like the other children, the ones from the ceremony. They washed them, they raped them and then they were gone.
He cried more as he wondered if it was going to hurt. They had used knives on him many times then sewn him back together, the needle proving far more painful than a razor-edged blade. It would puncture the skin fine, but as it dragged the thread through and pulled the skin tight, it was an irritating, grinding pain.
They might shoot him, it wouldn't be their usual dramatic style, but they had seemed so scared of late and it would make a tidy, quick job of it.
A stark realisation trickled into his eyes, pushing out the tears and replacing them with a blank stare. This would all be over soon. Maybe the gates of hell would greet him like

they had said, but to him he was already there. He had wondered why him, what had he done to deserve this, but then he was reminded several times a day that he was a demon. He was poison and needed to be eradicated, but they wanted to do it slowly. Years had passed and still he was chained and kept as a wild animal.

Jack shook his head. He was awake again, had he passed out? Or were these hallucinations he kept having? His eyes blinked the room into focus but it swayed, it wouldn't come to realization. His eyes felt heavy and he could hear voices, could hear Tanya speaking to him in his ear, but the voice morphed and now Father Moon's high pitched laugh filled his head. The darkness came again and, like before, Jack was transported away.

It was dark again but for the small tunnel of light he had deliberately set up for him to see out of. Jack was remembering a time when he wasn't being tortured but was still feeling pain that rocketed up through his body. He was tucked up in his bed, cover pulled up over his head and depression pinning him down. He had been stuck there many times before – the despair in his heart would bind him beneath the duck down duvet.

The small window he left for air became obscured. A beautiful green eye had appeared, followed by the tiny lips of his four-year-old daughter.

'Hey, Daddy, Mummy said your brain was poorly again, so I thought I would come up and take your temperature. I can be a nurse,' she said, bringing her eye back down to look in on him.

'Hey, darling, I'm ok, just need a little rest,' Jack said, his voice muffled from beneath the cover.

Again, his daughter put her mouth to the opening. 'But I want to look after you, Daddy. I want to help.'

A tear formed in his eye.

'Don't cry, Daddy. Do you need medicine?'

Jack sat up on the bed, wiping the tear away quickly, embarrassed that she had seen it at all.

'Look, darling, Daddy's just feeling a bit poorly, it happens from time to time, but it's not your fault. I'm sorry if I'm being a rubbish daddy, I will try harder, I promise. And it's my responsibility to look after you,' he took her hand, 'my little Flick Flick.' And he flicked her hand gently twice.

The detective's eyes flew open. Suddenly, he was himself again and it was confusing. Realities and memories were all getting in each other's way in his head, being tumbled over and over, colliding uncontrollably. Each time he was getting drawn in deeper, but right now he was strapped up, stripped, and his body was shaking in pain. He couldn't afford not to focus or would surely die there in that dungeon, at the hand of Father Moon, a pathetic excuse of an adversary.

His muscles had stretched now, become slightly more acclimatised to his positioning – still burning, but not enough to cloud his thoughts. He looked around the room as much as he was able. He could see the entire floor plan, but not much else, his neck still taking much of the strain. There was a small nursing chair, old like the floor slabs, and Jack's phone, keys and lighter lay on it. His clothes weren't there, nor was there much else, only a small occasional table.

Father Moon re-entered the room; Jack could only see up to his waist, which was more than far enough to spot a black leather briefcase hanging at the man's side. And then Jack realised what the table was for as the case was set down heavily upon it. The detective's heartrate doubled as the tell-tale noises of tools came from within it.

'Now, I don't do this sort of thing very often, so I wasn't sure what exactly to bring,' Father Moon said, flicking the latches open and lifting the lid. 'So, I just threw together some interesting tools. I pride myself on my imagination, if nothing else, so I am sure that we will get on just fine.' The priest pulled out a large mallet and pair of needle-nosed pliers.

'So, I will start easy on you and perhaps I will work my way up. That way you will have plenty of opportunities to tell me what I want to know. Because I think if I start at the top and work my way down with this,' he flipped the mallet over in his hand, catching it neatly by the handle, 'I doubt you will speak at all.'

The priest walked back to the case and threw the pliers back in, trading them for a large screwdriver. He pulled the rope a couple more inches and tied it tightly to its bracket. Jack's muscles were brought back to breaking point, the agony nearly causing him to pass out all over again.

The man in black spotted it. 'No, no, detective, you stay with me, there will be plenty of opportunities to faint later on, I promise you that.'

The priest knelt in front of Jack. He had picked up a large, flat-headed screwdriver and smiled as he held the tip on Jack's little toe, directly over the first joint.

'Deep breath,' the priest said sarcastically and brought the mallet down hard.

The back of Jack's head collided with a hard floor, his body thrown down by two men.

'The little bitch tried to bite me,' the one with a thick Welsh accent told his colleague.

The other man laughed. 'We only have to babysit a little while longer, they'll come to collect soon. Sometimes children need to be taught a lesson,' he said, his accent clearly English and his tone very much suggestive. 'I'm going out for fag anyway. Meet you in the car.'

The Welsh man nodded and closed the door behind his friend. 'You fucking bite me again and I'll smash your head in. Now, turn over, face down.' He started untying his belt.

Jack screamed himself back into the room with the

priest. He looked down at his foot. It was large, hairy, definitely his own, and covered in blood. He could see a small cable tie around the toe. It had slowed the bleeding but not stopped it.

'Ah, there he is. You had some sort of fit then, your eyes rolled back and everything. You know, I thought it would take much more than this to have such an effect on you, detective. Guess you're not as strong as I thought you were. Right, I take it you're ready to talk, otherwise I'll skip straight to the big toe.' The priest threw Jack's phone and other bits onto the floor and pulled the chair up close.

'Now, detective, why are you investigating the death of Father Lopez?'

Jack strained his head up, meeting the man's eyes. 'The timing of his death … it seemed too unlikely to be a coincidence, but I wanted to make sure that's all it was – coincidental.'

Father Moon thought on it for a moment. 'Coincidental with what? With you finding that boy in the hole? How did you conclude his involvement?'

Jack couldn't think, there was no option other than telling the truth – it may just be enough to keep him alive. He struggled to breathe and spit gathered between his gritted teeth, forming strings all the way to the floor.

'No, I sent him some information about my daughter's murder.'

The priest looked heavily agitated. 'You did, did you? What information?'

Jack lowered his head, unable to keep it up, the strength in his neck waning. 'Pictures. The church had investigated them. They had that symbol. The pope one.'

Father Moon stood up, clearly confused as he paced the room.

'You're lying, you linked us to the boy, to that teacher, and I want to know why. Who tipped you off?'

Jack shook his head. 'I'm not lying, I'm here because of my wife and daughter, that's it.' Shooting pains burned through his toe. He dared to take another look; he could see the tip sitting inches from his foot, it looked like a loose bit of meat.

'FUCK!' he shouted, more bouts of pain coming in relentless waves.

The priest rummaged through the case, looking for something specific before kneeling again in front of the detective.

'Now this time, it is really going to hurt. I warned you not to bullshit me,' his voice was quick and panicked, no bravado left, just fear.

Jack couldn't escape the fear he didn't think he could take anymore. He tried to wriggle his foot away from the man but he grabbed it and pushed something sharp into the base of his big toe. There was no screwdriver – it had been replaced with a wood chisel.

'No, please, I'm not lying.'

The priest shook his head and dug the chisel into the flesh so Jack couldn't move his foot. He brought the mallet up high once again.

MEDUSA

Jack felt a surge – he had run every last bit of power through his body with pure unconscious movement. His foot allowed the chisel to tear his skin as it forced its way up, following the knee. Jack felt his kneecap connect cleanly with the side of Father Moon's head, sending the man sprawling backwards, the mallet coming down on the face of the man wielding it. The priest's body collapsed in an awkward shape on the floor, a clear indication that he had been knocked unconscious.

Jack examined his situation. In all the action he hadn't noticed that he was now able to stand flat footed – either his muscles had loosened as far as they could go, or the rope had given a little. Even if the mallet had landed cleanly on his opponent's head, it wouldn't be long before he was awake again and then he really was in trouble.

This position was reminding him of something from when he used to box – he must have only been about twenty at the time, but his BPD would often store strange memories away only to bring them out unexpectedly. He remembered a kid who would flick his legs up over the pull-up bar backwards and would repeat this over and over. He had said it worked on his core and upper arm strength at the same time. It wouldn't be the same movement, but it *was* similar and hopefully possible.

'Come on, Jacky boy, been a while since you hit the gym, let's see if you've still got it.'

Jack bounced on his feet as much as he could before throwing himself forwards, trying to roll his body up through his arms. He managed to tuck his back through but his waist was another question. He fell back down onto his feet, slipping in the blood and pulling his weight on his arms with tremendous pain. He stifled a painful scream – he couldn't risk waking the man on the floor.

He gritted his teeth. 'Now or never, Jack,' he whispered. 'Now or you'll be dead.'

He tightened his abs, closed his eyes and bounced once again before throwing all his strength at the jump. This time, his hips and legs jammed up between his arms and his body finally relinquished into a more manageable position. He was still hanging from his wrists, but that was the only pain and he could handle it, hanging there for several minutes until he wriggled his legs through, finally righting his body.

Relief washed over him – even if he couldn't get his hands free, at least he was in a decent position to put up a fight now. He'd learned during his self-defence classes on the force that he at least had some decent kicking power.

He looked up at his bindings and laughed with comfort – his wrists were bound with more cable ties and attached to the rope with a bog standard climbing carabiner clip.

He'd expected to be at least handcuffed or tied tightly.

'Amateurs,' he said, unhooking himself.

Even the cable ties were an easy escape. Something that he had been taught many years ago was to bring his arms up and swing them down hard, bringing each elbow apart and past his hips. They had all tried it in the training group and with each attempt, they had snapped with ease, just as they did this time.

He scooped up his belongings and the set of keys –

they weren't his but they might come in handy.

He could barely walk and the cold stone floor stung where the tip of his toe should have been. Jack hobbled to the toolbox, grabbed the pillars and carefully cut the long end of the cable tie around his toe so at least he could fit his feet into shoes if he could find any.

He searched the room; it really was as bare as he'd first thought. He looked down again at his injury: blood spilled from both feet. His legs and upper body were naked and only his underwear had been left on. He sat next to the unconscious Moon and measured his feet up against the soles of his shoes. They were tricky to get off – he hadn't realised that they genuine army-style boots, laced up high. Jack slowly lowered his more drastically injured foot in first and tied it tight. The second one wasn't quite as painful.

He heard footsteps approaching.

He had thought about stealing the priest's trousers but was now glad that he decided on only taking the essentials. Jack stood behind the door. He had subconsciously picked up the mallet. He felt the weight of it in his hand.

'Shit, this might actually kill someone,' he thought before watching the door open slowly.

It was the fake flower selling man and he had just reached for his gun when the blunt tool rendered him as blacked out as the priest. Jack picked up the gun and headed out of the room. There was only one direction to walk in and the building was small so he soon came to a spiral staircase, his energy allowing him to scale it slowly.

'Come on, Jack, keep going.'

Rounding a corner, he came face to face with two more priests. Friend or foe, he wasn't taking a chance and fired the gun at the ceiling above their heads. They scattered like frightened cats, long clothing flapping behind them.

Jack looked at his phone, opened it with his fingerprint and started to search through his contacts. The phone bleeped – he still had no signal, the thick walls acting the perfect barrier. He heard shouting from up ahead, lots of voices, all sounding alarmed and aggressive. He ejected the magazine from the gun – there were only two bullets left. He fired them down one corridor and headed the opposite way, throwing the gun behind a propped-open door. He searched the next room for a way out, but it was small and empty with only one tiny stained glass window. His limp was growing, every step becoming more laboured than the last. He continued walking away from where he had heard the men's voices, doing all he could to just keep moving.

He turned a corner and the decor changed. This part of the building was newer, with thinner walls. He tried his phone again. It started dialling and rang.

'Jack, Jack? Is that you?' Tanya's voice sounded loud from the speaker.

Jack was breathing heavily now, his voice difficult to catch. 'Yes, it's me.'

'Where the hell are you? What's going on? We've been driving around for hours trying to find you.'

Jack heard more shouts, all in Italian, coming from somewhere nearby. He ducked into a room, this one with hefty double windows, easily man-sized.

'Hang on,' he said quietly into the phone before tucking it into his pants. He climbed the windowsill and looked down. A fifteen-foot drop onto a roof with a following eight-foot one to the street below.

He had barely needed an excuse to jump but just to make sure, the sound of boots running towards him was the final encouragement. He landed hard on the roof before giving himself time to examine if he had injured himself further, he skidded down to the bottom and fell the remainder of the journey.

If he had broken anything else, his brain had switched off his pain receptors and he half-jogged, half-dragged himself out onto the main street.

'Tan?' he said, taking the phone back out, grateful it was still in one piece.

'Yes, I'm here, where are you?' she said, her voice switching from concerned to focused.

He looked around. 'I don't know, I think I'm still in Florence, I mean, it looks the same.'

'Narrow it down, Jack, what do you see?'

Jack heard more shouting. He looked back in the direction he had fled – it wouldn't take them long to track down a man wearing nothing but boots and boxer shorts.

'Right, ok, I'm looking at a huge cathedral.'

'Jack, this is Florence, everything looks like a cathedral. Describe it to me.'

Jack searched around. People were beginning to stare at him and then there were shouts again. The detective's survival instinct sent him into top gear. He hobbled around a corner and spotted a bridge, one that was completely full of people. He attempted a run, trying to lose himself among the crowds, desperate for some space between him and those following.

'I'm on a bridge, there're shops,' Jack gasped into the phone, then heard screams from a woman being knocked to the floor. A couple of men were trying to catch up with him, both dressed all in black like Father Moon had been.

The detective made it to the end of the bridge and took a couple of sharp turns around the corners, hoping again to lose his assailants.

'Jack, where are you?' he had brought the phone halfway to his head and bent over double to reach it.

He looked down at his foot, blood poured from the boot now, leaving small puddles as he tried to take some more steps.

'I don't know. I can see …' He looked around, the landscape turning fluid like water. He fell to the floor, he could see blurry images of people all closing in on him.

'I can see medusa, her head. I can see her head cut off.' Jack succumbed to this newest hullicintion. He could hear Tanya's voice faintly from the phone lying inches away from his head.

'Piazza della Signoria. Ok, I know where you are, just hold on, Jack, hold on.'
But the detective was gone.

I LOVE YOU, JACK

The detective's eyes flickered gently, opening at their leisure. No more pain anywhere, no more tiredness, fully relaxed and tranquil. He had an almost irresistible urge to giggle.

'There he is,' a voice spoke softly into the air. Jack knew it well, so very well he didn't even need to look at who it belonged to, it stood out from the rest of the world like a large bird in flight in a plain blue sky and swooped down into his ears.

'My handsome man.'

Jack sat up and breathed in the warm, still air.

A smile hit his face now like sunrays bursting over the top of a hill. Jack couldn't help himself, he smiled back, his insides relaxing into place, his entire body cradled with love.

'I've missed you,' he said.

'I know,' Jessica replied. Her hand reached forward towards Jack's knee, almost feeling real, but also feeling very short of the real thing.

'I suppose I could have died and this could be hell – being tortured by imaginary version of you.'

Jack's wife's smile didn't leave her face, but it did look

less full. 'I thought that would be heaven, wouldn't it? Spending an eternity here with me.'

Jack shook his head softly. 'No, the real you would be heaven, my imagination can't even begin to produce anything like the real thing. You were too magical for that.'

Her warm grin returned. 'You always were a smooth talker.'

Jack laughed. 'No, I wasn't, I was bloody awkward and you know it.'

Jessica laughed too. 'Yeah, you're right. Remember when I taught you to tie a bow-tie for my work party? You were so anxious about getting it right you went to the toilets to tighten it and when you came back, your face had gone bright red. You would have choked yourself before letting me down, you daft prat.'

The two of them laughed, but Jack's ended first. He knew it wasn't real – he so wanted it to be but at any moment this would be ripped away from him and he would be alone in the darkness again.

'Why are you here, Jess?'

She looked at her surroundings that didn't exist and then down at herself. 'Why am I here, Jack?'

Jack dared to take his eyes away for a second. 'Because I'm … I'm lost, I think.'

Jessica shed a single tear. 'You always were.'

'And you always found me.'

She wiped away the tear. 'I'm here now, aren't I?'

Jack shook his head. 'No. No, you're not. You left me. It all went to shit and you left me. I needed you so much and you fucking left me.'

Her hands raised up and cradled his face. 'I didn't want to, I wanted to stay with you forever. I tried so hard to stay, Jack, I fought, but I just couldn't. It was my time to go, you see.'

Jack cried now. 'You should have fought harder, I needed you, I *still* need you and you're not here.'

She put her hands down, cupping them together,

ashamed. 'I'm sorry, Jack. Please don't hate me.'

Jack wiped at his running nose. 'I could never hate you, I still love you, that's why it hurts. It hurts so much. I just want to hold you again and I can't and it hurts. I don't know what I'm doing; I'm chasing shadows, chasing after an evil that ended a life I used to have and I don't know why.'

She didn't reply, just watched him as he hunched over and cried, wrapping his arms around himself, looking like a small child waiting for a parental hug, that reassurance that says the world is shit at times but it will be alright. A comfort that he would never know again.

They sat together for as long as he needed, his eyes drying as best they could, the heaving of his body slowing and becoming less rhythmic until he could finally breathe again.

'I'm sorry, Jack, it's up to you to move on. I'll always be in your heart, but that's not where the problem is anymore. That will be fixed with time and by new people, but it's your head that's holding you back.'

Jack just nodded, he couldn't argue, he couldn't blame. He was the one alive but he was the one not living. Jessica was right, she always was – whether she was real or not didn't even need to be added into this equation.

'So what do I do?' he finally asked her.

She shrugged her shoulders and again they sat a while in silence. The implausible quiet helped – it was the space between the words that gave them meaning.

'Aubrie Sellers,' Jessica finally said, as if answering a quiz question.

'Oh?'

'She seems really nice; I think I would have liked her. I think I met her once, didn't I?'

Jack nodded. 'Yes, she started not long before you died, I think you met at a Christmas thing.'

More emptiness. 'She is a good person, isn't she?'

Jack looked up at her. 'Yes, she is a good person, which

is exactly why it will never happen.'

Jessica looked back at him. 'You deserve to be happy, you know. How long are you going to punish yourself? This world isn't your fault, people get hurt, Jack, and it isn't your fault.'

Jack disagreed, 'Sometimes it is my fault, Jess, sometimes it is. She's a good person; she deserves a good person back.'

Jessica leaned in and kissed him. Jack's heart pounded with joy and sank with a lack of hope all in one movement.

'I love you, Jack.'

Jack smiled weakly. 'I know, I love you too. You're going now, aren't you?'

Jessica returned an empty, kind look. 'For now.'

THEY'RE DEMONS

Jack felt real light entering the backs of his eyes now; he could hardly bear it. His hands groped the air aimlessly, trying to bat it away.

'What's going on?' he shouted, bolting upright in a bed.

A burning pain rushed across his shoulder blades as he tried to straighten up on his arms.

'Detective, calm yourself, you are ok.' Father Camaldo placed his hands on Jack's shoulders, causing him to fight against them.

'Detective!' the priest shouted, holding him tighter. 'You are ok, we found you, you are safe now.'

Tanya came running into the room. 'Jack, it's us, it's us, Jack, you're ok.'

Jack's heart pounded. He couldn't focus, his mind pricked with panic. He gripped at bedding and kicked his legs.

'Jack O'Connor, it's Tanya Red, stop fighting,' the young woman said simply and with force.

Jack's eyes found hers, her head nodded and his pupils fixed on hers, his heart begging him into flight or fight.

'Jack, it's me, you are ok,' she said again, holding his forearms. 'Do you know who I am?'

Jack nodded, not breaking eye contact.

'Good, we are in a hotel room in Florence, you are safe now.'

Jack nodded again.

Tanya turned away very briefly. 'Father, please could you get Jack a glass of water?' She turned back. 'It's ok, Jack, you are ok.'

Again, the detective dipped his head with acknowledgment.

Jack drank with a tremendous thirst and lay quietly in the warm bed. It took a while before the adrenaline had subsided and even after that he could feel the ill effects it had on his muscles – like they had all been attached to electrodes for a few seconds and then completely relaxed immediately after. It had exposed all his injuries.

Jack sat silently. His head felt like it was swimming without the rest of his body. Tanya rushed about, changing icepacks on his shoulders, checking swelling in various places, trying to examine the injuries without causing him too much pain. She would occasionally have conversations with Father Camaldo in Italian; Jack wasn't sure if this was to spare him more anxiety of something else happening or because Tanya was worried that one of his ailments may actually be serious. She eventually took a seat beside him to speak with him, a large needle in her hand.

'I've got some morphine, I didn't want to give it to you too soon – we only have one dose and I wanted to make sure you weren't going downhill. You ready for it?' she asked, holding the needle up.

Jack rcognised that the needle in question was rather thick compared to his past experiences of hospitals.

'What the fuck is that, a rhino sedative?'

Tanya smiled with relief. 'And he's back. You had me so bloody worried, Jack.'

'Not as worried as I am that you'll stab me with that. The pain isn't too bad, just put the javelin away. Where the hell did you get morphine from anyway?'

Tanya put a cap over the needle and put it on the bedside. 'When we found you I realised that taking you to the nearest hospital would probably not be a safe idea, so we may have swung by a vet to borrow some supplies late last night.'

'A *vet*?' Jack laughed. 'If I were a dog they would have put me down a long time ago.'

Tanya didn't laugh at his joke, instead she was concerned. 'So what actually happened? I was trying to get hold of you for hours. We went back to find Father Moon and he had gone missing too. We thought something had happened to the pair of you.'

Jack laughed again. 'Who do you think did this to me? Bastard tied me up and used me as a punching bag, nearly broke both my arms, too. What is the damage?'

Tanya raised an eyebrow. 'Did he now? Well, wait till I find him. Makes sense why you sat up and tried to punch me, calling me a Bible-bashing bastard.'

Jack looked worried.

'No, it's ok, Father Vincenzo managed to get the chloroform on you pretty quick. So, we have twelve cracked ribs, your jaw looks like it's been re-broken and dislocated. Two hyperextended shoulders – probably came as close to being fully dislocated as they can be without actually popping out.' She pulled the cover off of his legs. 'Your ankle, well, that's pretty messed up, you hyperextended that, too, in three directions – a sort of triple strain. And then, my favourite: a third of your little toe is completely missing. Oh, and you stink.'

Jack gave a tweak of the head. 'Not too bad then. Can't believe he got a souvenir, that was my favourite toe and everything.'

Tanya shook her head. 'Not funny, Jack. What the hell happened?'

The detective explained how he was tied up and how he eventually managed to escape.

'So what did he want to know?' Tanya asked, checking

the bruising on his ribs for him once more.

'Just why we were there, so I told him – told him everything.'

Tanya looked surprised. 'You told him?'

Jack's eyes opened wide with offence. 'Yes, Tan, I told him – the psychopath was cutting my toes off! But he didn't want to know, I mean, he refused to believe it. He started asking me about the Pearce case.' Jack rcognised the confusion on his friend's face. 'I know, I'm as baffled as you are. There must be a link, but how or what, I haven't got a clue. I have an idea of where to start, though. Sophia – I think she didn't tell us everything— Actually, scratch that, I don't think she told us *anything*. If Father Lopez helped her escape something, I need to know what and who. It's the only thing I can see that might link missing children in England and our murdered priest in Italy. Help me up a minute.'

Tanya shook her head. 'No, you need to rest.'

'And I will, but right now I need a piss.'

Tanya helped him to his feet and he made it to the bathroom, limping and using the wall for stability.

'Jesus Christ,' he called from behind the bathroom door. 'What is this, a meth lab?'

He looked behind the shower curtain, revealing a large gas bottle, a bunsen burner and various other types of apparatus. Short of a beaker, he couldn't even guess what the rest of the apparatus was called. He returned to the bedroom.

Tanya was holding up the prayer beads.

'Don't worry, they're perfectly safe now but I had to get a bit more equipment than I first thought. I was getting results, but they were weak. We were right, though – cyanide. It had been put on with a type of lacquer.'

Father Camaldo re-entered the room. 'Ah, detective, it is so good to see you are alive.' The priest saw what Tanya was explaining. 'Ah yes, did you know how clever this beautiful young lady is?'

Jack raised his eyebrows. 'Yes, I have a pretty good idea.'

'You see, Father Camaldo here told me that Father Lopez would often pass the beads through his lips. This would have slowly broken down the lacquer and eventually poisoned him. It wouldn't be fast, but it would seem like some sort of illness, so no one suspected anything.'

Jack nodded. 'This was definitely that Moon.'

'How can you be so sure?' Vincenzo Camaldo asked.

Jack tried to rotate his arms. 'He has a soft spot for the dramatic – or maybe it's a hard spot.'

Father Camaldo seemed excited all of a sudden. 'Speaking of this dramatics, I feel I may have something to add to this – my letter.'

He waved the piece of paper. 'It would appear that Father Lopez has left us a clue.

Jack rolled his eyes. 'Great, that's all we need, the Davinci code, why not?'

After finding out how long he had been unconscious for, Jack insisted that they continue any further conversation in the car. Tanya put up a pretty good resistance but came to the agreement that time was of the essence and, after Jack agreed to have his ankle splinted, they were on their way. Jack was impressed at her handiwork with bed slats and duct-tape. He insisted on bringing the morphine – as much as he was putting on a brave face, he really was in agony.

Father Camaldo drove while talking them through the letter, now in Tanya's hands.

'Can you translate ok, my dear?' Father Camaldo asked over his shoulder.

Jack was surprised at the speed he was able to drive through the narrow streets and was even more in awe of a man who could disappear for five minutes and return with a rather flashy BMW, no questions asked. The detective assumed it was a church car he was loaning, but seeing as the priest had now spent hours alone with Tanya Red, he wouldn't be surprised if the man had actually hotwired it himself.

'Yes, fine, Father, what is it we should be looking at? It all seems a little regular. He says he misses the old times, traveling with you around Europe. How you both had your doubts about becoming priests and helped each other to find your paths towards God ...' She ran her finger lazily along the lines of Italian words.

'Indeed, but can you see how the writing changes on one word in particular?'

Tanya checked the letter again. 'No, where? Oh no, wait, yes, slightly italic on *Giants Causeway.*' Tanya guessed she would need to explain what that was to Jack. 'It's a rock formation in Ireland. Hexagonal rocks lead out to sea. They're a natural occurrence but don't look it; they're quite the tourist attraction these days.'

'Right, ok?' Jack replied, nonplussed.

'No, my dear, just the *Giants.*'

Tanya looked closer. 'Oh yeah. It's subtle, I'll give him that. But I'm not sure what it means, Father,' she replied, skimming the remainder of the letter.

The priest swung the car heavily to the right. 'On its own, it does not mean anything, but there was one other thing that confused me. He mentions several names, people who we went on sabbatical with. We took a year to write a book together. There was four of us, as you can see by the names mentioned. Only one of those names is wrong.' He spun the wheel, flicking the car swiftly down a tight left-hand turn. 'Reprobus. This name is a fabrication.'

Jack pulled himself upright, growling with agony. 'No shit, it sounds completely made up.'

The priest caught Jack's eye in the mirror. 'Sorry, detective, I will slow down. Yes, you are correct it does sound fictional, which you could argue to be true. The only time I have heard that name is in a hagiography.'

Jack looked at Tanya.

'Biography of a saint,' she said flatly.

'So what the hell has that got to do with giants?' the detective asked, squirming as the car once again turned heavily.

'Saint Christopher, he was reported to be a giant. Probably just a tall man but, nonetheless, in many pieces of literature he is called the giant. But note that, detective, his real name is widely believed to be Reprobus.' The car took one last swing around a bend and, to Jack's relief, they were now leaving the city.

'The rest of the letter is very accurate, except that we never visited the Giants Causeway while we were in Ireland.'

Jack felt still and steady, thinking about what the priest was telling them. '*He put the papal seal on it, he knew it would give them an excuse to read it, he knew that would be the only way it would get passed on — if they were confident it was benign. What harm could the dying letter of one friend to another possibly do? And, of course, that fuckwit Moon wouldn't spot the subtle clue, of course it would be too clever, too straightforward. I bet he tested it for invisible ink or hidden messages in the first letter in every sentence. He told you the name, he told you in plain writing and it bested you, you arrogant arse.*'

And then something hit Jack, hit him so hard in his mind it felt almost like an actual blow to the body – he even tensed for impact.

His grandfather had given him a Saint Christopher pendant when he was a little boy, telling him it would always keep him safe. If only he had managed to keep it safe, maybe he would have recognised it that few seconds earlier.

'A boy, a boy on his shoulder!' Jack shouted, sounding somewhat random.

'A child, yes, the Christ child,' Father Camaldo replied. 'He carried him over the river, bearing the weight of the world on his shoulders, and still he made the other side.'

'Yeah, well, I saw him— I mean, a wooden him. I

mean, in Father Lopez's bedroom there was a carving on the wall of Saint Christopher.' The detective looked at Tanya for reassurance.

She raised her shoulders. 'Could be something, I suppose.'

The rest of the journey was quiet. Jack could feel the energy in the car, all three of them thinking. The trip really had escalated fast, which was why Jack felt that maybe this last revelation had been wishful thinking. It was far more likely that the clues would be a computer password or a file name – if they were indeed clues at all. Perhaps the name was misremembered and the word in apparent slight italic writing really *was* slight. His BPD mind flipped from being convinced to utterly disheartened. He hated when the black and white clouded his vision, if he could only see the shades of grey in between the bigger picture might not get lost completely.

They arrived at the old church, the town was quiet and deserted just as before. Jack limped his way through the large oak doors as fast as he could. He almost expected the bells to be ringing again – it would have been handy to have Sophia there already rather than have to go looking for her.

The small bedroom was just how they had left it and, to his relief, the detective spotted the antique on the wall. He reached up and took it from its mountings, turning it over to see if there was anything written on the back, but it was painted a bright blue with nothing else to show.

He looked at the front again, but it looked just as innocent and unassuming – if not beautiful – as before.

Jack decided that perhaps this wasn't the best place to examine it and took it with him.

On leaving the church, Jack was surprised to see Sophia dismounting from her moped. She tore her helmet from her head and dropped it to the floor without a care, walking aggressively towards him. Tanya and Father Camaldo tried greeting her, but she burst between them and pulled out a gun that had been tucked in the back of her jeans. Jack put his free hand in the air, not to surrender to the girl as she may have thought he might do, but to indicate to Tanya that the situation was in hand. He threw the wooden picture to his friend and now opened his palms, facing the barrel of the gun.

'You come here again, and why? To take things now? It is not enough that people get killed, you must steal their things. You don't know what you are dealing with. People get hurt and now they will come for me. Everything that he did for me, everything he sacrificed, you have destroyed. Is this what you wanted? The only people I have ever loved are gone and they died because of you. This is your fault!' the beautiful girl screamed at the detective, her throat breaking with fury, the tears on her face leaving tracks.

'I'm here to help, I want to know what happened to Father Lopez, I want to bring them to justice.' Jack was struggling to understand, using his BPD's intense empathy to prod and probe at the situation, desperately trying to know what she meant.

'You do not care, if you did you would leave his name in peace, leave us to live our lives, instead you bring more death with you.' She waved the gun with little control, it was so loose it was almost falling to the ground.

Jack could see a new pain, he could feel it emanating from her soul. 'Who? Who else has died?'

The girl cried at the question. 'Just leave, just fucking leave before I kill you.'

Tanya had clearly had enough; she approached Sophia confidently. The brunette turned the gun on her, not realising that the redhead was well within reach of it. She grabbed it from the Italian with ease, knocking her hand away. Sophia flicked her hair out of her eyes and threw a heavy, hooked punch. Tanya ducked it and pulled the top of the chamber on the handgun back and ejected the bullet at the other woman's face. It hit her, causing her to stagger a little and step back, giving Tanya the time to flick the bottom of the firearm upward, the magazine sliding neatly out, it too striking Sophia somewhere up near her face. The younger girl's legs struggled to keep stationary, making an opening for the redhead to grab her by the throat and kick the back of her leg, putting her heavily down on her knees.

'That is enough!' Father Camaldo yelled, shocking even Jack, who watched Tanya release her sparring partner.

'No more fighting, not here, not now.' The detective was impressed by the authority in the other man's voice.

Tanya reluctantly let go of Sophia, offering her a friendly hand. The young woman stood up and walked away from her, collecting the pieces of the gun from the floor.

Jack took advantage of the lull. 'Sophia, you have to help us, I think Father Lopez may have discovered something big, something that might be able to help other children.'

She flicked her long, beautiful hair from her face. 'You cannot help anyone. I cannot help you. This is too big, they are too powerful. You need to learn when to let go.'

Jack's head dropped with frustration. 'You're probably right, but there are other children and they're suffering.' Jack paused, frustrated, his body becoming animated. 'You don't understand.'

Sophia laughed sarcastically with a sickening cough. 'You can say I don't, that I don't understand the pain, the pain I will never go back to.' She pulled her shirt over her head, leaving her top half completely bare, her small, firm breasts covered with angry red scars. She turned her back and pulled her hair over the front of her shoulder. 'Tell me I don't understand, tell me I do not know how deep the scars go. I know, I know better than any of you.' Her voice softened, close to a cry but not quite, 'I know what they are capable of and what they will do to me.'

Jack was appalled, the sight of her marked skin jarred

him to his soul. Her entire back was covered with scars running at all angles. Some were clear, deep wounds made with a sharpened edge, others were blistered and raised. Jack couldn't begin to imagine the pain that came along with these wounds made on such young flesh.

'I know, detective, I know what flames, I know what acid, I know what machetes do to these children and I will not go back.' She faced him once more. 'They are not human, they're demons. They take your soul and they cut that to pieces, too, as they cut your body.' Her hands ran over her breasts in front of him. 'They wanted my body. I was an innocent child, I was clean. How clean am I now, detective? Do you want me now, detective? Do you want to fuck me as I scream in pain, do you want to tie me down, cover my mouth so I cannot call for help while you choke my throat?'

Jack couldn't answer, his eyes betraying tears at the girl's revelations.

She pulled her top back on. 'I will not go back and I will not let them kill me. Father Lopez saved two of us. Another girl, one year younger than me, I loved her like a sister – we *were* sisters after what we had survived by each otherss sides. This morning they went to her village and they shot her in the head. You bring death with you, detective, and I do not wish to die.' Sophia looked past the detective now, fear in her eyes as her hand slowly rose, pointing a finger back along the road entering the town.

A large black Land Rover drove towards them, two clear, dirty clouds forming a wake behind it.

BLOOD DOUSING

Jack's mind raced and he took in as much information as possible. He saw Tanya take the gun from Sophia and tuck it away in the back of her jeans before picking the wooden Saint Christopher up. She hid it under the back wheel of their car. He watched as Father Camaldo shielded Sophia from view as best he could. He noticed the couple of townsfolk who had taken an interest in the shouting disappear back into buildings.

'Shit, nowhere to run. Not in the church, they'll surround us. The car won't outrun theirs either. We're on our own. You'll have to talk your way out of it, Jack. Come on, Jack, you're good at this.'

The four-by-four pulled up, a handbrake turn kicking up the dust on the dirt track road, clouding everyone's view of who would appear.

Two men, both dressed in black military gear, jumped out, high energy and large rifles trained on them.

'Sophia Florenzi, get in the vehicle,' one man shouted, aiming his barrel at her. 'Or we will shoot you.'

Father Lopez put his arms up, completely blocking the girl from view. 'She will not go with you.'

'Move, Father, or we will shoot,' the man in black replied loudly.

Jack couldn't see his eyes through his dark shades, but he wasn't going to try to spot a bluff.

'Who are you?' Jack shouted, desperately trying to move the attention onto himself. 'I said, who the fuck are you?'

The other gunman turned his scope on the detective with a precise, fluid movement.

'Sophia, get in the car or we will shoot you and your friends,' the first gunman spoke again.

'Hey, do you know who I am? I am a British detective. Hey, I'm talking to you.' Jack took a couple of steps towards them.

The second gunman tightened up. 'Step back, sir, or I will shoot you.'

'No, tell me who the fuck you are and who the fuck you work for,' Jack spoke to them like they were idiots, deliberately becoming the most threatening thing in front of them.

He took another step forward at the same time as the priest. A pop sound deadened the world to the detective. The whole environment went silent, his vision slowed and the scenes played out in front of him, his consciousness working on a different plane. He was nothing but a bystander watching a show.

Bright lights burst from the end of the first gunman's rifle and Father Camaldo lurched backwards, his confused hands grappling at his robes, futile energy expelled into the ether. Jack saw Tanya move down onto her knees with no sound whatsoever, her hands full and arms extended. She rolled to her side and two light-sounding thuds reached Jack's ears from her direction, barely registering at all. The detective turned his head slowly, his eyes barely keeping up with the movement, but still they were in time to see the two black cladded men fall heavily behind their vehicle.

Jack knew there was screaming, only it wasn't having the same effect as it usually would – it was too quiet and came to him as if through water. He stared at the priest now. He lay on the floor, resting on Sophia's legs where they had both fallen. The girl's face was covered in red splatter and tears. It was her scream that was slowly becoming louder, penetrating the thick atmosphere.

'Jack? Jack? Jack, for Christ's sake!'

Jack's eyes flicked up. They found Tanya.

She shook him by the shoulders. 'Jack, come on, come back to me, Jack.'

Sophia's scream burst into his mind, the hot air and dust were back on his face, he was there, he was with them and time was back to its regular pace.

'He's dying, help me, he's dying.' Sophia pushed at the priest's throat, blood gushing between her fingers.

Jack moved her hands. 'Shit.' He stood up and paced. 'Fuck.' He stopped and looked down, both women were trying to stem the flow. He shook his head, there was nothing more to do, nothing could save his friend and he knew it.

'Give him the morphine, Tan.'

She looked up at him, shocked at what he was saying.

'Just give it to him, take his pain away.'

'You're not even going to try?' she shouted back at him.

The priest's hands lashed out with panic, hitting the two trying to save him, connecting with their shoulders and faces.

Jack knelt down and grabbed his hands, holding them tight on his chest.

'Just give it to him now, it's a straight through shot, nothing we can do.'

Tanya did as she was told, laying the gun down and running to the car. She returned moments later with a small black pouch, which she unzipped. She removed the needle and stabbed it into the flesh of his upper arm. The priest's arm twitched, followed by the rest of his body. He coughed, sending blood clots feet into the air and peppering the girls and Jack in large ruby smears.

He jerked hard and all three tried to hold him still, his convulsions more powerful than their combined strength.

His voice started blowing through the hole in his neck, no words, just the last frantic noises of life trying to stay but being defeated. His death rattle was gentle, like a parent whispering goodnight to a child, the medication coursing through his veins now, his body going limp. Sophia cradled him gently, directing him on his journey. His chest heaved a couple more times before deflating for the last and Father Vincenzo Camaldo was gone.

Jack stood up, anger fueling his body, no pain in his muscles, just hate. He grabbed Sophia's gun and made his way behind the Land Rover to stand over the man who had shot the priest. He let rip, pulled the trigger over and over, screams getting louder with each thud of metal on flesh. The bang of the gun joined like a symphony in the projection of voice. Then the noise stopped, but his hand didn't. The empty chamber gave light clicks, his finger still pulling the trigger, still pulling until his finger fatigued. He turned the gun over in his hand. He saw the priest's face, saw the smile of his young friend Daniel, his colleague taken as she enjoyed a drink at the pub with friends, the green of his wife's eyes and finally the innocence of his daughter. He dropped to his knees and the butt of the gun smashed through the man's jaw as his arm swung violently, blood dousing him in the face but not deterring him. The jaw bone cracked and caved in on the face, the nose completely inverted. Jack's weapon rained blows down time after time, not seeing what was actually in front of him but the ghosts still swimming in his mind. His arm ran out of strength and he shoved the handle into the eye socket, screamed at the now shattered pieces, hating the mess beneath him and pushed himself up. He breathed heavily, like a fighter who had just won after many rounds, only he felt like a loser.

The two girls sat watching him. Even Tanya looked concerned. Jack took a moment and walked around aimlessly, then a noise brought him back to himself.

'Beagle one, gunshots heard, can you confirm you have target?'

Jack looked at the man whose body he had just violated.

'Shit, Jack, there're more of them. What now, Jack?'

He pointed at Sophia. 'Go. Get on your bike and go. Stay off main roads, take country tracks and go. What direction is that?' he said, pointing up at some local hills, more specifically at the woods.

Sophia looked confused.

'What direction is it, goddamn it?'

'Er, it should be north east,' Tanya replied.

'Beagle one, come in, beagle one, do you need backup?'

Jack picked the walkie talkie up. 'Go now, that way,' he pointed Sophia in the opposite direction, off towards the trees.

She ran to her moped, not bothering with her helmet. It took her a couple of attempts to kick start it; she gave one last look back at the bloody scene with a flick of that long hair and pulled the handle back. The bike sped off. She leant heavily on one side and flung the back wheel out and around a corner.

'Beagle one, no response, we are coming up on your six, going to approach target.'

Jack held the button down. 'This is beagle one, sorry for delay, signal interference due to the hills.'

There was a long pause for a suspicious amount of time – he didn't think they were buying it.

'Copy that, signal boosted. Do you have target?'

'Negative, target fled north east on foot. We took on fire, three armed men also on foot with target,' Jack replied. He didn't know if he was using the correct language.

The reply on the walkie talkie confirmed that he had been close enough and they were happy enough to believe him, *'Copy that, we have a bird here, will send it up. We are one point five clicks out, should be up and in place in five. Wait for further instructions.'*

Jack's body sank with relief. 'Copy that.'

Tanya ran to the BMW and grabbed the Saint Christopher artwork. 'Let's take theirs, I think there is a pretty good chance that ours is being tracked.'

Jack nodded, grabbed one of the rifles and jumped in the passenger seat – he knew full well that Tanya was a better driver than him.

Tanya jumped in and drove the large vehicle directly over the body of the second armed man, half for convenience, half with satisfaction.

'Where to?' Tanya asked, turning off the main road and taking a scenic route in the hope of not meeting the remaining armed personnel on the road.

'I don't know, I need to think and I need some painkillers, my head is killing me. Is the hotel room in your name or mine?'

Tanya smiled. 'Technically neither, I used a fake ID, should be pretty safe there. Dump the car outside the other hotel down the road just in case – should throw them off just enough.'

Jack grunted to agree, his brain couldn't be bothered to use more than a couple of words. 'We can take a proper look at our Saint Christopher then.'

A USE FOR YOU

Jack didn't notice the journey back into the city, not even that it was twice as long or that Tanya doubled back a few times to make sure that they weren't being followed. The suite was a welcome relief – it felt safe, which was an unusual feeling in itself.

Jack threw the painted woodwork on the bed and sat on a chair. He was tired. He was a beaten man.

'Shall I take a look?' Tanya asked, pointing at the small figure on the wooden board.

Jack was about to agree when a small vibration and tinkling of a ringtone came from his pocket. He kicked off the shoes Tanya had managed to get him, blood dripping from one of them – Tanya's stitches on his little toe hadn't stayed in place.

The detective answered his phone, reading *Unknown Number* on the face of it quickly.

'Yes?'

'Not a very warm welcome, detective,' the voice of Agent Charles spoke quietly back.

'I've had a bad day.'

A small chuckle came down the speaker. 'So I have heard. We need to meet.'

Jack lowered the phone and looked up at the ceiling before speaking again, 'Do we really?'

He heard a strange cracking sound. 'I am waiting at a restaurant one block down from your hotel called Ora d'Aria. You have ten minutes.'

The phone went dead.

Jack threw his phone onto the bed next to the taken artefact and walked to the balcony. He could just make out the restaurant in the distance.

'MI5?' Tanya asked, placing a gentle hand on his shoulder.

'In one. Good news is, they still think that we're in the other hotel. Bad news is, I don't have time to come up with a decent plan to keep us alive.'

Tanya looked over at the meeting point. 'Do you think they sent the armed goons?'

Jack chewed the inside of his cheek, deep in thought. 'No, but I don't have a clue who else it could have been. Ok, I've got an idea. I need you to dump my stuff and our little saint in the room I'm meant to be in down there— Actually, put it in the safe in the room, that'll be more convincing.'

To his surprise, she did as he asked, no questions asked. He tried his best to tidy himself up, pretending to use a mirror for its intended purpose.

It might be worth taking one last look at the old mug.'

The detective reached the restaurant just within his time limit. Agent Charles offered him a seat, scooping the white from a boiled egg with a delicate silver spoon.

'Jack— I can call you Jack, can't I? How is your investigation going?' The man maneuvered the spoon to get the last bit from the shell.

Jack gritted his teeth, it hurt his jaw, but that didn't matter. 'About as expected.'

The other man laughed. 'You expected to end up almost dead, did you? You have balls, Jack, I'll give you that. I believe you have exhausted your purpose here. Shame about Father Camaldo. I hear he was a good friend of yours.'

Jack took a deep breath, he wasn't taking the bait. 'He was a good man.'

The MI5 agent threw the spoon down with enough force to shock Jack. 'They all are, Jack, all good men die first, it's the toughened alley rats like us that survive. Good never lasts.' He pushed plane tickets across the table to the detective. 'Go home, Jack, there's nothing here for you, there never was.'

Jack took these words and tumbled them over in his mind. They sounded like the truth. Jack allowed himself an inward smile at the thought of an MI5 agent telling anything other than a complete fabrication.

'So why am I here? Why did you let me come if that's the case?'

Charles picked his teeth. 'Because I had a use for you.'

Jack looked around. He saw Tanya standing across the road, she gave him a small smile.

'A use for me?' Jack looked into the other man's eyes, he could see glee staring back at him.

Where's that come from, Jack? Why is he so happy? What has he manipulated here?'

'Moon,' Jack said blankly. And that was enough – it was just enough to give away the agent's tell. 'That's it, isn't it? You wanted Father Moon. No, you needed to find out who Father Moon really was. I flushed him out for you. Like a rat down a pipe.'

The agent clapped his hands. 'Clever boy. You were my pawn and you exposed a knight and I am the king. Moon was becoming a nuisance with some MI5 business; I needed to find him and eliminate him without getting my own hands dirty. You see, Jack, this whole thing is much bigger than you could ever imagine. Did you really think that I was going to let you come over here and play policeman? And I thought you were clever. You did what I wanted you to do and nothing else. You were my bait and I'm the fisherman. I caught a very big fish.'

'Were you watching me? Did you know Father Moon was torturing me, cutting my fucking toes off?' Jack's temper flared a little and he checked it immediately.

'We heard.' The agent waved his hand up by his ear. 'We still weren't sure of his identity; I had to be one hundred percent, Jack.'

'You bugged my phone?' Jack asked forcibly.

The other man laughed. 'Bugged? Don't be so antiquated. It's called hacking. We heard everything. I wouldn't worry about Father Moon, he will be getting much worse by this point, I promise you that.'

Jack noticed another figure coming into his peripheral vision; it was Casper Collingwood. He gave a nod to Agent Charles that obviously meant more than its appearance.

'Take the tickets, Jack. Go home, get a life actually worth living. Buy a jet ski, or I hear paddle boards are popular at the moment. We're done here, *you're* done here.'

'Just one question. Did you know Lopez was murdered all along?' Jack asked, looking closely at the other man's features, expecting a slight inkling of a lie to betray him.

'Goodbye, Jack, and good luck – something tells me you're going to need it.'

The agent stood up and left with his colleague, leaving Jack with his thoughts and remnants of boiled eggs.

Tanya sat next to him, placing a hand on his knees, looking at the table and the mess left behind.

'Boiled eggs? What a weirdo. So, how did that go?' She pushed the shells away from them, turning her nose up.

Jack nodded. 'They played us, done a pretty good job of it, too,' he answered, picking up the plane tickets to take a closer look.

'You don't think that they met us out here to make sure the room was empty so they could steal what I put inside the safe, do you?' Tanya asked ironically, laying her head on his shoulder.

Jack nodded again. 'I do indeed. And I want them to think that is exactly what they did.'

Tanya pulled away to look at him, confusion on her face. 'What do you mean? They obviously took the Saint Christopher.'

Jack gave her a broad smile. 'And Saint Christopher carried the Christ child across the water and delivered him to the other side.' The detective took his hand from his pocket and spun something on the table.

It remained unrecognizable until its pace slowed and it finally stopped spinning, still rocking slightly. It was a little wooden boy. He stopped the last of its movement, held it up, pinching the top half and pulling it off. Inside was a USB stick, which had been neatly hidden in a cavity.

'You sneaky bastard. When did you find that?' Tanya said, taking it from him.

'It came off in my hand right when Sophia pointed a gun at me.' Jack took Tanya's hand in hope of some reassurance in its embrace. 'Do you think she's ok?' Jack asked, not much conviction to his question.

Somehow, Tanya managed a comforting smile. 'She's a survivor, wherever she is, she'll keep fighting. Come on, let's get this back to the room – there's a computer in there, we can see what all the fuss is about.' She returned the embrace on her fingers with a tight squeeze and pulled him up to his feet.

Tanya settled in front of the computer and plugged the USB into a port, Jack leaning on the back of her chair for support. His toe was still bleeding so he left the shoe on this time – at least it aided in putting some pressure on it.

The computer fired up.

'Goes to show how impressive a suite this is – having access to a brand-new computer without it being tied down,' Jack thought.

Windows opened and Tanya ran the mouse around them like a pro – the detective's eyes could hardly keep up.

'Wow, huge files. Nothing fancy, though – Excel and

Word, mainly. Let's try this one.'

She double clicked and a file containing a large table, at least five columns wide and several pages long, opened.

The writing was small, they both leaned in.

'List of names, what's that next to them?' Jack asked, jabbing the screen with a keen finger.

Every name had a random word next to it and beside that some numbers and then over one column again parts of addresses, some of them just postcodes, others road names and a couple with the full mailing address.

'And what's that, money? In euros?' Jack wasn't sure what he was looking at but there was a lot of names on this, so many he dared not think about what he was unearthing. 'Open another file.'

Similar information came up again, only this time there were dates and more information than just a word or two in several of the columns and rows.

'Shit, look at that. "Fourteen-year-old male, brown hair, brown eyes. Thirty-three thousand euros,"' Jack read aloud, making himself feel sick. 'It's fucking order forms and receipts.'

Just as the penny dropped, so did the screen, turning instantly black, numbers and symbols flashing up and down, none of them remaining long enough to be read.

'What's going on?' Jack asked, panicking.

Tanya ripped the USB stick from the computer and then reached under the table to pull the Ethernet cable from the wall. It came out with a snap but still, her head fell into her hands and Jack's heart sank just as far.

'What just happened, Tan? Tell me we didn't just lose all of that information.' Jack knew the answer, but still waited in hope for her reply.

Tanya slammed her hands down on the desk. 'I'll have to see what I can recover when we get back home, but yeah, I think we lost it all.'

Jack stuttered, 'What? How? I mean, how can that happen? That's not possible.'

Tanya plucked up the courage to face him. 'I've never seen technology like that. I've heard it's possible but never known it put into practice. That's high-tech, Jack, that's MI5 and up. Maybe even MI5 would struggle to pull that off, to be honest. The number of computers they would have needed to piggyback to get that much power that fast …'

Jack stared at the computer. 'What do you mean? I don't understand, they tracked it down?'

She nodded slightly. 'Whoever it was, they knew what they were looking for and had one intention – to destroy it. They matched the searched content from every server around Europe, most likely, finding the corresponding data in seconds and attacking it. The information just …' She shrugged. 'Just ate itself.'

Jack's eyes looked up at the heavens for answers, his body giving him enough pain to match his mental anguish.

'I knew it was theoretically possible. If I hadn't been so hot-headed, I should have seen that coming, I should have disconnected it.'

Jack watched as Tanya beat herself up and decided to save her. 'There's no way you could have known; it's not your fault.' He almost sounded convincing but his heart wasn't in it – it had gone the moment those files had disappeared.

He couldn't take much more, he needed air, he needed pain relief and, above all, he needed to work out what to do next. If ever he had hit a brick wall before, it paled in comparison to this one. He walked out onto the balcony, holding the railing hard, feeling his palms trying to bend the metal beneath his grip.

Tanya joined him. She cuddled up to his arm and said nothing.

The silence was grating on him. 'He was a good man, I could feel it. Does that make sense?'

Tanya stood tall on her toes and kissed his cheek. 'Yeah, it does and yeah, he was a good man. A bible-basher, but a good man.'

Jack wanted to laugh, but he didn't have the energy. 'I've got to find out what's going on, I can't let him die for nothing.'

Tanya held tight around his bicep. 'He didn't, he stopped them from shooting Sophia. I bet he wouldn't have wanted it any other way.'

'Maybe.' Jack sighed. 'There is one other thing, if you wouldn't mind?'

'Hmm?' she replied, intrigued.

'My toe won't stop bleeding; you couldn't sew it back up again, could you?'

Tanya opened her mouth to answer, but a pulse of hot air took her breath away.

Like the beat of a huge drum, a pressure squeezed in on them, followed by an almighty explosion.

THE TEACHER

Tanya rocked back on her heels. Jack fell against the open door, just managing to catch himself and stay on his feet. Both grimaced with ringing ears, like babies had screeched directly on their eardrums.

Jack frantically looked around, trying to work out how much danger they were in, but that wasn't the case – the explosion had been some way down the road.

Tanya finally managed to right herself properly. Massaging her ears, she accidentally shouted at Jack, 'Isn't that the hotel you were meant to be staying in?'

Screams sounded out on the road below them, the odd bit of debris still hitting the pavement. Some people ran away from the centre of the commotion, others towards it, no one understanding exactly what they were doing. A large cloud of black smoke pushed its way up above the buildings.

'No prizes for guessing what room it would have been, either,' Jack replied, his face screwed in pain from the blast. There was still some residual heat in the air. He focused on a man running down the street, holding his face, blood drenching his shirt.

Tanya gasped at the sight of a woman limping out of

the smoke, most of her clothes ripped off, skin visibly burned a bright pink, even at their distance.

'The one I was standing in about half an hour ago, I wager.' She rubbed at her ears once again; the high-pitched noise relentlessly refusing to subside.

Vehicles screeched to a halt below them as more and more voices joined in with the fray, those who could shout loudest trying to take charge, directing stumbling bodies and those who had come to help.

The chaos reminded Jack of an ant's nest being drowned in hot water – panic-driven instinct, fight or flight in its truest form.

'I feel like we should help,' Tanya said.

Jack shook his head. 'Nothing we can do now, the police and ambulances will be arriving any second.' He kept shaking his head in disbelief. 'That was for us, you know. Well, for me at least.'

He tore his eyes away and returned to the room and took up residence in a chair.

Tanya entered through the net curtains moments later. 'Casper Collingwood. It must have been him. But a bomb, to get rid of us, that's overkill, isn't it? Like, literally.'

Jack played with the stubble below his bottom lip and raised his eyebrows in agreement.

Both jumped at a sound then the pair felt ridiculous in tandem as they realised it was just the detective's phone ringing.

He took it from his pocket and read the name out, 'It's McQuade, what does she want now?'

He was just about to answer when Tanya stopped him quickly, 'Probably best to destroy that after this phone call.'

He nodded and answered it, 'Ma'am.'

Her voice was harsh and rushed, 'Jack, you are in so much shit. Where are you? Are you still in Italy? Tell me you're on your way home.'

'Yes, should be back soon, what's wrong?'

'Everything, you are meant to be here for questioning on the Peters' case, the defence would appear to have a new angle from which to attack you. You really are in the shitter, not to mention me too for apparently sanctioning your shitting jolly. For one, I was told that you were no longer needed in court, and second, I was the one who didn't want you to go over there in the first place. The situation has turned really shit here, Jack; you'll be under arrest from the moment you step back on British soil. They've issued bail for you.'

Jack was confused. 'Charged with what?'

McQuade laughed. 'With whatever they please. I'm being kept way out of the loop on this one, but it's a real situation here.'

'Yeah, I kind of have a lot going on here, too,' Jack replied.

'Not as big as this, you don't,' McQuade answered uncompromisingly. She had her stern voice on, but he noticed a different tone in it – had he not known her better, he could have sworn it sounded like panic.

Jack listened as sirens signaled the emergency services arriving at the scene of the explosion. 'If you say so, ma'am. What do they want to question me over? He pleaded guilty, for Christ sake.'

'That's the problem, Jack, they've changed the plea and, from what I hear, they have built a bloody strong case – a case against you.'

Jack shook his head. 'This has got to be a joke, there's no way they think he can get off.'

'Well, no one here is laughing. I suggest you either get your shit together and get back here ready for a fight, or you don't come back at all. Either way, I may be losing my job over this so I couldn't give a shit. I've got to go.' She hung up the phone, leaving the detective perplexed.

'Sounds like an interesting conversation,' Tanya joked, sitting on the floor at his feet.

Jack explained about the exchange with McQuade. The

pair talked over the same subjects, trying to make sense of them, trying to find the link. It all started with Jessica and Felicity and spiraled, picking up mess along the way. A dead priest with information on what looked like a pedophile ring, only with MI5 breathing down their neck, too. And a Bristolian teacher who used to move children around, but with no seeming connection to Italy.

'Could Father Lopez have been part of some sort of secret organisation, then suddenly got a conscience? No, Jack, that's not right, he saved two girls years ago, think harder— no, feel harder, who was he, what did he stand for? The Church. No, that's who he stood for, *what did he know to be right? And Moon, why did he keep asking about Pearce? How did he know him?'*

Jack threw question after question at himself. It was too messed up, he needed to focus – or try to un-focus, maybe, let himself see the wider scope.

He watched Tanya. She sat at the writing desk, scribbling on paper, using the straight edge of the Bible to create tables and charts.

He looked over her shoulder. 'Is that what was on the memory stick?'

More sirens went by the window, distracting them. The noise had quietened, even though hundreds of people now gathered. The police and ambulance noises weren't like that of those in England. They played a solid, mournful note, it was harsh to hear but clearly signified the occasion.

'I have a photographic memory,' the woman replied, returning to her work. 'Only I didn't read much of it, just a few columns.'

Jack laughed. 'A photographic memory and I still get surprised.'

Tanya handed him the paper. 'That's about it.'

He looked at the rows and columns, some were filled out, most were blank.

He read the first and most complete line of words out, 'Falcon, Saint, Carpenter, Canine, Rosebud, Rosehip, Fuhrer,' Jack turned his nose up and then carried on,

'Teacher, Raging Bull, Alarm, Designer. What do you think, code names?'

'I guess so,' Tanya replied, but shrugged her shoulders, unconvinced.

'What do you think about these numbers?'

Tanya took another look. 'Well, they look a lot like bank accounts, but no way is there enough digits. And, look, Rosebud and Rosehip's look pretty much the same – only one digit different. Unless that's my mistake.'

'Unlikely,' Jack retorted. 'I think they are accounts, but not for a bank. And I think those particular two are probably related, or live together – or they could even be a couple, I guess.'

Jack took the paper back, he could feel something, something staring at him, daring him to spot it.

Then the warm trickle of recognition filled him, a glow of hope fueling his body with a strange energy.

'He *is* the teacher,' he said to the room.

Tanya looked confused. 'Who?'

'Pearce, he told me clear as day when I interrogated him, he is *The Teacher*.' Jack turned the information towards her and pointed at the name. 'And I wonder who Saint might be.'

'You think it's Moon?' she asked, not sounding convinced. 'Surely he could have gone for something like … I don't know, Apollo or Eclipse.'

Jack shook his head. 'Not grand enough for that arrogant prick. I would bet my last penny on it being him, I can feel it.'

'So, what, we have a paedophile ring spanning across Europe, now?' Tanya said, turning in the chair to face him.

'Would explain why MI5 want to claim it all on their own – would be a huge publicity boost for them. God knows they need it. Would also account for Moon being obsessed with Pearce.'

Tanya considered his words. 'Makes sense, I guess. The killing of Father Lopez, realising he was gathering information, making it look like an illness, arousing no suspicion. And then we turn up, a day after you arrest another cell in their organisation, asking questions that shouldn't need to be answered.'

Jack nodded excitedly. 'Completely coincidental, but they weren't to know that. They panicked, they couldn't let me get any further, it exposes everything, so Moon tries to kill me. The only reason Agent Charles even let me into Italy was because he knew that Lopez had been killed, he just didn't know by who. It was obvious my timing would flush someone out of the woodwork, and it fucking kills me to say it, but it was bloody clever plan.'

Jack noticed something troubling Tanya, he stayed quiet to let her speak, 'But why would MI5 try to kill you? They got what they wanted; they think they got the whole lot on that memory stick, not knowing you still had it. Seems a bit risky.'

Jack thought on this. 'You're right. And why send a virus to destroy the information on the USB? Unless … unless it wasn't them.'

Tanya's eyes widened. 'You think the Church has the power to pull off a bombing and the most sophisticated hack known to man? Jack, come on, I know you don't like them—'

He interrupted her, 'They certainly have the finances, but no, I'm sure sweeping things under the rug is more their style. Not carnage.' He pointed out the window, where more loud emergency vehicles had joined the melee.

Tanya threw her hands onto her hips. 'Then who?'

The detective waved the piece of paper. '*Them.*'

WHAT DO YOU WANT FROM ME?

Jack turned on the hotel TV and found the news while Tanya packed her bag and got one of her fake IDs ready. He was impressed at the secret compartment in the bottom of the handbag – completely x-ray proof, not that he understood how it worked.

The hotel's TV was already set to have English subtitles on. It did have English news channels, but they were obviously off the pace.

'At least three dead and many more injured. The killed victims to be confirmed and named so far are an English policeman, Jack O'Connor, his fiancé Tanya Red, and a priest, Father Richard Moon. Families have been informed and police say the death toll is likely to rise.'

'One, I'm a detective, two, like you would ever be engaged to anyone, let alone me, and three, what family exactly have they informed?' Jack looked at Tanya. 'Do you have any family?'

Tanya zipped up her suitcase and blew her disheveled hair from her eyes. 'I have a sister I see about twice a year and my dad's still alive – just. My mum left when I was about five, remember?'

Jack smiled. 'Sorry, you know what my memory is like.

I remember now, I tried to track her down when I was trying to put you away. I think she had run away to Peru or something, wasn't it?'

Tanya pulled her case to the door. 'Something like that. My dad always said she had a fancy for black men, that's why she left. What the hell that means, I don't know, racist bugger. Right, I'm off, are you sure you'll be able to get back ok?'

Jack stood, limped over to her and gave her a kiss on the forehead. 'Yeah, I'll be ok, I've got a few favours I can call in.'

Tanya didn't look impressed about leaving him on his own. 'I'll get some ID sorted for you by the time you get back. Just … I don't know, try to stay out of trouble for a few hours, maybe?'

Jack laughed. 'You can't hurt someone who's already dead.'

'Here, it's clean, you should be able to make as many phone calls as you want on this without them tracking you, just don't phone—'

Jack took a phone from her hand and interrupted her, 'Any close friends directly, they'll be monitoring their calls. Tan, I'm a detective, give me some credit, please.'

She left reluctantly, leaving Jack to figure out who the best person to phone was.

He opened up the home screen and dialed Yeovil Police Station.

A young officer answered politely.

'Hi, sorry, I have called the wrong number, can I be put through to Bristol main office?' The phone went quiet then he heard classical music, followed by another voice. 'Hi, yes, can I be put through to CID, please?' Again, Jack waited until someone answered. 'Sorry! I have been put through to the wrong department yet again,' he lied, 'I need to speak with an officer Nitin Kapoor.'

It took a while for this one to connect – it always did, he was awful for answering his phone. Then Jack realised that the news may have gotten back to Bristol by now that he was supposedly dead.

'Shit …'

The phone was answered and the first thing that came to Jack was to put on a Dutch accent to disguise himself.

'Sorry, please, can I be put through to pathology?' he asked, his own voice sounding strange even to himself. If he had been watching from the other side of the room, he probably would have been laughing at his own attempt of sounding like he was from the Netherlands.

Nitin was a good officer, he wouldn't just put any joker through. 'Can I ask what it is concerning?'

Jack rolled his eyes at the thought of having to do the ridiculous impression again. 'It is regarding the Pearce investigation, we have evidence that he may have been in the country and need to confirm some things with your pathology department.'

Even Jack knew that sounded like nonsense, but hoped his luck would finally start turning.

An unconvinced voice came back, 'I'm not on that case, so I don't know too much about it, but I do know the pathologist you need. I'll put you through to her now.'

Jack held his breath and then sighed loudly as the phone got patched through and started to ring.

'Dr Sellers,' a quiet, defeated voice said.

'Aubrie, it's me,' Jack replied, instantly needing to hold the phone away from his ear to protect it from a scream.

He heard other people in the room with Aubrie showing concern and coming to her aid.

'No, sorry, it's fine, just had some … some good news, that's all. I won a … I won a holiday. Sorry, I'll take this outside,' Jack heard her say to the others in her company. 'Can you hold a minute and I will go somewhere more private?'

Jack registered that she had directed that at him. 'Yeah, sure.'

'Thank you, won't be a minute.' The phone went quiet

before erupting again, 'Jack, you sodding, *sodding* arsehole, you're a sodding arsehole, do you know that?'

Jack grimaced. 'Yeah, you mentioned.'

'You shut your mouth, you sodding prick. No, you're an arsehole, you don't even deserve to be a prick. Do you know what you have just done to me, do you know what I have just been through in the last hour?'

Jack answered cautiously, 'I take it that you heard I was dead, then?'

Aubrie laughed sarcastically. 'You think? And lo and behold, even without the help of your medium friend Florence Keilty, here I am speaking with you from beyond the sodding grave. What are you sodding playing at?'

Jack didn't answer.

'That wasn't rhetorical, Jack, I mean it, I literally stopped crying for two seconds and you phoned me up like it was nothing. I can't handle this, I think I need to see the doctor for a prescription of Prozac.' Aubrie breathed heavily, obviously trying to calm herself down.

'Aren't you a doctor, can't you just write your own prescription?' Jack asked.

'Don't you sodding start with me, Jack, don't you dare,' she replied, again going back to inhaling and exhaling loudly.

Jack gave her a chance to come to terms with what had just been asked of her emotions before explaining his predicament of being technically dead and needing to get back to Bristol.

The conversation took twists and turns as the pathologist wanted to know more and more with every passing detail that Jack divulged.

'So, what do you want from me? I can't just drive to Florence and pick you up.'

'I wish, but no. I need you to get in contact with an old friend of ours, I'm pretty sure he does business out this way, or if he doesn't, I'd like to think my name would intrigue him enough — after hearing I'm dead, anyway,'

Jack replied, going on to give her the details of who to contact and how, and also where Jack would be able to meet them.

Aubrie was just about to hang up and start immediately trying to arrange his transport back to Britain when a thought occurred to the detective.

'Aubrie, I need a couple of lists. All the children that are suspected of being linked with Pearce and all those whose bodies have been found. I'm trying to work out who we still have missing.'

Aubrie answered, but not willingly, 'Ok, but don't you have bigger things to worry about? If you're found alive, you'll be dragged up in front of the Peters defence and if you aren't found, what the hell are you going to do next? You can't be dead for the rest of your life.'

Jack tried not to laugh at how ridiculous that sounded – he thought it best not to displease her any more than he already had.

'It's ok, I have a plan, just need to sort some things out first,' he assured her.

'To be honest, Jack, head office has been monitoring me really closely on this one. As soon as I've completed any work, they've taken it from me and given it to the investigation team. They didn't like me having any copies, they only let me after I argued with them for about half an hour. I'll try to get it for you, but since you left it's all gone a bit cagey here.'

Jack thought on this for a minute. 'Is that young kid … what's his name, Timmins? Is he still on the case?'

'Yeah, I think so, he's become a bit of wonder kid since you two found that boy,' Aubrie answered. 'Jack, do me a favour, won't you? Stay out of trouble for a bit?'

'Why does everyone keep saying that to me?'

SCREAM FOR ME

Jack sat, waiting on a wall outside the main train station in Florence, Firenze Santa Maria Novella. It made Bristol's Temple Meads station look like the set of a post-apocalyptic dystopia. He had only taken a quick look around inside the actual building as the amount of CCTV cameras started to make him feel uncomfortable. He was sure that whoever was looking for him would most probably now assume him dead, but on the off chance that he had been spotted, he wanted to play it as safe as he could.

A small colourful lorry, with images of healthy farm foods across its side, pulled up in front of him.

'Detective O'Connor, fancy meeting with you here,' the creaky drawl of Yanislav Ivanovic, real name Luka Alkaev, gloated from the driver's window.

I knew he wouldn't be able to resist coming himself.'

'For once, it is good to see you, Yanislav. Is this my taxi?' Jack asked, banging the side of the lorry.

Yanislav gave a harsh smile, showing the many scars around his mouth. 'It is, how you say, a car share. When we get to France, you will be accompanied by others.'

'Fine by me, as long as you can get me home I am not

bothered,' Jack replied.

Yanislav spoke to a colleague sitting in the cab in another language. The man grunted, hopped out and opened the rear door of the lorry.

Jack was instantly overwhelmed by the smell of fish, then he fully realised that the lorry was chilled. There were a couple of blankets waiting for him and several empty boxes that Jack quickly decided would make good insulation beneath him. It was going to be cold – uncomfortable, maybe – but very doable.

The journey through Italy was uneventful, even pleasurable at times – those times being the ones where Jack fell asleep with exhaustion.

The rear door didn't open again until France, where several men, all of different looking origins, started climbing in hastily.

'No, no, wait, get out!' Yanislav shouted. He then shouted in another language, but the words sounded like exactly the same sentence.

Even Jack clambered down, rubbing his legs back to life and pacing, his body temperature coming back up. He watched a couple of men climb in. By the look of their tattoos, they were gang members rather than mere migrants. Then Jack was shocked – right at the back of the lorry compartment, the men pulled away a false wall. There was a small cavity, barely a few feet wide and right below the cooling system.

'You must go in there,' Yanislav told them while pointing. He lit a cigarette, his body language all that of someone waiting to have a confrontation with the detective.

'Is this a joke?' Jack said, doing all he could to keep from slapping the roll up from the man's mouth.

The gangster took a long drag. 'No one here is laughing, detective.'

Jack and three other men maneuvered themselves into

the small space, while two other men pushed the fake wall back into place, leaving them all in the dark.

A loud bang came from the other side of the partition. 'Remember to stay quiet,' Yanislav called gleefully. 'That means you too, detective.'

The journey began uncomfortably and only got worse, the turns pushing the strangers against each other and the bumps clattering their knees on the back wall, not to mention the cold. Jack could feel his lips tightening, resisting against the shakes of his freezing body. A small light behind him began sparking in and out of life. One of the other men had started trying to light a plastic lighter.

'No, stop,' Jack said, sounding like the typical Brit speaking to a stranger of unknown origin. He always wondered if his ignorance towards recognising where someone was from by their appearance or accent made him more or less racist.

'No fire, gasses.' The detective started pointing up at the refrigerating system inches from their heads.

The man shook his head. 'Cold.'

Jack pulled his blanket awkwardly from his shoulders and offered it to him. 'Take this, but no fire, too dangerous.'

The man tried to refuse, but Jack insisted – they were close enough now that he could force it onto the man's shoulders.

Another man spoke unexpectedly from Jack's other side, 'The gasses aren't the problem. The oxygen level is low in here. Even if he did manage to get a flame, it would burn out remaining oxygen in a couple of minutes.'

Jack managed to turn and angle his body towards the new man. His muscles actually ached from fighting back the uncontrollable spasms.

'I am an engineer back in my country. I worked on systems like this. My name is Omid. You are a detective.'

Jack shook his hand, the cold shivers doing most of the work. '*Was* a detective, I think I may have got the sack.'

Omid smiled. Jack could tell that he didn't have a clue what he meant but was being as polite as feasibly possible given their current situation.

It wasn't that Jack wanted to be rude and not speak for the remainder of the journey, it was that it was taking all of his effort to stay alive. His body shivers became violent and then tipped over the edge into tightness and cramps. He tucked his fingers as snugly as he could under his armpits, concentrating on his heart rate. The muscles in his chest were trying to move by themselves, looking to race out of control. He watched the plumes of breath leave his mouth, studying their shape as he tried to keep his mind from panicking. A few times it tried to work out how far they had travelled, working backwards from the time on his phone, how fast they were likely to be going, subtracting from the miles until their destination. His brain started struggling to compute then began taking little side streets away from his main train of thought, randomly diverting its way as the synapses missed fire, the intense cold now taking full effect, slowing the world down.

Jack's eyes closed under the pressure. *Just a little sleep to refuel, just rest the cylinders for a short moment.'*

His fingers ran over small indentations that he had made. Grooves in a skirting board, a specific pattern, spelling out the initials F.O. The second initial was squarer than he would have liked but maybe one day, long after he was gone, they would find his marks and know that he had been there, that he had existed at all. He tucked the small shard of glass away quickly as two men opened the heavy iron door.

'You don't need to keep moving them, I told you he has been dealt with. He got lucky in the first place, he didn't have a clue what he was looking at. No, the detective has been eliminated.' The two men stopped speaking to look down on their captive, detest across their faces.

'But we should keep the plan the same. Would usually go to The Teacher for disposal, he has links down this part. I've made other arrangements, however, for this one. They'll be here in a day; you can stay while they do the deed and help with all the lifting. Have you got the plastic sheeting?'

The other man nodded. 'Yeah, loads of farming suppliers around here, I managed to get silage sheeting, it's about forty meters long, but it looks far less suspicious buying in bulk like that. And we've always got spare then, too,' he joked.

His friend laughed. 'Very true. Until he arrives, then, just carry on as you were. Might as well have a bit of fun with this one,' he pointed at the young body on the floor, barely conscious due to lack of food and water. 'Before it's too late. Not sure if they'll even last the night.'

The first of the men walked over to the helpless child on the floor and kicked him hard in the calf muscle before leaving the room, just giving enough time to his friend to pat him supportively on the shoulder.

The second of the capturers took a deep breath, rolling his head around, his neck clicking with the strain. The light clink of metal echoed as if it had been a church bell in the victim's ear. The tell-tale call of a belt being undone followed by the harsh sound of friction between leather and thread as it was pulled through its loops.

The child lay there, waiting for their fate, there were too many uses for that belt that they had experienced to be able to predict where exactly the pain was about to come from.

I'm the child, it's me, I'm scared,' Jack spoke inside his head, but then he was lost in the moment again, becoming nothing but a spectator, observing the interaction. He was watching it like a horror movie, only he couldn't pause it or escape it, his gaze was fixed.

The belt tickled its way up the child's leg, slowly touching the sensitive rear of their thigh, tickling up to the buttocks, stopping on a cheek.

Then the man thrust his weight violently onto Jack's back, the detective becoming the victim again, feeling the pain as if it were real and right now it most certainly felt tangible. He felt as the man scrabbled his hands together, pulling them through a loop made in the belt, the shard of glass falling unnoticed. The detective had moved from being an onlooker to becoming a star in the show – a show he desperately wanted to end.

The man leant down into Jack's ear. 'I want you to fucking scream for me, because this is going to really hurt.'

The belt was tied tightly around the detective's wrists, his mind willing his body to fight back, but his limbs didn't resist. None of his body did, not when the erection could be felt pressing in the crevasse of his backside, nor when the underwear was sadistically tugged down to his knees. Jack wanted this boy to scream and fight, he wanted to transfer his energy to him, give him the fight that he had, but he couldn't. He was stuck somewhere between himself and this helpless child, not feeling a part of either while experiencing the pain of both. All he was able to do was be a passenger to the hell. He felt the man force his legs apart.

A naked penis started to probe near his genitals.

'Please, please, scream, please fight, please, just do something. Don't let them do this to you.' The voice in Jack's head was desperate, it wanted to help this child, but just as much – and he was ashamed to admit it – he wanted to escape the hell himself. He didn't want to feel the penetration.

F.O.

A sharp pain spiked on the side of Jack's head, like a bucket of cold water dropped over him. He was shocked back into reality. He could feel his own body weight, his large frame, now laying on the ground, not the broken, emaciated one of before.

Bright light offended his senses, he breathed heavily, the wet mist that had been there before no longer existed. He was back to himself and he was alive, two things he didn't expect to happen.

'Detective? Are you alive?' Yanislav's voice spoke blankly and somewhat disinterestedly.

'He's raping him then they're going to kill him,' Jack replied, not able to consciously form sentences yet.

The gangster laughed. 'Is that right? Well, he won't need this,' he replied, as Jack vaguely recognised a blanket being pulled from another man and placed over himself. 'You had better get yourself warmed up and go and stop them, then, detective.' Yanislav walked away, his outline, which had been shadowing Jack from the sunshine, disappeared and the detective was left alone.

Jack lost track of time; he knew there had been men

and a lorry that had driven away. It was a while after that he realised the metal lighter in his pocket was pressing harshly into his skin. He pulled out the small metal box, fiddled with the lid and flint, desperately trying to get it lit. The flame was small, but the heat grew quickly, bringing life back into Jack's hands. He sat up and observed his surroundings. He was in a small batch of woods, the sound of speeding cars the only accompanying sound to the birdsong. The woolen blanket was giving him shelter from a small breeze and insulating his body heat, his muscles slowly feeling renewed.

He should have felt relief, but the hardened dead body of the engineer lay peacefully a little over ten yards away. What really made him angry was that he knew that Yanislav could have gotten rid of the body anywhere – he hadn't let the other men out at this stop, for example – but no, he had wanted Jack to see it. Just another game, one man's life, a father maybe, a son, but still, it was nothing more than a game to the Polish gangster.

Too many people have gone, faces that swum in and out of his mind, the clearest of all of them always those of his wife and daughter. It took a while for him to find the energy to leave the secluded spot but, covering the dead man completely with the blanket, he headed to the road to hitchhike.

Of all the people to have stopped and picked up a dirty, unkept, clearly dangerous man, it had been a woman verging on the age of antique. She hadn't even been going to Bristol, but insisted on dropping him there after discovering that Jack was a police officer – the same as her son. Jack hadn't recognised the name when she told him, but managed to pretend that it registered somewhere in his mind.

Waving off one of the kindest women he had met, Jack was surprised that the city hadn't changed. Not one thing seemed different. The same grey roads still cut between valleys of uncompromising, unforgiving structures, all built with purpose, with that being their main function and aesthetic their last.

Not that he had much time with his own thoughts – the woman had liked to chat – but Jack had managed to come up with something that resembled a plan.

It took several hours, but after buying a handful of street magazines and a high vis jacket from the pound shop, along with a baseball cap, Jack could wait unnoticed as a rag salesman pretty much anywhere. He sat on a small wall, watching bike racks, waiting for a specific police officer.

'Timmins?'

A man in a cycling helmet, ankle clips and illuminous strips turned around slowly.

'Sarge? You're meant to be— I mean, you're dead, aren't you? What's with the clothes? Seriously, though, you were killed on holiday in Italy. Is it really you?'

Jack was frustrated already – being dead wasn't as fun as he thought it was going to be.

'Yes, it's me, no, I'm not dead, I was set up. I think it's a cover-up.' Jack took in his surroundings suspiciously. 'Can we go somewhere and talk? Right now?'

Officer Timmins turned and looked around. 'Oh yeah, course. Hang on, I'll lock my bike back up.' A few minutes later, the two men sat in a coffee shop in the impressive Cabot Circus shopping centre.

'So, no one knows you're alive? Wow, you're like a spy or a superhero or something!' the young officer said excitedly.

Jack felt a billiard ball of regret settle in his stomach – perhaps the faith he was putting in this young man was misplaced. 'It's not as cool as you might think. If the wrong person finds out that I'm not dead, they'll make sure that I am, and I should imagine it will be much more painful than a quick hotel room explosion.'

A waitress placed two cups of warm drink on the table in front of them.

'Right, yeah. And you came to me?' the younger man said, surprise and glee emanating from his voice.

'Who else? You helped me find that boy and I think this all might be linked. You're a good officer, you should remember that,' Jack said. He wasn't playing to Timmins' ego to manipulate him – which he could have done quite easily – it was more that he could see someone who had been beaten down by life and needed a confidence boost. If he had someone he respected tell him he was worth a damn when he was younger, maybe he wouldn't think so little of himself every day.

'Well, I've been told that I'm a crap officer lately. After you left, outside resources were brought in to evaluate our station's performance.' Timmins took a long sip of his drink, getting cream across his top lip.

Jack rubbed the thick stubble on his chin. 'Is that right? Are these the same people showing a lot of interest in the Pearce case?'

Timmins nodded and took another sip. 'Yeah, they want copies of everything. We have to debrief with them at the end of every day, too. McQuade is losing her shit with it. Every now and then she just swears at the wall but calls it Jack.'

The older man laughed. 'Is that right? I'll be sure to remember that one. Well, the Pearce case is what I need to talk to you about. How much of a good officer are you? I mean, do you leave everything at the door?'

Timmins looked a little confused. 'What, you mean emotionally?'

Jack tried not to show frustration. 'Well, that is always good to keep in mind, but no. I meant paperwork.'

Timmins smiled. 'Of course I leave all my paperwork at the office, it would be completely irresponsible of me to take it home. No, I make copies onto a memory stick and take that instead.' The young officer picked up his laptop bag and took out his computer.

'That's my boy,' Jack said, slapping him on the

shoulder.

The detective waited for the home screen to fire up before moving around to sit by the policeman.

'I'm so glad you're not dead, sarge.'

Jack smiled. 'Me too.'

'Otherwise, I would have no one to go to with this. I found something out. I don't know what it means, but it's pretty weird.'

Jack had for a moment thought that the young lad had been glad for Jack to remain breathing because he looked up to him as a mentor, but no, of course not, it was because he had no one else to talk to.

He clicked a couple of files and opened some images, photos that had been crudely taken directly from paper copies.

'Did you take these?' the detective asked.

'Yeah, on my phone, had to be quick. Seriously, sarge, the place has gone into like lockdown. We were told that if we made any sort of statement to the press, we would be suspended immediately.'

Jack shook his head. 'What the hell is going on? How is the lad, anyway? Is he still in a coma?'

Timmins shrugged his shoulders. 'No idea. Don't think they would tell me if he was ok or not.'

Jack's hands went up to his cropped hair and rubbed at it, desperately trying to help his brain make sense of it all, then something popped back into his memory. The carved letters that he – or rather *someone* – had been carving before being raped. He felt as though he had half been watching someone scrape them into the wood and half actually doing it himself. There was a barrier of grey confusion to where his mind ended and this locked up child's began.

'Sarge, you ok? Shall I show you what I've found?'

Jack looked at the man, but at the same time saw straight through him. 'Yeah, in a minute. I need something first, I need a list of all the children victims that Pearce has been linked with but are still missing, can you help with that?'

Timmins chewed his lips in thought. 'I'm not sure, I have some of the lists, I'll have a look.'

Jack remembered the letters in the wood, F.O. He could almost feel the splintered strands of rotten timber beneath his fingertips.

'No, I don't have of the confirmed deceased. I have … hang on a moment. There, a full list of suspected children that he may have come into contact with that are either missing or declared dead.'

'Wow,' Jack couldn't hold in his surprise at how much longer the list had become.

'Who are you looking for?' Timmins asked, rolling the list up and down.

'I don't know,' Jack said flatly.

Timmins looked confused. 'Ok, what about year range? That's how it's catalogued, going back to nineteen seventy-four.'

Jack sighed. 'I don't know that either, but not that long ago. Nothing past eighteen years, at the most.'

The young officer nodded and scrolled the list about halfway to the top, still leaving three whole pages. Jack breathed heavily and started concentrating on the names. One beginning with F caught his eye.

'Stop, no, carry on, wrong last name. Stop, there, look. Freddie, Freddie Owens, *F.O.*'

MASS GRAVE

Jack nearly fell off the front of his seat as he got a good look at the name. 'Have you got any other information on him?'

Timmins brought the computer closer to himself. 'I don't know, some of the kids didn't have any information, not even addresses. Wait, yeah, I've got this.' The next file that opened was a Word document, clearly not a photograph this time.

'Oh,' Timmins said, disheartened.

Jack sat back. 'I take it that's it?'

The page was almost blank, just a few contact details below which Jack read *investigation notes unknown.*

'There have been a few with no notes, just like this. Apparently, there was a bad flood in one of the buildings, lots of old records damaged,' Timmins told Jack as he looked through more file names, just in case they had missed something.

'You don't say?' Jack replied sarcastically. It never did cease to amaze him how often records went awry. At least six cases, high profile ones at that, seemed to lose the odd piece of evidence mysteriously, or a statement wouldn't quite make it to the save button.

'Is it ok to show you what I found, sarge? I did a little digging,' the young officer asked timidly.

Jack had tipped his head back to rest upon the chair, he pulled it up with effort.

'Sorry, yeah, of course.'

The young police officer smiled half-heartedly and started tapping the keys. 'Well, I tried to look up Pearce a bit more, see if there was any old media or local journals, maybe. Turns out the name Pearce isn't easy to track. I came up with tons of stuff, a lot of it with paedophilia, too, but nothing directly linked to our Pearce. But I did find this; it's an old newspaper clipping from an online archive. Now, he looks very young as this was from nineteen-sixty and the image is a bit grainy, but I would bet my bike on that being him.'

Jack looked at the article on the screen and his colleague was right: it was very grainy and he did look incredibly young, but still, it surely was Pearce.

Jack read the first paragraph aloud.

'Father O'Flaherty has finally managed to raise funds for the roof of one of Ireland's many children's homes, Tuam care home. With the help of the village residents, such as local teachers Mr. Pearce, Mr Hacker and Miss Leach, a former child from the home and another local priest, Father O'Donald, pictured right, the work can now begin on repairing and correcting the faulty roof. The fair on the green brought people from all around Ireland together, raising just under ten thousand pounds for this tremendous cause, making sure that this local man of the cloth will go down in the town's history as a hero.' He swallowed, sounding like he was trying to digest the words.

'I can't read any more of this, can you give me the long and short of it, please?'

Timmins clicked the button. 'Just see this a second.'

Another newspaper clipping popped up with a headline much darker than the previous, giving the desired effect of holding his attention.

Jack also read this one out, starting with the striking headline.

'Mass grave of nearly eight hundred babies and children uncovered in Ireland.' He looked at the young officer. 'What the fuck.'

Timmins nodded, leaving Jack to read on.

'A mass grave containing the remains of babies and children has been discovered at a former Catholic care home. On the site of the former mother and baby unit, a large unground structure, thought to be the original sewer and wastewater system, was divided into twenty chambers, all full of remains.'

Jack pushed the laptop away. 'I can't read this right now.'

The young officer leaned across and turned the laptop off. 'Do you want me to tell you about the home?'

Jack shook his head but said, 'Yes.'

'Right, ok, well, it was a home for mothers to have children out of wedlock, mainly. Things being as they are in Ireland – no abortions, I mean – what they would do is take the women here and then once they'd had the baby, they'd take them away from them.'

Jack knew all this but didn't have the fight to interrupt him.

'Well, I looked into it a bit more, this home in particular. It was like a business, they used to bring families in, line the kids up and then they bought the one they liked the look of. It's sick, it's like shopping for a hat or something. But the mortality rate was ridiculous and not just when the babies were little, the age range was all ages, up to like nine or ten. Anyway, they didn't keep records of …' the young man searched for the most politically correct words. 'Their sales. They didn't even keep accurate birth and death records. No one has a clue how many babies were born there – it must have been thousands.' He stopped, waiting for his excitement to infect Jack.

'So, he could have been in there, selling kids to

whoever he wanted, with no one to stop him. And now we know where he got his septic tank idea from,' Jack said, taking a deep, heavy breath.

'Precisely, he's just recycling what he learnt there. They gave him all the skills he needed. I think you were right, sarge, I think Pearce was used to dispose and maybe move the kids around.'

Something poked Jack's curiosity from across the shop, an uncomfortable movement. He had learnt that most people make up a certain range of movements in various settings. In a coffee shop, for instance, the slow, almost rhythmic movement of the cup being lifted to one's mouth and sipped before being placed back down was like the natural flow of a river. You don't need to be looking at the exact spot of the river to see a disturbance on the surface, you just become aware of it, just as Jack had become aware of this. A man lifting his sleeve up to his mouth a couple of times in repetition, in short, jerky motions.

Jack was looking directly at him when a waitress stood between them, blocking his view.

'Complimentary muffin, sir, on us. Oh, and you've been made. Back of River Island in five minutes.'

REFUSE TO STOP FIGHTING

Jack looked up to see Tanya smiling down at them. She gave him a wink.

'Enjoy, sir,' she said, walking off to play waitress at another table.

'Who was that?' Timmins asked, gazing at her, adoring her from behind just as much from the front.

Jack stood, picking the cake up. 'Don't stare, just act normal.'

Two large men at the other table got out of their chairs. Both modelled the same short hairstyle – they could have been twins had one of them not been slightly stockier with his stubble shaved into a goatee.

Jack turned, straightened his cap and looked the young policeman in the eyes. He had to be very clear with what he was about to say.

'Don't panic. They're going to take you. They'll ask a lot of questions, just answer them and you'll be fine. I can't come with you. Do you understand? Just tell them whatever they want to know.'

'Wait, what? Who's going to do what?' Timmins stuttered. He was some yards off the pace.

Jack turned back around; the two men were right in

front of him. He pretended to be half startled and fell into the first man, giving him a good shove into the one behind, both falling back onto an innocent bystanders' table. Coffee went flying and so did Jack's feet, straight into top gear.

Jack had never been a very good pickpocket. He had worked on a couple of cases targeting gangs of pickpockets in central Bristol in his early days on the force and a few of the officers would often practice the techniques on each other – sometimes as a training exercise, other times just for the hell of it – but he had never thought that it would have come back to help him in a situation like this. As the two men righted themselves and chased him out of the shop to where the heavy canopy of glass stretched above them, Jack raised his newly acquired gun.

He shot off several rounds at the windows above them, the falling glass giving him that crucial couple of second's head start that he needed. He could have done with a couple of *minute's* advantage – the men had looked in pretty good shape so even if he hadn't recently had part of his toe painfully removed, he would have struggled to get away. The escalator was clear and he could hardly feel his injuries as he jumped down the bottom half. He knew exactly where River Island was located – it was the shop where he bought most of his work shoes. He rounded the shopping centre's long, sweeping corner and ran into the shop. He grabbed a large hoody from a rack. It was in the women's department, but black was always good and then he spotted a white baseball cap. It was similar in style to the one he had on, but it was the opposite colour – that should be enough to fool them, if needed. With the same train of thought, he also snatched a thick woollen scarf from a display box labelled sale.

'Where's the fire exit?' he asked a girl behind the till.

She screamed a couple of inaudible words in return, staring at the weapon in his hand.

Jack looked at it, not understanding her problem before remembering what he was holding.

'Oh, crap, yeah, it's fine. I don't want to shoot anyone, I'm just on the run.' He emptied the magazine, dropped it into the sale items and threw the gun amongst some women's shoes on a shelf. 'Ok?'

The girl nodded and pointed towards the fitting rooms. 'It's that way, I'll show you.'

He followed her through a *Staff Only* door and headed down a corridor, pulling off and on clothes as they walked. They reached the fire exit and Jack kicked it open, his hands still finding their way out of the sleeves.

'Wait,' the girl said quickly, startling the detective. She reached up to the scarf and organised it neatly for him, so it now covered his mouth. 'That's how they're wearing them, you look weird otherwise.'

'Thanks,' Jack said automatically.

A car screeched to a halt a few meters away on the road; it was Tanya in a black saloon.

Jack peeked out, checking both ways before leaving.

'Fuck the po-pos!' the girl called after him, making a gun sign in the air with one hand.

'Friend of yours?' Tanya asked as the man in disguise jumped in the car.

Jack pulled the scarf down. 'That's what I do, make friends wherever I go, I'm a people person.'

Tanya laughed and smacked the gear knob into first, spinning the tyres on the spot and then racing off.

'How did you find me?' Jack asked, but then soon realised the answer as he pulled the phone she had given him out of his pocket. 'Fuck sake, can people stop tracking my phone?'

'Hey, it's lucky I did or you would be locked up having the crap beaten out of you again. Anyway, how much help was the young lad?'

They swerved in and out of traffic, heading up towards the Bristol Downs.

'Young lad? He's about the same age as you, you know. And, yeah, I think I have a name for the kid I keep seeing in these, like, visions,' Jack answered honestly.

Tanya gave him a worried look. 'What kid? The one in your dream? It's just a dream, Jack.'

Jack knew it had been coming. He didn't want to argue about it, but it was all he could think about now. 'I don't think it is, Tan, I think this kid is out there, being hurt, being ...' He took a moment to gather the courage to use the word. 'Being *raped.*'

The pair fell silent. Tanya drove, concentrating on the road, not even looking at Jack, not until they eventually parked in a quiet spot at the far side of the fields, bushes along one side and far open fields stretching across the other.

Tanya gently turned the ignition, unclipped her belt and turned to face him. 'What are we doing, Jack? I thought this was about Jessica and Felicity? Then it moved on to Father Lopez and now you want to go around chasing ghosts with absolutely no idea of where to start? You need to sort your head out, Jack, this can't go on.' Tanya's eyes were full of pity and confusion.

Jack knew it sounded like madness, and perhaps that's what it was, but he didn't care. Everyone wanted him dead, he had no doubt lost his job, he had no friends other than Tanya and Aubrie and, even then, he wasn't completely sure of their intentions. This was his life, he had no one else to live it for anymore, so why not be mad? At least he would be fighting for something he believed in. If he was right and seeing events in his mind that were actually true, a doctor would just dose him up on drugs, and if he was wrong, it would equal the same outcome anyway.

He turned to look at her. 'I'm not asking you to believe me, only for you to help me. But if you don't want to, or you can't, that's ok, too.'

Tanya looked away, obviously enraged. 'No, you're not asking for me to help you, you're asking me to enable you, like drug addicts or alcoholics. *Trust me, just one more drink will help, it's what I need.*' She did a mocking male voice and, for the first time, Jack saw a hint of a little girl in front of a parent. She continued, 'Vincenzo is dead, Jack, that girl Sophia is probably dead, too. Jesus Christ, Jack, I killed two people in Italy, do you ever stop to think about that? Think about what everyone else must go through for this, for you to pay penance for a past that isn't your fault? You need to let it go, Jack, you need to forgive yourself. The guilt just keeps building up.' She placed a hand on his leg. 'I love you, Jack, I know you know it. I play the role of being untouchable, but I hurt, Jack. And I hurt for you. You need help.'

Jack had been listening up until this point. The last sentence had been a trigger, he shoved her hand away.

'I'm sorry I'm not good enough for you as I am, but I didn't ask to be either. I don't want people to get hurt because of me, I don't want any more suffering, but I can't just ignore it, Tan. I won't ignore the injustice, I can't let innocent people be shit on. If I'm not what you think I should be, then you need to stop looking for something that isn't there. If I don't fight for what I believe to be right, then I don't have anything worth fighting for anymore. And I have been to that place, Tan, I've stood there with my demons and screamed at them in the face and all they do is laugh back. That pain is unbearable, the torture from inside, hating your very being. You can cut off all my toes and it wouldn't fucking compare. And where are you then, huh? Where are you when my only chance of release is at the end of a rope or an empty packet of pills? You don't want to help me, fine, but don't tell me you love me until you've stood at the edge and held me back from jumping because until then, Tan, you don't even fucking know me.' Jack ripped at the door handle and got out of the car, pulling off the hat and scarf and tossing them into a bush. Tanya stood up to follow him, but Jack faced her and pointed at the bushes to their side.

'A young girl died in those bushes, there. Murdered by one of my own officers and I didn't stop him. Tell me how to forgive myself for that, and then tell her family to move on, too. I refuse to stop fighting. I refuse.'

He walked away, glad that Tanya hadn't tried to follow again. He knew a quiet spot ideal for thinking and right now it was only big enough for him and his hate.

YOU'RE NOT, I AM

The view was like none other in the city, an unrestricted scene looking down at the gorge with the suspension bridge in the distance. If you knew the right bushes to pass through, it was easy to find, but not many did know them. Jack stood on a rock, its flat top perched at the top of the sheer face of the cliff. Jack only knew of it due to the two bodies found, on two separate occasions, at the bottom — it really was an ideal spot to jump from. There was not much of a breeze, owing to the surrounding trees and rock formations, but enough fresh air to fill his lungs. The line of traffic on the road below was a stark reminder of how quickly the city was growing and how overcrowded it now felt. Tail-to-bumper red lights heading in and out no matter how many times they adjusted the layout of the roads.

A small breaking of twigs sounded behind him.

Jack couldn't be bothered to turn around, he knew who it would be.

'That's the last time I track it, I promise,' Tanya said, standing directly behind him.

'And where would I be if you didn't,' Jack answered, his voice calm and hollow, the anger subsided and back in its place, deep inside.

Tanya sat on the rock beside him. 'At the bottom of one of these, I would imagine. Is this what you meant by standing on the edge with you? Because you're right, I don't like it. I'm not afraid of heights, but bloody hell, that's a long way down.'

Jack laughed. 'I could do it, you know, step off, cause no more harm to anyone else, stop the pain inside of me.'

Tanya slid her hand against his and linked her fingers between, locking them with his. 'I know. I'm sorry. I was wrong. Us that get hurt along the way,' she pointed at her chest, 'we decided to be here. We chose to stand at your side and we know the consequences. But I see it now. You don't really have a choice, do you? It's either fight or jump.'

Jack took a deep breath and shrugged his shoulders. 'And I don't know which is better.'

Clouds moved over them, the traffic queues slowly snaking their way into the centre. It must have been at least twenty minutes before Tanya spoke.

'So, how do we find this kid? What have you got on him?'

Jack sighed. 'Nothing. Not even a full address. When I was having that sort of vision thing, I saw him carve his initials into some wood and I felt it, Tan. I could touch them, I know it was real. The only link I have is Pearce; I need to get in and speak to him.'

Tanya laughed. 'He's in custody and you're a wanted man. There's no way you'll be able to get anywhere near there.'

Jack smiled cheekily. 'You're right, but *you* could. You like playing dress up, how about as a sexy lawyer? Or maybe just a regular one?'

Tanya returned the smile. 'That could work, you know. But I think we will need a little bit more help.'

Jack was intrigued. 'Who do you have in mind?'

Tanya's smile broadened. 'I know just the person.'

Aubrie Sellers freed herself from her scrubs. It hadn't been a particularly messy day, but there was some microscopic fiber work and the cotton material caused less static, making it slightly easier than if she was in her civilian wear. She walked down an empty corridor towards her office, paperwork in hand, fully engrossed as she entered through the doorway, giving extra emphasis to how startled she became.

'Dr. Sellers, I presume,' Jack said, a warm smile greeting her.

She dropped the paperwork but didn't care. 'Jack!' She walked over and hugged him. 'So good to see you. I didn't think you would make it back. Yanislav actually got you here, did he?'

'Just about,' Jack answered as they disengaged.

The door behind Aubrie closed, someone had been standing behind it.

'Aubrie,' Tanya said coldly.

'Miss Red,' Aubrie returned the ice dagger.

Jack eyed them both. 'You've met, have you?'

Tanya straightened the dress she was wearing. 'Only the once.'

Aubrie turned back to Jack. 'What's going on, Jack? You shouldn't be here. Everyone is looking for you.'

Jack smiled weakly. 'Don't have a choice, I'm afraid, and I'm sorry, but I need your help.'

The pathologist laughed meekly. 'Why doesn't that surprise me? Got any more gangsters in lockups for me to cut apart?'

Tanya walked over to sit on the desk beside the pair. 'Thought you liked hanging around by the lockups?'

Aubrie ignored the comment; she wasn't going to start a sparring match with Tanya – she knew she would lose.

'What do you want? I can't access any case files anymore.'

Jack was confused. 'What? Why not?'

Aubrie rolled her eyes. 'I told you, it's all pretty much on lockdown. That's not strictly true, I *could* access them, but would need permission and then every page I open, I assume, is being logged. Not sure what type of can of worms you've opened, Jack, but it seems to have some higher powers spooked. This is coming in from above McQuade's head. She's pretty much a spare part at the moment and will be until they have you.'

Jack nodded. 'Yeah, I expect that means dead or alive.'

'Well, if you had been a bit better at espionage, they would think that you still were dead. Might be able to get something actually done, then,' Tanya interrupted.

Aubrie looked from Tanya to Jack. 'What? They know you're alive? How?'

'They must have seen me on CCTV meeting with Timmins or something,' the detective replied in a manner that automatically signaled that he wanted to move on.

Aubrie disagreed, 'No, I've had a tail on me several times in the last couple of days, I think they were probably already following him. Just hit the jackpot, pardon the pun, when you turned up. Funny how they didn't tell anyone here that you're alive, then. I saw McQuade earlier; she was still in shock over your death. I had to pretend to be too upset to talk about it and hide in the toilets. Oh, and guess what? I have literally just finished up on the eighth body from the Pearce case today. Just bones, this one, must have died at least fifteen, maybe twenty years ago.'

'A child, I assume?' the detective asked.

Aubrie nodded.

Jack lowered his eyes to the floor – yet another child he couldn't save.

'I need your help, Aubrie, we know that someone linked with Pearce is holding another child – alive – and we have to save them.' He hid the lie somewhere amongst the truth.

Aubrie's eyes scrutinised Jack's face, looking for a tell. '*How* do you know that?'

Jack opened his mouth but couldn't brave the words, couldn't face the truth of telling her. A woman of nothing but science, she would laugh him out of the room and out of her life, no doubt.

'He can't tell you,' Tanya interrupted.

Aubrie looked directly at her, daring the other woman to stare her out. 'Oh really, and why not, pray tell? No evidence to show me? Is that why?'

Tanya stood up, obviously affronted by the attitude of the other woman. A little staring competition never worried her, she practically invented them. 'Oh no, he has evidence, don't you, Jack?'

Jack nodded, it felt less like lying if he didn't use words.

Tanya continued, 'But he hasn't even shared it with me because he doesn't want us to come to any harm – like Father Vincenzo. He's dead, Dr. Sellers because he knew too much, so he'll probably be passing under the knife of your Italian counterpart as we speak.'

Aubrie looked back at Jack. 'Is that true? He was killed?'

Jack nodded again. He hadn't liked the fact that Tanya had used the man's death as a means of bending Aubrie in the necessary direction, but it really was necessary and he couldn't let his conscience get in the way just now.

'So, what do you want from me? I have only got the autopsy notes here, even then I've had to make copies on the sly,' the pathologist said.

Jack straightened himself up. 'I need to speak to Pearce. I need to get him to tell us who or where the child is being kept.'

Aubrie laughed. 'Well, you can't go in there, you'll be arrested, most likely.' Then a look of panic swept over her. 'Oh no, you're not expecting me to do it, are you? I can't speak to him, I won't know what to do or say. They won't let me, anyway, I don't think—' She was trying to convince the other two hurriedly.

'That's why you're not, I am,' Tanya said clearly.

HEAD TEACHER

'Place your bag there for me and step through the metal detector.'

Aubrie and Jack listened to headphones hooked up to a laptop. Jack had been surprised at the efficiency with which Tanya was able to acquire quite sophisticated equipment. She hadn't even made a phone call, but a mere couple of texts and a twenty-minute drive around Bristol and they had all the tech needed for espionage. They could hear the security guard rustle through Tanya's bag, the sound quality of the receiver was that good.

Tanya thanked someone unseen by the two and her high heeled steps echoed off the walls.

'If you could just wait in here a moment, he will be brought through shortly,' another man's voice told Tanya and, in turn, the two hooked up to the laptop in the car outside.

Tanya pulled out a heavy chair and sat down.

'If you can hear us, give a small cough,' Jack told her, which she did immediately.

They all waited apprehensively, a short rustle coming through the headphones as Tanya positioned the piece in her ear more comfortably.

Jack put his hand over the small microphone that was plugged into one of the USB ports. 'Did you have any difficulties arranging this?' he asked Aubrie.

She smiled. 'No, there's a guy here that's been asking me out for a while, got him wrapped around my little finger. He's not really my type, but he's sweet enough. Should stop leading him on, really.' She looked at Jack, an uncomfortable look betraying his feelings. 'The big bad detective isn't jealous, is he?' she mocked.

'I am, actually.'

'Can you two focus, please? We have a job to do here, you know,' Tanya's voice came over the speakers.

Just then, they heard the sound of Pearce being led into the room, he too scraping a weighty chair on the hard floor a little before taking a seat.

'Who the fuck are you?' the accused's opening gambit was meant to shock the woman in front of him and he grunted when he recognised that it hadn't.

Tanya slowly lifted a notepad from her bag and cleared her throat. Taking her time was a good way of keeping control of the situation, pacing it uncomfortably for him. Jack was impressed.

'Mr. Pearce, I am here to ask you some questions and help you,' Tanya said clearly and calmly, clearing her throat with a small cough.

Jack could see her now, peering over the top of the glasses that she had insisted on wearing, along with the wig, that *made her the part*.

'You're not a lawyer so I'm not answering shit. I think we can call this conversation over.' The man began to stand but was caught off guard by the laugh of the woman in front of him. He sat back down; she laughed a little harder.

'Sorry, but it was funny how you even thought for a moment that I would be your lawyer. No, I'm something much more important than that,' Tanya's voice sounded jovial and, more importantly, convincing.

Pearce was hesitant. 'Did they send you? Because they said they wouldn't, they said I was on my own.'

Tanya opened her notepad. 'And who would you be referring to? Your group of paedophile friends? What do you call yourselves, a gang, a gentleman's club? Intrigue me, why don't you?'

Pearce examined her hard.

Jack listened carefully as the conversation went blank, then the teacher finally spoke, 'You know exactly what they call themselves, did the Syndicate send you or what?'

Jack and Aubrie quickly looked at each other, the word *Syndicate* had not only finally confirmed their suspicions, but now the thing had a name.

'Would you like me to be from the Syndicate?' Tanya asked, but Pearce didn't reply. She gave a small laugh again. 'No, I'm not from them, in fact, I'm from the other side. You see, Mr. Pearce, I am a negotiator. I may be your only means of staying alive.'

Tanya was playing along to an agreed story put together by Jack. The detective knew that the man they were questioning was not a fool, he knew that one small slip up of information and claiming to be a part of his little group of friends would come crashing down. So, they agreed to play it closer to the truth, play it so to tell the teacher that they were not on his side, but also tell him that this is exactly what he needed anyway.

'While you are most definitely going to be incarcerated for the remainder of your life, that life will not last long without the proper protection. I have the means to ensure that where you are kept is far out of reach from harm, but I will need something in return.'

Now it was the time for the man in the room to laugh, Pearce sounded maniacal. 'Oh, my dear, you are very misinformed if you believe that there is anywhere safe for me. Do you really believe that they do not possess the power to get at me anywhere you might be able to hide me? Tut tut, and I thought you may have been one of the clever ones. You know what's really funny? They have ways of making me forget, they don't even need to kill me. They can render me harmless and stick me in a hospital somewhere where no one would be interested in speaking to me ever again.'

Tanya cleared her throat again, obviously a little thrown at the man's reassignment. 'There is something I would like to ask you and if you choose to help, the court and her Majesty's Prison Service will look much more favourably upon you.'

Again, Pearce chuckled. 'Fire away, I could do with one last laugh.'

Tanya swallowed. 'We believe that,' she ran her finger over the word she had jotted down on the paper, 'the Syndicate is holding a young boy – a child by the name of Freddie Owens. If you can provide us with information of his whereabouts, or anything leading to his safe return—'

The teacher interrupted, 'If they're holding him, they would not be needing me, would they? Surely you know what my job was, by now. I cleaned up their mess and got paid for it.'

Jack covered the microphone again. 'What was the main cause of death of the children?'

Aubrie put her hands to her throat. 'Strangulation or asphyxiation, most likely in plastic.'

Jack thought for a minute, he listened as Tanya spoke, but didn't hear what she said. He needed to get to Pearce, needed to push his buttons, get him really speaking. If he could annoy him like last time, find that way to burrow under his skin so he would lash out in anger …

'Ask him how many children he strangled,' he told Tanya through her earpiece.

Tanya paused mid-sentence and again cleared her throat. There was no clear segue, so she just went for it, 'How many boys did you have to strangle to clean up their mess? Surely that's *your* mess, isn't it?'

Pearce had been speaking meaninglessly under his

breath, mocking what Tanya had been saying, but stopped and redirected the conversation, 'If that's what I needed to do, I did it, so what.'

Jack thought for a second and Tanya waited for her instructions.

'But you don't need to, do you, Pearce? You chose to strangle them, you could have just shot them, or stabbed them, even, just let them bleed out,' Jack said and, in turn, Tanya, word for word.

Pearce didn't reply.

Jack whispered to himself, 'What is he, what is this man? Empathy, come on, Jack, empathy. The ability to understand and share the feelings of another.'

'Teacher?' Aubrie said quietly, ensuring not to be heard over the microphone.

Jack shook his head. 'No, that's what he *wants* to be, trying to prove himself every time he killed. So, if not a teacher … Ask him what it was like having a father who was a head teacher. It's a punt mind, Tan.'

The pair in the car heard her ask him the question and held their breaths.

'What's that got to do with anything?' the man replied, clearly on the back foot.

'Yes, got you,' Jack said, allowing him a small fist pump. 'Ask him if it hurt when his dad strangled him.'

'Fuck you, you fucking bitch,' they heard Pearce spit in response to the last question.

Jack smiled, he was in, like a hacker finding a back door to a website and sending in a virus to disrupt the software. He told Tanya what to say next.

'They don't actually need you anymore, the Syndicate, you know that, don't you? They've got someone else in to get rid of Freddie Owens. Even they think you're a waste of space, just like your father did.'

Pearce launched himself at her; Jack heard what sounded like a table being shoved across a tiled floor and the rush of people entering the room.

He could just about hear what the man was screaming, 'I'm the best they had, whoever they're using will get them caught, mark my words.'

'Who is it? Who is it, Pearce, who is going to get rid of the boy? Where are they going to do it?' Jack heard Tanya asking, but he could also hear at least two other voices restraining him.

The sound went quiet, like the earpiece had been covered over.

Ten to fifteen seconds passed before it kicked back in.

Must have been interference,' Jack told himself.

'Do the right thing,' they heard Tanya say.

Aubrie looked at Jack who shrugged his shoulders. They listened as Tanya got up and left the room before pulling the headphones off.

'Well, that was a great waste of time, the fucking bastard didn't even care,' Jack said slamming the laptop shut, almost shattering the screen.

It was only then that Jack noticed Aubrie. She was an odd shade of white and green and looking straight out the window past his shoulder.

With a foreboding pain in his chest, the detective turned around to see the barrel of a gun pointing through the glass, directly at his head.

ALTAR

Jack gazed at the black barrel and followed the flow of the arm up to the man's face, where he found a small goatee beard. The detective pushed the button releasing the window down slowly.

'Oh hey, you found your gun ok, then?'

The man grunted and was forcibly pushed out of the way by another man, who swung open the car door, grabbed Jack by the scruff and extracted him from the car.

'Looking good for a dead man, Jack,' the MI5 agent Casper Collingwood said, straightening the other man's jacket.

'And you still look like a stuck up, rich, posh prick,' Jack replied.

Casper smiled. 'That's because I am a rich, stuck up prick.'

'You missed out posh,' Jack replied with a smile designed to annoy.

'Just get in the car, Jack,' Casper replied, pointing at a black four-by-four.

The car was plush and the man with the small beard drove. It was only in this confined space that the detective realised the bulk of the man whose pocket he had previously picked. Jack felt lucky that he hadn't managed to get hold of him – he could have squeezed the life out of him as easy as a bunch of flowers.

'What now? You used me as bait for your priest, tried blowing me up, chased me down in the middle of Cabot Circus, what more do you want from me?' Jack said, making himself comfortable. His injured toe was becoming incredibly painful again. The pain relief had worn off.

'Tried blowing you up? That wasn't us. I thought that was you. Do you know the shit I've been through trying to clean that up? Managed to tie it to a small group of terrorists, thank God. Do you really think you're worth that sort of hassle? If it had been linked to us, there would have been an all-out EU enquiry,' Casper spoke while punching in a message on his mobile. 'And as for Florence, that's done with now, that's left behind. This is something altogether new.'

Jack laughed incredulously. 'Left behind, along with the end of my toe. Were you listening in on that?'

Casper looked down at Jack's foot. 'That explains the limp and yes, of course we were listening. You know you scream like a girl, don't you?'

Jack didn't give him the satisfaction of a response, instead he changed the subject, 'So what do you want from me now?'

Casper composed another text before speaking again, 'I want to be given any task other than babysitting you. Again, I'm only here to ensure you comply. You know, you're quickly becoming nothing but a chore.'

'You're hardly a barrel of laughs yourself. How about you stop the car and I disappear for a while?' Jack said, chancing his arm.

Casper looked him directly in the face. 'You don't even realise how much shit you're in, do you? Have you not realised where we are going?'

Jack took notice of their route for the first time – they were heading to the centre.

'You're going back to court, detective, to stand as a witness on the Peters case again, only this time, it's a little more serious,' the MI5 agent told him happily.

'I don't like the sound of this, what's happened that I need to stand again?' Jack asked, examining the other man's face for a tell.

'Oh, only a change in plea, change of defence and change of jury. So, to be honest, detective, I think the technical term for describing your situation is *royally fucked.*' Casper gave him a weak smile.

Jack's eyes narrowed. 'You called me *detective,*' Jack said happily, before addressing the main issues. 'All this change and they send an agent to bring me in? What the hell is going on, Collingwood? Who cares enough to interfere with this?'

Casper shrugged his shoulders. 'I couldn't say. But this case has suddenly gone very high profile; you'll be on the front of all the papers tomorrow, you lucky boy.'

The car pulled up to a melee of people outside the old stone building of the courthouse.

'You have,' Casper checked his watch, 'twelve minutes until you are due to stand. Go to the toilet, clean yourself up and take a minute to consider your future – I think you'll need it.'

Jack didn't move, his brain was racing through the situation, trying to understand what was going on, watching the occasional flash from the cameras of the paparazzi.

He breathed heavily, telling himself, '*Whatever is about to happen, is going to proceed regardless of my actions, so I should stop trying to think about how best to change it. Sometimes you must become the leaf on the river rather than forcing your way to become the dam.*'

He turned to the agent. 'Did you take that wooden painting thing from my room in Florence?'

Casper looked up from his phone. 'You mean the orthodox wall-mounted altar? Yes, I took it. There was nothing on it. I examined it for hours, whatever you thought you were getting, you were wrong.'

Jack looked out of the window, up at the building. 'If I don't get arrested today, can I have it back?'

The agent tucked his phone away, looking intently at the detective. 'Maybe, I'll see what I can do.'

A strange silent agreement came between them, almost like a slither of friendship. Jack gave the other man a thankful nod and ventured from the vehicle.

Voices erupted on seeing him, all shouting different questions and blocking his path to the doors. By law, they had to let him through, in practicality, it was like fighting a rip tide – being pushed every direction except the one he wanted to go in.

Falling through the door, he was immediately searched, ushered upstairs and led around to the small café area. The shutters were down but all the self-help machines were lit. Standing in front of one was his superior, McQuade.

She picked up the dull brown cup, walked over to Jack and handed it to him.

'No, thanks, I feel sick enough without that muck,' Jack said, looking around at the empty room.

This was normally a space open to the public – not a good sign that it had been cordoned off.

McQuade raised her brows and took a sip. 'Suit yourself. Hope you've had some food, you're going to need your strength in there.' She took another sip. 'Good to see you alive, Jack. I didn't believe it when they said you were dead – knew it would take more than a little explosion like that.'

The door behind them opened and a woman dressed in long black robes, her hair tied up and thick-rimmed glasses addressed them. 'Detective O'Connor?' the clerk asked.

Jack nodded, a lump stuck in his throat making it difficult to speak.

'You're just in time, they are ready for you in court

four.'

The corridors only had a few people in them as Jack made his way to the courtroom. He wasn't surprised – he knew exactly where they would have gone. He climbed the stairs at Bristol Crown Court and stood outside the labelled doors.

Courtroom Four.

Jack took a deep breath and pushed them open.

FALSE CONFESSION

Jack was led to the stand by the clerk, read the promise to the room and then began to notice the situation in all its mayhem. The gallery in the room was full to the point of some people standing, along with the viewing gallery up on the floor above. Dozens of faces were looking down through the glass like tourists at an aquarium.

Peters sat at the back behind thick glass. He had taken to styling his moustache into a handlebar one with small curls at the tips. He smiled arrogantly, like he was the only one in the room to know what was coming.

Jack shifted uncomfortably on the spot, stroking his clothes down, trying not to look quite so disheveled. It had been a long time since he had felt so off balance.

'Hello, Mr. O'Connor,' a man in a fine, pristine wig addressed him. 'Nice of you to join us eventually, my name—'

'*Detective* O'Connor,' Jack interrupted purposefully. He wasn't going to be intimidated any more than he already had been and he wanted this man, and the rest of the room, to know it.

Years ago, he would have shrunk under that sort of pressure but, to his surprise, he seemed to be able to summon a fight out of nowhere these days.

'Indeed, my mistake. *Detective* O'Connor, my name is Jeffery Robinson, I represent Mr. Peters. As you have been tardy for the last few days, I will just try to bring you up to speed. I am Mr. Peters' new representative and, as you may or may not have been informed, my client has changed his plea so we are re-examining everything in the case. I believe by appointing us, we have narrowly missed a case of gross miscarriage of justice.'

Jack wasn't listening. He looked at the government prosecution lawyers, at their moth-eaten wigs and robes that were visibly torn. They were a stark contrast to the man standing, speaking from an iPad. They even had bits of what looked like scrap paper for their transcripts.

Jack turned to a large man to his right who sat up much higher than the rest of the room. 'Is this common practice, Your Honour? To change lawyers, plea and even jury midway through a hearing?'

Peters' lawyer stopped in his tracks and the judge visibly jumped at being addressed so out of turn. He had looked more interested in something out of sight on his own desk, almost as if disturbed from writing a shopping list.

'Well, no, it is not common practice, but it is not unheard of. Clients often have disputes with their representatives and are more than within their rights to change firm if they wish. As for the jury, it transpired that one of the previous twelve had known the defendant and, as such, had to be dropped. If you had been here previously, you would have known that the defense put forward a case for unfair biased. As the case had already started and the known juror interacted with the rest of the jury, it seemed prudent to start with a clean slate. If you have any qualms, detective, with how the law works, I would suggest getting your own lawyer and starting a case yourself, but if you are happy to proceed, perhaps we could continue with the case at hand.' The man was asking a rhetorical question but waited facetiously for an answer regardless.

Jack responded with just a nod and turned back to the room. The mutterings couldn't have been less distracting if they hadn't been there, Jack was in a zone. He wasn't sure what zone it was, but he was there and he was ready for a fight.

The lawyer smiled mirthlessly. 'Thank you, Your Honour. Now, detective, regarding the evidence given previously, we have to consider it null and void – not only due to the circumstances presented to you by His Honour, there, but also due to the fact that you manipulated the truth.'

Jack wondered if the lawyer had learnt to be that smarmy or whether it was just a talent that happened to coincide with his given profession.

'You see, detective, your statement regarding gaining the warrant before running a trace on my client was factually inaccurate. The statement of officer Nitin Kapoor exposed this. So, if you feel the need to massage the truth in future, please refrain from doing so.' The man smiled and raised his eyebrows at Jack, egging a response.

Jack's teeth gritted, frustration brewing somewhere in the back of his BPD mind.

The man tapped the iPad several times and walked over to Jack.   'Please, detective, could you tell me what you see in this picture?'

The judge interrupted, 'It is not necessary to approach the witness, if you list the piece of evidence, my clerk can put it on the screens.'

The lawyer nodded. 'Picture twenty-one C, please.'

A few moments later, the three large televisions around the room displayed an image of a tree. Jack recognised it as the one that had the large bloody handprint on from the first crime scene in the investigation.

'Again, detective, please could you tell the jury what is in this picture?'

Jack took a deep breath. 'It is the handprint of Mr. Peters and the blood of the victim on a tree, found beside the body. The handprint is a couple of feet up the tree, most likely from where he pushed himself up off the ground, stabilising his weight on the trunk.'

The man in the wig smiled and nodded. 'Indeed, detective, and this handprint has indeed been confirmed as that of Mr. Peters. Can I ask how many other handprints were found at the crime scene or, indeed, at any of the other crime scenes?'

Jack didn't know where he was going, but he knew he was being led somewhere – somewhere blindfolded.

'On the victim's neck a couple of fingerprints were obtained by pathologists,' he responded.

'None on the other bodies, though?' the lawyer wanted clarification.

'No, he had been very conscious, most likely wearing leather bike gloves,' Jack extrapolated.

Robinson smiled eagerly. 'I am not interested in your most likely, I am going to speak about pure fact. The fact, so far, is that there is one clumsy handprint and a couple of fingerprints throughout this entire investigation that just happened to be belonging to my client. Doesn't this strike you as odd? Not one mistake at any of the other crime scenes, except one – the first one, the one that happened to be where my client was first on the scene. You see, detective, my client has explained, in your absence, that he accidentally left that handprint there after being called to the crime scene. He has informed the jury and those present here that the two fingerprints found on the victim's neck are from where he checked her pulse.'

Jack interrupted with an incredulous noise and the lawyer smiled weakly.

Damn, he had expected me to do that,' Jack chastised himself.

'He has also explained that he tripped and his hand caught him, keeping him from falling directly onto the body, but that had inadvertently got covered in blood. He had not realised this until he had already righted himself, as you say, against the tree. Does this not sound more plausible, detective? More reasonable than a very fastidious killer, one who knows police procedure inside out, making such a rooky mistake?'

Jack didn't answer, he was beginning to understand where this was going.

'I mean, if my client had killed the victim, his DNA would have been on the body. Or do you suggest that he killed her, then took his glove off to touch the victim before standing up against the tree?'

Jack inhaled a lungful of hot, dank air. 'I would not begin to question the method of a madman. Like you said, it's the evidence that we have. The fact that Peters then went onto the system and changed his details would imply a guilty conscience to me.'

Robinson shook his head. 'Not guilty, detective, but a scared man. Isn't it true that you have never liked my client, that you have always been short with him and never attempted at building a productive work relationship with him?'

Jack didn't respond, instead he stared intently into the lawyer's eyes, trying to work him out.

'He was frightened, detective – frightened of you. So, on making this, granted, rather large mistake, rather than feeling comfortable enough to tell his superior, he instead did all he could to try to cover it up. By, as you say, going onto the system and changing his details. Not the criminal mastermind you are attempting to paint him as, but a clumsy human being. We have records of a login happening just hours after the victim's murder which, we put it to the jury, was the occasion at which my client changed the details. If he is this callous murderer you are leading us to believe, detective, would he not have had the foresight to change his details before committing the crime?' The man's tempo increased, building up to his killer legal prowess blows.

'Peters admitted to killing the victim; he gave a detailed account—' But Jack was neatly interrupted.

'Indeed, he did, detective – as detailed of an account as any of the officers on the case would have given. Nothing that he would not have heard around the station. Of course it was detailed, that's what detectives are trained to do – pick up on the details. Unlike murderers, who disconnect from the truth, from the fact and see what they want to see.'

Jack shook his head. 'He admitted to murdering her, to me, to other officers, on record.'

Robbins looked gleeful. 'And if you had been where you were meant to be, detective, you would know that the reason for the change of plea is the fact that my client gave a false confession.'

DEATH SONG

Jack heard the words, but his insides tightened, forcing them out, trying to make it all unreal.

'Of course my client knew the details, of course he admitted to the killings while cornered by you in a dark park. He was dressed as a character from the game, yes, his fragile mental health already failing him and that's when you made your move. You knew he was vulnerable and you pounced, you tracked him down in the park, told him that you knew he did it, you knew he was responsible, telling him how he did it and why and he just nodded and agreed and, for added measure, detective, you stabbed him. There were no marks on you, were there, detective? No defensive wounds, not even a scratch. Now, my client says it was The Fair Assassin, did you plant that in his mind, too?' The lawyer's pace quickened with excitement.

Jack could see the thrill on his face, his tight eyes not blinking. 'This is ridiculous, he had the weapon on him, the only reason he was there was to murder,' Jack replied, looking at the faces around the room, making sure that they weren't believing this bullshit. But none were nodding in agreement with him. The jury looked bored while he spoke, looking down at the notes in front of them, one or two making amendments of their own. His gaze rose up to the public gallery, nearly all were press and nearly all were scribbling furiously on notepads.

'I am so glad that you mentioned the weapon – the weapon that you used to stab my client.' The man in the wig had slowed down again, he was calm, as smooth as the polished shoes he wore.

'Tell me, detective, in figure nine on page eighteen, there are details of where some identical weapons used in the murders were being held. Can you confirm the location of these weapons, please? The page will appear on the screen.' And it did, again on all three televisions.

There was a small description of the knives, scribbles in black ink, followed by several lines of different code. Beside that was a picture.

'That top code beneath the description is the log number, it tells you the station and department filing it. This is evidence information,' Jack answered flatly, he didn't want to betray that he had no idea of where it was leading.

'That's correct. These knives, I believe, were filed in evidence several days before the murders started, as the date indicates there. Now, I am not sure if you are aware, but two knives were checked out from evidence, one of which made its way into your hands, mid-investigation. Is that correct?' the man's tone was now one of reassurance.

Jack felt as though he had taken his hand and begun leading him down a dark path. He wondered at what point he was going to let go and leave him there to fend for himself. 'I was unaware that two had been taken, but yes, I had one. It stayed at my private residence at all times.'

The man nodded. 'That is more than fair, perfectly safe there. But the other one, can you tell me who you asked to retrieve the weapon from evidence for you?'

Jack, still blinded with ignorance, answered, 'Yes, it was Officer Peters.'

'Precisely. So, we have one weapon in your possession,

and one in my client's. I have a burning question, however – why would my client take one of these weapons if, as you would lead us to believe, he had already been murdering people with one of his own? What possible use could he have with two?' the wigged man asked Jack earnestly.

Jack shrugged his shoulders. 'I couldn't begin to second guess the mind of serial killer.'

'So, you're telling me, my client, intelligent enough to avoid capture, intelligent enough not to leave a single trace of DNA other than on the tree and neck that we have our alternative explanation for, was stupid enough to take a weapon from a police station that he already owned? He wouldn't even have had that weapon in his possession if you hadn't asked him to retrieve one for you. Can you understand how out of kilter this is sounding, detective?'

Jack didn't answer, again he looked around the room. He couldn't believe that they were buying this bullshit, but they were. He didn't know what to say, everything he suggested they would have an answer for.

'I followed the evidence, it led me to Mr. Peters. He admitted the crime and I caught him in the act of looking for a next victim. I'm not sure what you want me to say,' Jack said, even in his own head he sounded pathetic.

The barrister picked up some notes. 'I don't see any evidence that you say you could have followed, detective. You were only led to my client because you sought out his whereabouts via his mobile phone – illegally, I might add. Even the connection you seem to have made via the motorbike is simply fanciful. We have spoken to the man who claims to have seen the motorbike in question, on the night of the murder of Officer Smith— wait, sorry, I mean *heard* the motorbike. Most of the officers were indeed at the pub that night with her, except one or two. One of whom is my client, who has already admitted that he was indeed out on his motorbike that night – he was out looking for a murderer, as it so happens. More than you were doing, I dare say, detective. Now, as far as I am aware, it is not illegal to be out riding a motorbike, nor is it illegal to dress as a character from a computer game. The latter is unusual behaviour within common boundaries, just as admitting to a crime that you did not commit it, but that is all it is, detective: unusual behaviour. Now, my client has admitted that his mental health has been rather unstable and he is asking the court to appreciate the work that he has already started in rectifying his behaviours. He is seeing a therapist and has been asked to go voluntarily into a secure unit once this farce is over.'

Jack watched as the man began to pace the room, addressing only the jury now. He watched as his over-animated arm gestures lulled them into his fairy-tale, and then Jack heard it.

A loud screech – something like a seagull but not quite animal enough. He looked around the room frantically to see where it had come from, wondering if someone had screamed in anger, but no one else was showing signs of hearing anything.

The noise bleated again, this time louder, as if right behind him. Some people had noticed Jack looking for something, they watched him turning and looking over his shoulder.

Two people who had been typing on laptops looked back at him, anxious to know why they had suddenly become of interest to him.

And then the noise sounded again, even louder than before and from a new direction – up above.

The barrister was still speaking, but his words faded away. The room was slowly becoming silent, the air thick and heavy in Jack's head. Then something beat against his eardrums, a deafening scratchy sound, like an iceberg ripping in half.

Jack cowered in the stand; the volume had scared him so he could hardly stay on his feet. Then it sounded again, as loud as foghorn inches from his face. He closed his eyes but it wasn't darkness that greeted him, it was images, swimming through his vision.

'What is this?' the detective screamed, still not able to stand. His entire body tensed and then the pictures in his mind focused. He could see a man pulling reels off a roll of tape. That was the noise damaging him so, scaring him, making his heart beat at full capacity.

Then Jack realised he couldn't move his hands, they were bound, and he went to speak, but his lips were stuck fast. He was being prepared, being readied for execution and that realisation was setting in. Jack felt hands that, somewhere deep in his mind, he knew weren't there, but it was so deep he couldn't recall it. He panicked as strong hands bound his knees, forcing him to fall over.

Some voices in the distance could be heard, all shouting his name, asking him if he was ok, one shouting that questioning was over, but he wasn't there with them. No, he was in a dark room with a man about to kill him. He was immobilised and powerless. He felt his body being dragged by the feet. He tried to kick his legs, but there was starvation and dehydration coursing through his body, making him weak and powerless.

His body was being moved with effort across hard concrete, but then slid easily as it felt as though he was transferred onto a sheet of ice. The man didn't speak but walked around him, working methodically, more tape in his hand ready. A cover of some sort wrapped around his feet, then tape was applied, locking the ankles together even tighter than they had already been. He had now lost the movement of his feet, unable to extend and bend them at the joint. Then his knees, the man placed his weight down so that he could pull the plastic tight, giving a neat finish.

The screeching noise was becoming a death song as he pulled stretches of tape off and applied them. Jack tried to roll around, giving some sort of last fight, but his strength was pathetic against the other's. His hands, which had been taped down by his hips, were now being covered. The claustrophobic intensity was becoming overwhelming. It didn't take long until he was neatly parceled up to his shoulders, the thick plastic heavy on his chest, his breathing limited as his chest didn't have enough room to rise and fall.

Jack opened his eyes. There was a mass of people rushing around him. He was draped over the arms of a large police officer who was carrying him, removing him from the courtroom. He saw a throng of people rushing into the corridor, trying to catch up with him and his helper. His eyes darted around, not able to focus in what felt like brilliant sunlight. They walked through a set of doors, flagged by two more officers who promptly stopped anyone else trying to follow.

Jack could hardly make out any sound, his eardrums still vibrating from the torture, but he did manage to make out a familiar voice.

'It's ok, she's with me,' he heard Dr. Aubrie Sellers say as she and Tanya Red burst into the room.

'Jack, Jack, you ok? What's wrong, Jack? Can you speak to us?' Aubrie spoke, panic trembling her voice.

She was on her knees in front of him, trying to look into his eyes, trying to test them for a reaction. She pulled out her phone, turned on the torch and pulled at his eyelids.

Jack saw the burst of light, then darkness fell, like a blanket being pulled over his face that pressed down.

Jack fell to the floor, clawing at his mouth. He was being suffocated, plastic now applied to his head and taped tight.

LAST GOODBYE

'Don't scream,' a muffled voice said in Jack's ear.

Then the detective fell to his knees, twisting at the waist with panic, suddenly feeling bound again. His hands reached up to his mouth and clawed at the air – the air that he couldn't inhale. He jerked up and down, clashing his head on the hard stone floor, his wild legs kicking the seats behind him. Aubrie and Tanya wrestled with his body but he couldn't feel them, they didn't exist, only his bindings and coverings seemed to be real.

Jack's eyes watered, the veins bristling as blood rushed with the sheer force of his violent contortions. Small, red lightning bolts appeared in the whites of his eyes, vessels bursting and his pupils expanded to their parameters.

Jack's panic raced through his body, signals misfiring in his brain, desperately trying to find the right combination to unlock his predicament, allowing him to breathe, giving him a chance to survive. But carbon dioxide now recycled through his cells, oxygen levels depleted and acids formed. He was shutting down. He was dying. A few last attempts at pulling the suffocating plastic away from his mouth, but with no more vigor than a tired child pulling at bed covers.

That's where he could be, in his bed— no, not his bed,

that was empty now. Maybe, as he died, he would drift away into Felicity's bed. She had always enjoyed sharing it with him – she loved that a big man was in a pink bed made for girls. Sometimes, she would make him wear an Alice band in his hair, so that it would fool the fairies that watched.

She had so many stories and they flowed from her mouth with ease – she didn't even need to think, the words would just follow each other in beautiful patterns.

'I thought it was me that was meant to tell the bedtime stories,' Jack had said to her while they were flying the bed halfway between Bristol and Disneyland.

'You have had a hard day at work, so I'm telling them to you tonight, Daddy,' she had replied, sitting up, ready to play parent.

'Ok, well, how about I get to choose who's in this one?' Jack said, sitting up himself and grabbing her around the waist, making sure to tickle her as he cuddled her in.

'No, Daddy, I'm the parent tonight. I want to tell the one about the little girl who could fly,' she replied, fighting him off and straightening up her pajamas.

Jack punched the air over-enthusiastically. 'Yes, my favourite!'

'Daddy, shush and listen.'

Jack couldn't remember the story, not a single word of it, but he didn't need to. It was her face, the smile that he had wanted to see.

Maybe there is a heaven, maybe I will get to see her.

He often told her that she had the smile of an angel. It was crazy, but that cliché of someone lighting up a room with their presence must have been written for her. Her warmth, her generosity. Then Jack felt guilt trickle down his throat. She hadn't learnt that from him, she had somehow gained her inexplicable kindness *despite* him.

His mind wandered to think back on the times where

his Borderline Personality Disorder had left him bedridden with depression. He couldn't have hidden it from her, it consumed him, which wasn't too bad until Jessica had to go on long trips for work – three or four days in a stretch. That's where Felicity would find him wrapped in the covers, still in bed, some show about antiques playing on the television. After making herself some breakfast, consisting of yoghurts or biscuits or something else easily attainable without an adult present, she would crawl into bed behind him. Cuddled up to his back, playing with his hair, she was somewhere between child and carer. He would never have asked her to look after him, but the way that she empathised and understood people, it was clear that she had inherited his Borderline Personality Disorder. Something else for Jack to punish himself for – couldn't have just gotten his fat toes, no, she had to be infected with the very thing that Jack spent all of his life battling. It was hard to think about. As someone once asked him, if he could have a button that would turn his Borderline Personality off for life, would he press it? He had said no, it was part of him, it was the very worst, but also the very best. But would he wish it upon someone else, someone he loved more than himself? No, it would feel like a punishment. Sometimes his emotions felt so intense it was like he could understand the entire world at once and then half an hour later believe that the world in its entirety was against him.

So, while this little girl told her father that she was there to look after him, it only fueled the self-hatred that had placed him there in the first place. But what he wouldn't give to feel her delicate hands stroke at his hair and wipe the tears from his cheeks. What he wouldn't give to have his life brought back into the light by that incredible, tangible, true smile.

Her voice whispered to him, he heard the gentle tone like song carried on the wind.

'I love you, Daddy. I miss you, Daddy. Save me,

Daddy.'

And Jack was gone. The spark of life that had been flickering there, just on the edge of the horizon, danced its last goodbye. His body rolled over onto its front, sharp stones daring to bruise his skin, the last reminders of being alive, his face hitting them hard.

FLORENCE KEILTY

The plastic on Jack's mouth caught a sharp stone that had stopped it from falling all the way beneath him. It was supporting him. Jack's brain gave one last rev, one last hope. Heavy and barely functioning, it formed a thought.

'Don't fight against the binding, push down hard, force it onto whatever it's snagging on.' His neck forced his head down, pushing and scraping towards the earth. It was caught, the thick plastic was stretching thin under the pressure. He forced his head up and down on the rough edge, still no oxygen in his muscles, pain everywhere like concrete was encasing him, forcing every movement under immense pressure. One last shove of his face against the jagged rock and the sheeting gave, a hole created just around his nostrils. Finally allowing a small amount of fresh air into his lungs, he tried to sniff hard, but this caused the stretched, now delicate material to be sucked up. He shortened the breaths, taking short panicky ones, the pain in his head slowly subsiding with every intake of oxygen. His brain felt light, as if it was being relinquished from a substantial depth of water. He still couldn't expand his chest to its fullest, but by controlling his terror, he could feel the life slowly seep into his cells. He was alive –

nothing more than alive, but that was a start. He closed his eyes. The fight had exhausted him, he had used more than all of him, it had taken him to a point far beyond his own existence and yet he had managed to find his way back. But he was so tired. His eyes closed and he rested, from the inside out, with sleep.

'Hey, darling,' Jessica spoke softly as if wakening him ready for work. 'You scared me there for a minute, I thought you had given up.'

Jack blinked his eyes, the expectant contrast between dark and light not appearing. He knew he was dreaming and, for now, that was ok.

'I think, therefore, I am,' he muttered.

Jessica smiled at him. 'Bit early for Descartes, isn't it?'

Jack rubbed his eyes, again nothing happened. 'We're in my head, not sure it's too early for anything here.' He looked around, they appeared to be in their old bedroom. 'And yet, no whisky.'

'Now, now, there's always time for whisky later. Just here to say I'm proud of you. You were dying, you know.' She placed her hand over his. Jack could feel it, but it was not enough.

'Yeah, I was having a weird …like, dream – weirder than this one, I mean. I was being murdered and it was real.' Jack removed his hand from his wife's.

'So, not a dream, then?' Jessica said, standing up next to the bed.

'I don't know. I think it's real, just not for me. Someone else is in trouble. I don't know what to do.' He tried to look her in the face – the face that he fell in love with. But his imagination just couldn't get it right. It hurt seeing a poor imitation and he looked away.

'Will you forgive me one day?' Jessica asked, walking away now, heading through the door.

Jack watched her. 'One day.'

She turned, blew him a kiss and slammed the door.

The loud thud assaulted his eardrums, his eyes flicking open to light – real, harsh light this time. His hands rushed to his side, pushing against the seat he was sitting on, panic driving his muscles to act out.

'Jack. you're ok, Jack, calm down, you're ok.' It was Aubrie this time, holding his arms still by the wrists, a tight grip forcing him to stop flailing.

Jack's pupils darted around the room, focusing as and when they could.

'I died, I thought I died.' He stopped fighting against Dr. Sellers and she relinquished his hands, they went straight for his mouth. He needed reassurance that there was nothing to restrict his breathing.

'We thought you had died, too, and I'm not convinced that technically you didn't. I couldn't feel a pulse anywhere for about a minute. Then all of a sudden you came around,' Aubrie answered, again taking one of his wrists, this time much more gently to feel a pulse.

'Where are we?' Jack asked, he knew he should recognise it, but everything in his mind was still a little fuzzy.

'The club. The press broke their way into the room we were in and started taking your pictures. McQuade, is it?' Tanya said, looking at Aubrie, who nodded in agreement. 'Well, she helped us get you here. Told the boys not to let anyone in. Not the most inconspicuous place …'

Jack nodded, it had been a good idea in his mind. It was less than two hundred yards from the court and Tanya had her own private security blocking the entrance.

'I think you had a seizure, Jack. We're going to have to get you tested for epilepsy. I think maybe the stress induced it,' Aubrie said, sitting back in her chair, obviously satisfied with his recovery and exhausted herself from the whole vent.

'No,' Jack replied bluntly.

'I'm sorry?' Aubrie said, clearly taken aback.

Jack stood up, swayed and sat back down. 'No, it wasn't a seizure. I was experiencing a murder. Freddie Owen's murder. But he didn't die, he survived – only just, though.'

Aubrie laughed, but only slightly. 'Jack, you're feeling the effects, it's ok just give it some time, you'll be ok.'

'No,' Jack said again, exactly the same tone to his voice. 'No, I won't, not until I find him. I saw him, I *felt* him. Could feel his body being wrapped in plastic and then his head. I was choking. We were suffocating together.'

Aubrie went to place a hand on Jack's knee, but against his usual character, he slapped it away.

'I know what you think, I know you think I'm crazy, that I'm losing my mind, and that's fine. Maybe I am, but I also know that this kid is alive – just. And I'm the only help he's got and that's not a lot. So, if you're going to tell me I'm mad one more time, that's fine, just don't get in my way.'

Dr. Sellers was affronted, her hand clearly red where he had hit it away with some force.

Aubrie spoke quietly and clearly, 'Jack, I wouldn't dream of standing in your way, but I can't listen to any more of this.'

Jack scoffed at her.

'Just listen,' she begged him. 'This started with Jessica and Felicity, right? Then the priest in the Florence.'

'Father Lopez,' Jack interjected.

'Yes, Father Lopez, where you nearly got killed – several times, I might add. And now it's linked to the Pearce case. Are you really telling me you stumbled on all three of these things that somehow are all linked? There's physically over a thousand miles between the cases, yet you seem to think they go hand in hand. Doesn't that sound like too much of a coincidence to you?'

Jack stared at her blankly. He didn't care about a single word she had just said.

Aubrie turned to Tanya for support. 'Please, tell him,

tell him he needs help – professional help.'

Tanya shrugged. 'Perhaps he does, and yes it does seem too good to be true, but he's asked me to trust him,' Tanya looked in to Jack's eyes, 'and I trust him.'

Just then, a hand reached into the room and yanked back at a curtain, exposing a third woman standing there. She was a short woman, somewhat portly, wearing a long cream coat, a bright purple hat and carrying a full wicker cat basket.

'Mrs. Keilty, what the hell are you doing here?' Jack said, standing up to greet her.

Aubrie stood too. She sidestepped Jack and gave Mrs. Keilty a polite hug on the shoulders before turning back to the detective. 'I'm sorry, Jack, I can't stand by and watch you do this to yourself.' Tears slowly emerged, she nodded and made her way out.

'So, this is the famous Mrs. Keilty, I have heard so much about you,' Tanya said, shaking her hand.

'All rotten, I hope, my dear,' she replied, smiling.

Jack laughed. 'Seriously, what are you doing here? It's a long bike ride from Glastonbury.'

Mrs. Keilty looked around the room, her nose turned up halfway. 'Don't see what all the fuss is about. They tried to turn me away to start with, then the cheeky buggers wanted ten pounds to get in. I told them where I would stuff ten pounds worth of coppers if they didn't let me in. Anyway, I came looking for you, dear, heard on the news you may be in a spot of bother. Came down to the courtroom, couldn't get in for love nor money, then, as I was leaving, I saw these young ladies drag you up here. You didn't look well, dear, very peaky, I must say.'

Jack smiled warmly, his rage with Aubrie all but forgotten. 'Well, it's lovely to see you. Thank you.'

'No bother, dear, I got me a bus card, so I wanted to try it out, anyway,' she replied, placing the cat basket on the table-cum-dancefloor and making herself comfortable on the bench seat.

'No bike today, then?' Jack asked, sitting beside her.

She shook her head. 'Nah, sold it, dear. Turns out it was a collectable. Got a pretty penny, too.'

Jack felt the warmth of relief wash down him. She was a face that smiled without judgement. He needed her presence at this moment, needed something to neutralise the anger.

Then, a curiosity arose, had she been seeing what he had? Could she shed some light on where the boy could be found?

'I'm glad you're here, I could do with your help. Tanya, would you mind giving us a moment in private?'

Tanya initially seemed a little bit shocked to be asked to leave, but was happy to shut them both away behind the curtain.

'Shush, Jasper,' the older lady said as the cat started meowing with unrest. 'He's not been well, been losing too much weight, that's why I brought him along, don't want him to be on his own – you know, if the time comes.'

'Speaking of time coming,' Jack said tactfully, 'have you seen any more of your visions? Anything with children in?'

Mrs. Keilty smiled warmly. 'Jack, dear, I haven't seen anything since the last time we spoke about. I don't want to see anything, now, I'm shut off from all that now, dear. I think maybe you should be, too.'

Jack sighed. 'I thought you would believe me, at least.'

Her hand settled on his. 'Oh, I do, dear, I just think you work better when your head is on straight. Sorry, dear, but you are not one of those who can survive with a muddled mind.'

Jack nodded. *Damn, she's right, my head is muddled. I'm not sure where to go, or what to think from one second to the next. I need to get it together, iron out the mountain of creases – even if I am seeing the truth, I'm not doing a damn thing about it.*

'What does your doctor friend think? She's a clever lady,' Mrs. Keilty asked earnestly.

She had only been there a matter of moments and

already he was feeling the comfort that came with her presence. It was like taking diazepam, but without the side effects. It was like she was the mother of the world and she could look after everything and make it all ok.

Jack took a deep breath. 'She thinks I'm making connections up when they're not there – seeing what I want to see.'

The old woman nodded. 'And your other friend? Is she clever, too? What does she think?'

'She's the smartest person I know and she seems to let me trust my gut instinct.' Jack raised his hands in the air, torn from one side of the psychotic room to the other.

The woman nodded, looking past Jack and into outer space. 'Well, they're both much smarter than me – and you, I dare say. Sorry, my dear, but they are women, so it's probably true. How about if they are both right?' She left the question in the air like a balloon slowly falling to the ground, neither one having the ability to keep it afloat.

Jack rested his forehead on his hands while Florence Keilty fed her cat some snacks through the bars in the cat box.

'She's right,' Jack thought, *'goddamn it, I know she is, I just can't see why. If Aubrie says I'm losing my mind, she's got to be right, so if she says this is all too much of a coincidence, she's got to be right about that, too. But does that mean my gut instinct is wrong?'*

The curtains pulled back in the room, almost at the same time as the ones in his mind. Something was there, it had always been there, but his judgment had been clouded.

'Carla just phoned, the garage delivered your car to the house in Clifton by accident. She said you need to come and collect it as they left it on double yellow lines,' Tanya said, raising an apologetic hand to Mrs. Keilty for interrupting them.

Jack smiled. 'Well, we had better go and get it. Are you ok finding your own way home, Mrs. Keilty? Only I have somewhere I have to be.'

The older woman stood up. 'Of course, dear. I help,

did I?'

Jack grabbed her by the shoulders enthusiastically. 'You certainly did. It turns out it was all too much of a coincidence to be true, but that doesn't mean I'm wrong and I know exactly who I need to speak to.'

TIME TO GET THE TRUTH

Jack threw his new and improved Ford Capri around on the ring road roundabouts. It had gone in for a tune up but the young lady working there, being a boy racer and engine nut, had managed to convince him that some disc brakes could be fitted no problem after Jack moaned at how unsafe it was to drive at times. It had taken twice as long as promised and since then his enthusiasm for safety had flipped on its head.

Fucking BPD, why can't I stay constant just for one week, is that too much to ask?'

He knew it would pass and he would go back to the extreme of actually wanting to stay alive for a while, but right now, if it hadn't been for Tanya being in the car, he could have quite happily flipped it on its roof and ended it all.

'Bloody hell, Jack, not bad for an old man,' Tanya joked as Jack kicked the back end out, negotiating a small roundabout with some tyre smoke matching their screeches.

Jack didn't reply, instead he tested the brakes again on a tight, left-hand turn. The mood in the car was becoming intense, Jack could feel the hesitance in her voice, he could soak in her anxiety and spit it back without saying a word. His BPD was in full flow, understanding her every thought and manipulating it with the tiny, stiff body movements and grunts for answers. Manipulation was a key factor in Borderline Personality Disorder – getting people to do what you want, think what you want and say what you wanted to hear. It certainly wasn't deliberate – it was another of those survival instincts. You learnt patterns in people, gained knowledge of how to get your needs met subtly. Like, if a child sees you eating an ice-cream, they'll often tell you how much they like ice-cream, instead of just asking for some. Jack could feel inside his mind when he started to act on these adolescent levels, but by now it was so highly tuned, it was more like a weapon than anything. He could aim it and unleash it on most people – even Tanya was susceptible. The closer you got to him, the more at risk you were. He knew how dangerous this could be on relationships – especially friendships.

He decided to end the tension for her and bring the car to a sharp halt, leaving streaks of rubber on the road and the smell of burning in the air.

'Where did the pictures come from, Tan? How did the pictures of my dead wife and daughter make their way into your hands?' he said, not even bothering to turn his head. He didn't need to look at her; he could feel the guilt in the air.

Tanya made a faint noise as she realised where his recent anger had steamed from.

'Don't bother lying to me because I'll know. Just tell me where you got them. Or did they come *to* you?'

Tanya undid her seat belt and turned to face him, her hands trying too hard to touch him but hovering near to his arm with fear. 'They were left for me at the club by a courier, with a note. I didn't think you would believe me if I told you the truth, or you would be too suspicious. I tried my best to track down who sent them, really I did. Then I examined them and they seem to be legit. I was only trying to help, that's all.'

Jack breathed heavily, filling his lungs with familiar air — familiar as it came with a slight smell of the interior of the car. There weren't many places where he felt safe anymore, safe inside his own head, but this was one. The hard, worn rubber steering wheel, slightly clammy under his hands, almost molded to his exact grip. The feel of the hard headrest on his ear, not like the soft plush ones of new cars, no, this one let you know it was there to protect you, not for comfort. He pulled on the handbrake, its stiff, reassuring clicks telling him that's it, he was stopped and he could sit there and rest while the rest of the world carried on without him.

'You should have told me. I've been played like a pissing chess piece, being moved around the board at the whim of someone else and not knowing why. But I think I'm beginning to understand.' He thought for a moment and took out his phone. 'Can we access any confidential files on this? I mean, could you find a way around any of those firewalls or whatever you call them?'

Tanya looked relieved at the change of conversation. 'I could probably access a fair few websites, yeah. Why, what did you have in mind?'

Jack pursed his lips, calculating. 'I just need to make a phone call first.'

Ten minutes passed, Tanya was still surfing the internet, but Jack had found more than enough information to quench the thirst of his hunch.

He twisted the keys and turned the engine over. 'Time to get the truth.'

The new apartments along the docks in Bristol were situated half a mile down the river from Jack's boat. He hadn't realised just how swanky they were. The large windows preserving some of the identity of the factories of the building's past stood in two rows of arches, but even the large number of glass panes couldn't illuminate the two-bed flat in the gloom of a Bristol evening.

Jack watched the dark outline of the home owner from a seat at the glass dining table as they walked through their kitchen, not yet having had time to hang their coat up.

He kept a close eye on them as they placed a satchel onto a kitchen island and headed for the fridge, only then being fully brought into relief by its illumination.

Jack, in the comfort of the shadows, knowing fully well he couldn't be seen, cleared his throat.

'It's not in there.'

IT'S BUSINESS

The occupant slammed a salad drawer back into place and banged the fridge closed. The detective placed a small handgun down heavily, giving it a satisfying clank on the glass.

'How do you do it, Jack? Honestly, how do you get into people's heads and know exactly what they are thinking? You know what they are thinking before they do. It's a great talent, I must admit. Probably why you make such a good detective.'

Jack shrugged. 'Just a gift, I guess, or a curse, depends how you want to look at it. Got any whisky?'

His commanding officer smiled and walked to a cabinet not far from the table. She pulled out a large decanter and two glasses.

'*She really is living it up,*' Jack thought at the sight of the expensive, antique glassware. Then she opened a drawer and pulled out a large cardboard file, full beyond its capacity with paperwork.

'You going to kill me with that thing?' McQuade asked, pointing at the gun.

Jack stuck his finger in the trigger guard and spun it slowly. 'Nah, I'm not much of a killer,' he said, sliding it along the table. It scratched its way up to the paperwork that McQuade had placed down.

She raised an eyebrow. 'Really? That's not what I heard. I heard you left a man's face looking like a plate of minced beef in Florence. Didn't know you had it in you.'

She smiled and took the top from the large glass container and poured them both a healthy measure.

Jack forced a lump from his throat and looked out of the window.

'Yeah, well, not my finest moment, but in my defense, he was already dead, I just …' He paused to think. 'Took out some frustration on him.'

McQuade lifted her glass and saluted him. 'Still, using a man's face as a stress reliever … got to hand it to you, Jack, you never do cease to amaze me. Took you a while to get here, though, thought you might have figured it out a little sooner.'

Jack swilled the drink in the glass. It wasn't the same without ice. 'It wasn't easy, you played it very well. Just enough to be nearly nothing at all. But when Aubrie told me it was all in my head, that the coincidences were just too convenient, where I would usually assume it was me with the issue, this time I thought a little more outside of the box.'

McQuade gave him a mock round of applause, still holding her glass in one hand, before taking a large sip of the light brown fluid. 'That's the good stuff, savour the taste, won't you?'

Jack took a small sip.

'You don't understand why, yet, though, do you? You don't really get it yet, do you? If you did, you wouldn't be here talking, you would be cuffing me. Calling for backup, questioning me down the station. But you don't even know what the questions are, yet, do you?'

Jack barely recognised her, she was so different, all pretense gone, this felt like a performance, but it wasn't. The McQuade from before was the act. She had portrayed someone else all these years and now look at her. Calm, confident in her ability – she had no fear of him at all.

'Where to start, where to start?' she said, taking another sip.

Jack downed his drink, he wanted to feel it burn as his emotions matched it inside of him. 'How about you start at the beginning, start at when I got dragged into this, start at Felicity and Jessica's murders. I assume you know all about it, assume that you helped orchestrate it?'

McQuade stretched her neck out and clicked it loudly, she then took one large sip of whisky, emptying the glass before slamming it down.

'No, I didn't have anything to do with that. I mean, did hear about it, but I was working in the north west at that time, it was before I was needed down here. It was one of the reasons I was relocated – to make sure you didn't fuck anything up. I managed to keep you busy for the most part. Such a handful, though. I was essentially running two parallel lives by that time.'

Jack hit the table. 'Boo fucking hoo. My wife was murdered in front of my child, who was then stabbed to death right after. Give me some fucking answers. What had I done? What did I do to deserve that?'

His commanding officer shook her head. 'Was nothing to do with you. A low-level detective in the Bristol department, do you really think that it was anything to do with you? Come on, Jack, you're smarter than that, think about it.'

It was Jack's turn to shake his head now, he just couldn't understand it.

They destroyed my life, how could it not be about me, how could it be anything but personal?'

'Think, Jack, think,' McQuade said, urging him to work it out. 'Think who I work for. What's in their main interest?'

Jack's mind raced and then started down a path of thought that, deep in his gut, he knew was correct. He could feel that he was slowly pulling the cover back for the big reveal.

'To not get caught. To remain a secret.'

The woman opposite him nodded and poured another half a glass from the decanter.

Jack's head dropped with the knowledge. 'Jessica, what did you do?' He wished for her to be with him so badly, but she had never felt so far away from him as she did now. 'It was her story, wasn't it? She found something, she was going to publish it, she told me not long before she died. She said she had a huge story, life-changing. Tell me, what did she know, exactly?'

McQuade's shoulders raised and fell casually. 'Don't know. Enough to be killed over, though. I heard she was a talented journalist. Shame I never got to meet her.'

Jack's head fell into his hands. 'She was an amazing writer, yeah. I asked her so many times to take up an office-based role – she was offered deputy editor, but she turned it down. So stubborn, I joked that it would be the death of her. For Christ's sake, Jess.' Jack rested for a moment before finding new energy. 'And Felicity? Just a collateral damage thing, was it? My daughter, murdered for no goddamn reason?'

Alison McQuade pursed her lips, interested in the last question. 'No, that was a mistake. That wasn't meant to happen. That's one of the reasons why I was brought down here – to tidy up the mess. To try to manage you. They saw you as a threat right from the word go; you should take that as a compliment, coming from them.'

Jack's mind soaked in the information and turned it over; it just wouldn't add up. None of it was making any sense.

'But the marks on their bodies, the Arabic, what was it?'

McQuade pushed the cardboard file towards him and numerous pictures accidentally slipped out. The detective picked up one from the top. It was an image of a small boy, no older than eight or nine. His limbs were tied to a table, a blindfold hid his eyes, but his mouth said enough. Panic clearly captured on his trembling lips. And on his chest, wet, burning wax in the shape of a cross.

'McQuade, what the fuck is this?' the detective said, nearly retching with the uneasy motion in his gut.

She looked over at the picture, only looking remotely interested. 'That one is of a little boy receiving an exorcism. Carry on, look at that one there,' she said, pointing at another photo that had fallen on the table and was easily discernible.

Jack picked it up and turned it the right way up. In the picture were two small wrists, both with holes going right through.

'That's stigmata, that one. There's a few of those, easy to produce. Ah, look,' McQuade said, leaning over and pointing at yet another image.

Another child stared up at the camera with a fixed gaze. Long, dark hair framed her face, a peaceful expression of reminiscence in her features. It didn't fool Jack, though; he had seen enough dead bodies to recognise a person who had no life left in them.

She was naked and blotchy except for the luminescent diagram on her torso. It was a picture of a pentagram, adorned with small images and Arabic symbols, all lit under ultraviolet light.

'It looks like Jessica and Felicity's pictures. I don't understand, what are they?' He wanted to unsee it, but still he couldn't pull himself away – the macabre had gripped him.

McQuade took a small sip. 'Fake, that's what they are. Some lightly fabricated nonsense. I mean, the children are real, but all the other stuff is a load of nonsense. Keep looking, if you like. Should be about thirty different cases in that lot.' She saw the confusion on his face, it was written clearly. 'It's busin,ess Jack, like when companies fudge their numbers to attract new investors. Only this time it was to make sure that the Syndicate didn't lose a load. You see, Jack, the Church was turning and they were a huge part of the income. So something had to be done.'

Jack dropped the picture in disgust. 'You tortured children for that? But why? It's sick, you know it doesn't make any sense, don't you? You know this isn't normal behaviour for human beings – if you are even human.'

McQuade stood up and walked back to the unit again. She opened a drawer and produced a book. She threw it onto the table, taking a nonchalant walk to the chair before sitting back down.

Jack read the title on the heavy leather-bound book.
Identifying Demons

BRING IT DOWN

'What is it?' Jack asked, thumbing his way through the pages. 'Looks like a cookbook or something, full of recipes for how to abuse children.'

'It was the master plan of one of the handlers,' McQuade said before explaining the term. 'This is like a hierarchy system. The handlers are some of the most powerful, but it probably goes above that. Not too dissimilar to the police force, I guess.'

'Probably?' Jack asked, confused at her lack of knowledge.

McQuade gave a fake laugh. 'Come on, Jack, switch on, unanimity is the key to this – I only get told what I need to know, and even then, that's more than I want to know. Look, this business, with the priests, it was big money, I mean, it must have been to warrant all of these.' She pointed at the large pile of evidence. 'The Jesuits didn't want children anymore; there was too much heat on them, there were investigations coming in at all angles, they bottled it. But what they *did* want were demons.' She pointed at the book.

Jack laughed sarcastically. 'And, what, you gave them demons, did you? You made all this up to sell children.

You made products for your prospective buyers.'

'We were selling them virgin, possessed, demonic children and they lapped it up. Used them in rituals or whatever,' McQuade said, waving an uninterested hand in the air.

Jack stood up. '*Or whatever?*' He swiped at the paperwork, throwing it against the window, spilling the contents across the floor. 'They are *children*; they are innocent children, not a prize fucking cow at the fair.' Jack turned away from her; her face made him feel sick. 'Just carry on, tell me, before I change my mind and do something we'll both regret.'

'It was supply and demand and there was a demand, Jack. Dozens of kids every year, up and down the country. We were a fucking conveyor belt, kids going out and money coming in.'

Jack finally took a look at her, seeing her face for what it was for the first time. 'This is a joke, surely. You're sick, you know that?'

She nodded back at him. 'I know, Jack, I often wonder if I'm a demon, if the devil's work is done through me and I do believe that to be true. I'm far beyond any help, now, but there are others that are not. I was hoping you could save them, Jack, was hoping you could put an end to all this. Please tell me I wasn't wrong.'

A hint of the old McQuade shone through, the woman he had thought he knew.

'The photos … you left them for Tanya, you knew she would give them to me, didn't you?'

McQuade nodded. 'Weeks ago now; I left them at the club for her. I wondered if she had even got them at one point, but then when you asked about investigating Father Lopez, well, I knew there was something in it for you.'

Jack thought about that; it didn't make sense to him, even less sense than everything else from their conversations.

'But surely you would have known he would be killed if

I sent the pictures to him? You must have known he couldn't have helped me?'

McQuade now shook her head. 'His death and you sending him the pictures, I believe, was an unhappy coincidence. I certainly had nothing to do with it and, as far I can tell, neither did the Syndicate. It's all a bit of a mystery, to be honest.' She sipped her whisky.

Jack was unnerved by her lack of compassion; it was so far from any normal boundaries, he couldn't understand how to compute it.

He scorned her with a look for her choice of lackadaisical language.

'Do you really think you would have been left to roam around Florence if it was the Syndicate who killed him? Father Lopez was a threat, sure, he had been trying to gather evidence for years, but he was nowhere near proving anything— well, not that I know of, anyway. That's why he was moved away from Rome – because he was becoming a nuisance. Probably why your friend Vincenzo suggested sending the pictures to him, he probably knew his reputation. Put out in Florence where there were no connections – or so we thought. Turned out another priest had gotten wind of money passing hands and decided he wanted a cut. I think he tried to get Lopez to give him information and when it didn't work, he killed him. So, when you came to me, asking to go over there, I convinced my handler to let you go and find who it was trying to muscle in on the business.'

Jack sat back down. 'You let them use me as pawn, let them … let me be tortured. I've had half of my fucking toe cut off, Alison, this all part of your greater plan, was it?'

McQuade smiled so sweetly Jack became even more annoyed, his teeth firmly gritted together. 'Why do you think I forced you onto the Pearce case? I needed you to get mixed up in it, needed you to get so dirty in it all you wouldn't stop until you were clean. You need to bring it down, you need to bring the whole fucking thing down.'

Jack shook his head. 'No, I'm not having it, I don't believe you had any intention of trying to help these kids. I mean, you could have tried to do it yourself, you could have just come to me, brought me evidence, sat me down and told me about the whole damn thing. You could have told me exactly why my wife, my child – my poor little Felicity – were killed.'

McQuade looked away.

Jack could see some sort of shame hiding behind her eyes, it was a hard screen to see through, but there was a glimmer of something and then he got it. 'Ah, I see, I see you, Alison, there's the truth. You thought you would be able to get out of this untouched, didn't you? If I fail, nothing can be traced back to you, if I succeed, you come out on top, head of the police force that brought the Syndicate to its knees. You're unbelievable, you really are.'

McQuade waved a lazy arm around again. 'Well, that's by the by, now, isn't it? I'm a dead man – woman – standing, now you know the truth.' She took another sip of spirit. 'How did you work out it was me? I mean, you couldn't have been sure?'

Jack kneaded his forehead, grabbed his drink, downed the remnants and slid the glass back, requesting a top up.

'Your father – or stepfather. I phoned the hospital. He's changed his first name, but kept the surname, interesting choice. Then I searched the internet for you. Not easy, but I had some help, doubt I would have found anything had I not. Adopted at four by your father, name changed at twelve. A name you gave yourself?'

McQuade laughed. 'Now that would constitute a choice, a privilege I have never been afforded. No, it was to help me stay hidden. My father's mother's maiden name. His Scottish roots, he was very proud of them. He was very close to his mother. She died when he was nineteen. He struggled to let go.'

'And as long as he had you, he never had to, right? He stole you from the orphanage?'

McQuade shook her head. 'No, no, he paid for me fair and square. That's how he knew he owned me, and when you own something, you can do as much as you like with it. You can play with it, break it, beat it …' she paused and rubbed her upper arms. '*Burn* it. I was never a human to him, not really. And once I was an adult, I had to do as he asked and, in turn, as the Syndicate asked. He didn't touch me anymore – not out of pleasure, anyway. I guess he stopped loving me – a woman's body not perfect enough for him. So I try to please him in other ways, try to make him love me again, show him how much I can do. I can produce forgeries of demon photographs, I can keep police commissioners and cardinals and even judges out of prison. The one on our friend Peters' case is indebted to me. Press were going to have a field day with images of him with young boys as he stood over them, pissing on them, dressed as a goddamn Nazi. I've seen it all, been a part of it all, and now I'm done.'

Jack slammed his hand on the table, part of him hoped it would smash, would cut him, take his emotional pain for these children and turn it physical. 'No, you don't get to just opt out, you don't get to just escape untouched while this suffering goes on!' he shouted at her, his voice burning in his throat.

McQuade stood up. 'Untouched? *Untouched?* Oh, I've been touched, Jack, in ways that you couldn't possibly imagine. I have felt pain worse than having a toe cut off. I've been to that abyss where everything is black and dying looks like your only saviour. Not once, not twice, but for days upon days, lasting years. The only thing that kept me alive, gave me hope, was that my father loved me. Love from your abuser being the only thing good in your life, now, what sort of life is that? Yes, you've been used, Jack, but haven't we all?' McQuade's chest rose and fell, matching the passion in her voice.

Jack went silent, he had nothing to say to that. Their conversation was somewhere he couldn't recognise. How could he say anything when his ignorance was the only thing keeping him from dying inside?

'They're demons,' he finally spoke quietly. 'Sophia said it, and she was right.'

One single tear ran down his commanding officer's face, that's all she would allow. 'Yes, Jack, they are, and I love one of them, but it's time to stop them.'

Jack sighed. 'You may love him, but if I found out that he had anything to do with Felicity or Jessica, you know I will kill him, right?'

BRISTOL'S FLOATING HARBOUR

Jack allowed her a few moments to think and finish her whisky.

'They're moving a child, I need to know who is moving him and where they have taken him,' Jack said, his voice sounding uncompromising.

McQuade looked shocked. 'But how? How could you possibly know that?' She looked away again, worried that Jack could see into her mind through her eyes.

'They're moving all of the children from Bristol, they've cut me out, I don't know anything. They already suspect that I'm too close to you. I can't help you, Jack, if it's one kid you're trying to find, I can't help you.'

Jack punched the table again. 'For fuck sake, Alison, there is a kid lying in a ditch somewhere, half dead, and you won't help me? Who would they use instead of Pearce to dispose of a body, to kill a kid and dump them?'

She pointed at the paperwork. 'There, on the inside cover, I made a list of known Syndicate members who have flown into England since you left. One of them is probably being used.'

Jack opened the file; he found a list of names, about ten in total.

'You need to help me narrow it down, Alison; you owe me that, at the very least. You wrote these down because you knew I would need them, come on, give me something.'

But Jack was interrupted by a vibration in his pocket. He retrieved his phone and answered quickly. 'Yeah? Ok, thanks,' he said, then tucked it away again. 'Six men, all armed, have just arrived at the entrance downstairs. We need to go.' Jack stood up, collected up the paperwork and began his walk for the door. 'Well, come on, we need to go!' he shouted at McQuade.

'No, I'll slow you down. Just go, I'll be fine.' She picked up the gun from the table.

Jack looked at the door then back at her. 'Who is your handler? Tell me that, at least.'

McQuade stared at him, her eyes now trembling, tears dropping from her cheeks to the glass tabletop. She stood slowly and raised the gun at him.

'Goodbye, Jack, I'm free.' She turned the gun around and placed it against the side of her head.

'No!' the detective shouted, but his voice was drowned out by the sound barrier broken by the bullet leaving the barrel of the gun.

McQuade's body landed heavily on the glass, cracking it slightly, but still holding her up from the ground.

Jack, stunned, watched as a pool of dark blood spread its way outward from his commanding officer, filling the table to its edges before creating a small, red waterfall effect to the floor.

He heard footsteps approach the door – they must have heard the gunfire and determined that they should abandon stealth for haste.

Jack ran through to the bedroom. He had scouted emergency exits quickly when he broke in. The fire exit was an internal staircase, so a window and large drop would have to do. He looked out, seeing the hard cobbled street glistening in the moonlight. It was too far. Even if he had been fully fit, with all ten toes, it was much higher now than he had anticipated. He would have to go to plan C.

He raced back into the apartment just as gunshots hit the front door, clearly disabling the lock. He picked up the loose gun and fired shots towards the direction of the armed men, not with any hopes of hitting them, but just enough to give them second thoughts of entering. He hoped this would give him the precious few seconds he would need. He took out his phone, swiped up for a camera and placed the paperwork down on the floor. He barely had time to take one picture of the list of names when the door swung open.

Jettisoning the gun, he picked up a chair and threw it at the large glass window, shattering it completely. He was a good eight feet from the water and didn't have time for a run-up as two shots hit the wall beside him. He jumped, stretching his torso forward, praying it would be enough to clear the railings and land safely in Bristol's floating harbour. He held his breath in preparation, his left foot contacting with the metal barrier, breaking a bone but not his fall. He entered with a splash. The icy cold flooded his senses for a moment, but the sound of more gunfire refocused him. Coming up for one more gulp of air, he submerged himself again. The pitch black water hid him completely and, even if it hadn't, Jack knew that even the largest bullets could only penetrate a few inches into water. This had always bugged him when watching action films — not that he had time to let it irritate him now. He swam several meters away under the surface before allowing himself another quiet breath.

Sirens now began, scaring away his attackers. Once again, he had been on the brink of being murdered and, again, he had narrowly escaped. He began to wonder just how long it could last.

The cold now became apparent. He swam hard towards a pontoon, trying to free his muscles from their tightness. He pulled himself from the murky water, just his shoe missing where it had been struck on the way down. He felt the bones in his foot and something burned, most likely a break, he surmised. He pulled the phone from his breast pocket, expecting to see a dead screen but, to his amazement, it looked as good as new. He opened it and dialed Tanya's number.

'You ok?' she said quickly as she answered the phone.

Jack winced as he tried to stand up straight and looked around. To his amazement, he didn't appear to be in any immediate danger.

'Yeah, I'm fine, I'm about two minutes from Bristol Bridge, can you pick me up?'

Jack waited on some steps just out of view of the road, as Tanya arrived at a stop.

'I had to jump in,' Jack said, filling the passenger seat with his sodden body.

Tanya laughed. 'Yeah, I guessed. Get you, Jason Statham. Right, let's get out of here before you get into any more trouble. You should have *seen* the amount of undercover cop cars that turned up, I think they may have actually been MI5.' She pushed the car into gear and put her foot down. 'Did you get anything? Take your clothes off, you'll freeze to death,' Tanya said, pulling into a parking space on the fringes of Bedminster.

Jack fought with his trousers to pull them off in the cramped space of the car.

'Well, I know why Jessica and Felicity were killed. Jess was writing a piece on them – sounds like she was going to expose the entire thing. And, as for our missing child dying in a ditch somewhere, well, she wasn't as helpful as I had hoped. She gave me a list of people who may be moving our Freddie Owens. Had to take a picture of it. Hopefully, this phone is still working after my little swim. Managed to phone you Ok.'

Tanya unclipped her seatbelt and helped him pull his

shirt off, so he was down to his underwear. She leaned over to the back seat and found an old coat of his to throw over him.

'It should be fine, I got you the new iPhone, it's waterproof. Well, up to a certain depth, anyway, and as long as you weren't free diving into sea caves, I think you'll be fine,' she said, taking the open phone from him and scrolling through the pictures.

'Well, you have a small job lot of names, which one is our man, though? I mean, we could do a simple Google Search, but I doubt it would come back with anything. If I had time to set up some equipment and a few days, I'm sure I could track all of them.'

Jack shivered and tucked himself up into the coat. 'Well, we don't even have a few hours, let alone a few days …' his voice trailed off as his speech slurred. A searing pain rushed to his head and his body temperature plummeted. Jack could feel his breathing become shallow and fast; there was no warning, he was suddenly ill. He was suddenly close to dying.

Tanya leant over and pressed against this neck, desperately looking for a pulse. Jack slipped in and out of consciousness, everything turning black and then a collage of colours once more. He was so confused, a voice was in his ear, but it may as well have been speaking to someone else – speaking to someone else in Chinese.

'Jack, you are suffering from hypothermia!' Tanya shouted as she climbed out of the car and opened the boot. She found an old blanket. It had oil stains on it but it would have to do.

Jack felt the weight of it but none of the warmth – it was there, but his body was not accepting it.

Tanya took her top off, so she was down to her bra, and she slid her small frame under the cover and wrapped it as best she could around them both. Slowly, Jack felt her breathing pressing against him, his own breaths wanting to match hers, something for him to focus on through all the murky reality.

A few_moments passed and the Bristol lights became true once again. He could see buildings, he could smell the shampoo in Tanya's hair, he could feel her breasts, barely covered as her body became tangible.

Seeing him recover, she grabbed behind his neck and kissed him. It was the first time he had felt an embrace of love since Jessica and he kissed her back. Her full lips spread against his as their tongues met. He wanted to feel her against him, wanted her completely, his life now driven into a passion for this beautiful creature.

Tanya pulled away. 'I'm sorry, I didn't mean to, I just— I thought you were going to die,' she said, sitting up. 'Yet again.' She laughed and tucked her hair behind her ear.

Jack straightened up, quickly grabbing the blanket and covering himself as he realised he had an erection that impressed even him – it looked as though it could give the gear stick between them a run for its money.

'No, it's my fault, just been a long time since I've kissed anyone like that. I just felt alive for a moment – more alive than I have in years,' Jack replied, glad that his blood flow was now heading away from his genitals. 'Hardly the time or place, I know.'

Tanya looked back at him. 'You went into full hypothermia, then came out of it. I mean, in seconds. That's not normal, Jack. You really frightened me. I've seen you in trouble before, but you looked dead your face had such little life left in it. I know the water was cold, but you weren't in it for long. Unless your toe is infected and your body went into toxic shock or something?'

The detective shook his head. 'I don't think it was me, I mean, I know that sounds crazy, but I think it's Freddie, I think he's the one dying, I just sort of felt it.'

He recognised the skepticism on her face. He couldn't bear to look at her, he hated for her, of all people, to think he was mad, sick and needing help like an old man – like McQuade's father, locked in a home where he couldn't bother anyone. Perhaps that was his fate to come.

'Ok, so what do we do? You have your list, how do we follow it?' Tanya said, clearly ignoring the uncomfortable space he had just put between them.

Jack was grateful for this; he was running out of energy and he needed his friend, now more than never. He just needed someone to support him, no questions, just a crutch for his weight to lean on and carry on moving.

An idea came to him.

'I need to narrow it down, I need to find a common theme I can use. I need some sort of link between Pearce, our paedophile teacher, and one of these men. They've brought someone new in to replace him; there has to be something connecting them. We have to go to the police station. I think it's my only hope.'

Tanya laughed, she looked at him and then laughed again. 'Oh, wait, you're actually serious.' She laughed for a third time. 'Ok, well, do you think you ought to get some dry clothes first, at the very least?'

'If we had time.' He looked down at his pants, grabbed the coat, pulled it on and zipped it up. 'This will have to do. I'll put my wet trousers back on when we get there.' He picked them up and squeezed the bottom of one of the legs. Water drained out like a tap. 'Maybe.'

SEEN HIS NAME

Jack walked into the station barefoot, cold and leaving puddles behind him. He had decided that the sodden trousers were better than none at all.

He grabbed Timmins from his desk, almost literally pulling him into the nearest quiet room. Several people gawped at Jack for a plethora of different reasons. Some were wondering why he was stomping his way through with nothing on his feet, others because they still thought he was dead and then the last few because they assumed he had been sacked.

'What's going on, sarge?'

Jack looked around through the window in the door and pulled a lever, shutting its small blind. 'I have a list of suspects linked to Pearce and a missing child. I need to narrow it down and find one of them. Got to find which one is most closely linked with Pearce. I'm going to need your help.'

Timmins smiled. 'Of course, sarge, but it won't be easy. Is it just the two of us? Just because, I mean, ninety per cent of the paperwork is *actually* paper. Can't just document search it.'

'I appreciate that, but, yes, it's just the two of us. I have nothing to narrow it down and we are on a time limit of about two hours ago,' Jack said, pulling a chair and turning the computer on for the other man.

'Right, ok, yes. I will go and get the files,' the young officer replied, sounding as unconfident as a police officer ever had. But, before he had a chance, the door swung open heavily, crashing back on its hinges.

'Jack, what the hell are you doing?' It was an officer from Jack's team, Nitin Kapoor, but he had never referred to him by his first name before.

Jack didn't like it, he was being treated as a civilian and, right now, that just won't do. 'I'm still your commanding officer, you do realise that, don't you?' Jack stood up to meet the other man's eye level, ready for a confrontation.

'No, sarge, you've been suspended. If you come here, we've been told to arrest you.' The intruding officer sounded less sure of himself with each word leaving his mouth. It didn't help that the way that Jack looked gave the impression that he really wasn't stable enough to be arguing with.

'Under whose orders?' Jack spoke forcefully, refocusing the man's attention on him.

'McQuade, sarge, she said it was for your own safety, sarge.'

'Ah, yeah, she's dead now,' Jack said with deliberate, casual ease. 'So that makes me the commanding officer in this station at present. So, could you get a small team together and go to her apartment to sort that out? You need a large forensic unit, there's bullet holes everywhere and lots of blood. Can you also get out of Officer Timmins' way? He's got a lot to do and precious little time. Thank you.'

Jack watched, almost amused, at the face of Nitin as he tried to process all of the information. It clearly did not compute but he was not about to argue if the information was true.

'Uh, yes, of course, sarge. There *was* a reported

shooting not long ago, was that her? Is she really dead? Did you say *lots* of bullet holes? Did someone shoot her, then?' Officer Kapoor asked, scratching at his head below the rim of his hat.

'No, she shot herself. I was there, I will give my statement later, I'm a bit busy at the moment.'

Officer Kapoor turned on his heels to leave, then turned back. 'Yes, sarge, of course, I'm on it *right away.*'

'A bit harsh, but he deserved it, coming in here with his back up like that. Only enough room for one miserable bossy bastard around here.'

Jack got as far as logging onto the computer and copying the names out from his phone to post them when Timmins came back, his arms fully laden with two large, cardboard boxes.

'All of that?' Jack asked, eyeing the vast amount of information being heavily dropped onto the desk.

'No, there's another two boxes, but I thought this would be a good place to start,' Timmins said, pulling three or four files from the box and spreading them out on the table.

Jack rubbed at his stubble, his anxiety tipping over into anger.

'Why has this got to be so damn hard?'

The pair started thumbing through paperwork while Jack let Timmins simultaneously do various computer searches. Every page consisted of names, none of which were the same as their list.

A knock at the door barely took their attention, but the voice saying his name definitely caught the detective's ear.

'Jack, I heard … I heard you were soaking wet with no shoes and McQuade is dead.' It was Aubrie. Her voice gentle and weary.

He put the paperwork down and looked himself up and down. 'Well, I had one shoe, but I thought that looked weirder than no shoes, so I left it in the car.'

Aubrie's eyes widened. 'Is that really all you have to

say?'

The detective picked up the folder again, frustrated with her already – not for anything she had said, but for what she was about to say. He could predict her too well these days.

'McQuade is dead. She told me that Freddie Owens is being moved. It's a long story, but she was involved and now she's taken her own life, so I'm left to try to find this kid on my own. Except for Timmins, here, I mean. But she gave me a list of names and I have no way of working out who any of them are or which one it might be. Even then, if I work out which one it is, I still have to find them and get them to tell me where the kid is. And right now, I can't afford any distractions,' Jack said before shoving his nose back into the work.

'So, what are you doing? How can I help?' she asked, looking like a child repenting for annoying their parent.

Jack felt relief; he didn't have it in him to have another argument with his friend.

'I need to work out who on this list is the most likely to be our killer. They're all Syndicate members and all came back into the UK in the last few days. I figured that if they were bringing in someone to replace Pearce, there should be a connection between them.'

'Does there have to be, can't it just be a random Syndicate member?' Aubrie asked, playing devil's advocate.

'No, there doesn't have to be, but there *must* be, there just must. Otherwise, I have a dozen people to find with no means of doing so,' Jack replied, his voice empty and hopeless.

'Eleven people,' Timmins interjected before ducking back down again into the paperwork after realising that being pedantic wasn't much help.

Think, Jack, think, there has to be a link,' the detective encouraged himself. He threw the paperwork down and lifted his head to the ceiling. 'What am I missing?'

'Throw some questions at me, see if we can bounce

some ideas around,' Aubrie said, loosening her shoulders with a whip of her head.

Jack shook his head. 'What the hell am I meant to ask a pathologist?'

'I don't know. Ask me how they died. Do your thing when you see into the killer's head. There must be something we can do,' the doctor in the room said, some desperation now coming to the top of her speech.

'How were they killed?' Jack asked, but only to himself. *'What would that tell me? Tell me who killed them, sort of.'*

Then, something did click in his mind, one cog meeting another, giving the initial shove to get a motion going. *'Maybe that is almost the right question.'*

'How were the children killed? Have you completed all of the pathology reports now?' he asked Aubrie, a small flicker of hope shining through confused fog.

'Most of them. All were suffocated,' she replied quickly.

Jack bit his lips, then said, 'There's something here, I can feel it. Suffocated *how* exactly? All in the same way?'

Dr. Sellers shook her head. 'No, some were strangled and some asphyxiated – most likely in the plastic they were buried in.'

Jack nodded. 'That's it: two killers, one strangles, one doesn't.'

'Now what to do with that information?' Jack asked himself as he stood up to pace the room. 'At the sites where there were multiple bodies, were both types of murder found?'

He watched as Aubrie closed her eyes to think. 'Yes, at two, I believe. One in north Wales, in Abergele. I only oversaw the pathology unit there from my office, but they did good job. And the second one was north Gloucester, I can't quite remember the village now.'

'Right, ok, let's focus on these two locations, look for one of these names, something has to flag. Start on the files we have logged on the system, see if we can get lucky.' Jack jabbed his finger, poking the list of names as hard as he could without doing damage to his bones. He often did things that would be on the verge of causing himself harm, as if in punishing his body, perhaps the world would bring some relief to his mental pain.

Aubrie hovered in the doorway. Jack could feel her reaching bursting point with questions. He didn't mind, at least she wasn't doubting him and he would answer all of them – as soon as he found this child.

Timmins stood up and clapped his hands, pushing the chair so quickly and with so much force it toppled over backwards.

'Boom, get in. We have a match, look.'

And Jack looked, slowly moving in on the computer, hesitantly, almost afraid to approach in case he frightened it away.

There was the name *O'Donald*. Jack stared at it and it stared right back at him, daring him to remember. But remember *what?*

'Why do I feel like we have read these names together before?' he asked the room, not really expecting an answer but receiving a shrug of the shoulders from Timmins anyway.

'Because we fucking have!' Jack shouted. 'You included,' Jack said to the young officer, a wash of panic coming over him at being addressed. 'The news report, the one you showed me. Goddamn it, we've seen his name *and* his face. He worked at that care home, the one in Ireland, what was it called?' Jack thought for a second, but it came back suddenly, almost catching him off guard. 'Tuam Care Home. Oh, and guess what else?' Jack turned to Aubrie, ready to drop a bomb on her. 'McQuade's stepfather was the priest there, that's where he found her.'

Aubrie shook her head, the realisation of what Jack was telling her too hard, too true to comprehend. 'It can't be. She can't— that's not possible. She can't have been in on all … all of this. She just can't have been!'

Jack raised his eyebrows. 'Well, she was. She was, they brainwashed her.' Jack wasn't sure how to explain it, it was all a bit too crazy to keep inside his head, let alone say out loud.

'She was abused and used; I don't think she could help it. They're so powerful, these people. She was lucky to just survive herself. She wanted me to bring an end to it, she wanted me to expose it all.'

Aubrie gazed at him, almost in wonder but verging on disbelief before asking, 'So, how are you going to do that?'

Jack shook his head. 'I don't know, right now I've got to think about Freddie Owens and how I'm going to find him. If I can find this guy, I might be in with a chance.'

Jack hadn't noticed Timmins, who had picked up the chair and was sitting back at the computer, or how his fingers had been furiously punching at keys. He only noticed when the young man spoke, very quickly and very excitedly.

'Got him for you, sarge, he's booked on a Ryanair air flight in three hours, flying out of Bristol airport. And, as far as I can see, he hasn't checked in yet.'

Jack looked at the screen in amazement. 'Have you hacked the airport systems?'

Timmins flicked his nose with his thumb and ignored the question, sniffing his way past it.

'Good lad,' Jack said, slapping him on the back. 'I've got to go.' Jack turned to Aubrie.

She looked embarrassed and he knew why. She had doubted him; she had been so sure that he was ill.

The detective squeezed her elbow and gave her smile, one that told her that all was forgiven.

REALLY GOING TO HURT

A tall, thin man, his body in better shape than most others of his age – looking stronger than most people his age, too – stepped out of a taxi at the airport drop off zone. He waited as the driver retrieved his bags from the boot, placing them neatly on the footpath near to the doors. He paid the man, giving a substantial tip before putting a cigarette to his mouth and watching the car pull away.

A hand from the corner of his eye offered a light, it had shocked him a little, but the old fashioned lighter was so impressive with its large, dancing flame that he gave a nod of thanks and cupped his hands around it, igniting the end of the tobacco.

'Don't see many lighters like that anymore,' he said, in a thick Irish accent.

'No, this was given to me by a friend, it has an interesting engraving on it, look.' The man held it out in his palm to show him.

The Irish man's face was impressed. 'Jesuits. Haven't seen that in a while, either. I've worked with a few in my time. Good people.' He sucked heavily on the cigarette and blew deliberately away from his new friend.

'Yeah, me too – recently, anyway. Couple of them died,

unfortunately.'

The man smoking took a longer drag still. 'Yeah, well, even men of the cloth can't hide from the reaper. As hard as they try. You flying out today?' he asked, pointing with the fag towards the doors.

'Me? No, I'm here on business, unfortunately. I'm a police officer, you see — well, detective, actually.'

The man took a small puff on the cigarette, trying to keep his cool, but his grip on the butt had clearly tightened. 'That's exciting, what you doing here, terrorists or something?' he asked, unable to meet the other man's gaze, his cool Irish accent hiding the anxiety quite well.

The other man laughed. 'No, no, nothing like that. A missing child. Young lad, his name's Freddie Owens, went missing a while back.'

'Is that right?' the smoker said, throwing his cigarette down on the floor and stamping it out quickly.

'Yeah, that is right.' The other man noticed the smoke still coming from the burning end where it hadn't been extinguished fully. He stood on it, twisting it with his foot into the ground until it was nothing but flaky pieces. 'Now, I suggest you put these on, or I'll cut your fucking throat.' Jack handed the tall Irish man a pair of handcuffs.

He returned the request with a smile and said, 'Oh, I'll put them on, but we both know you're not going to do a thing like that. Not while you're still a detective, and all.'

'Behind your back,' Jack said, before O'Donald could click them into place in front of himself. 'And do you know what? I'm not sure I want to be a detective anymore, I think I would rather be more like you today. I fancy killing someone, just to see what it's like.'

The cuffs were on; Jack gave them an extra couple of clicks each for his own satisfaction.

'You going to gut me right here, detective, are you? Going to let all these holidaymakers watch my eyes roll back and hear my death rattle?'

Jack turned him around. 'No, first of all, you are going

to get in that car,' he pointed to his Capri, 'and then I am going to take you somewhere very private where we can talk as loud as you want to or, should I say, need to? And you're going to tell me where the child is. Now, I know that was a lot of information for you to take in, but did you understand all of it?' Jack asked sarcastically, leading him to the car.

The man struggled free for a second and twisted to face him. 'There'll be no need, detective, the child is already dead.'

Jack grabbed his arm and twisted it uncomfortably. 'We'll see. Right now, I would also be worrying about your future, because it's not looking pretty.'

He forced the man into the backseat of the car, got a second pair of handcuffs and connected the first pair he was already wearing to the buckle of the seatbelt – Jack had seen enough kidnap scenes in movies to recognise how much of a threat a large opponent could still pose from the back seat, handcuffs or no.

Jack pulled up to a warehouse, following directions text to him by Tanya. Its large, sliding doors were open and he slowly drove the car inside, its headlights gradually revealing the Irishman's imminent future.

Jack hadn't spoken to the man on the way there; he wanted him to sweat as much as possible, make every second agonisingly long. The Irishman had tried to spark up conversations, a false bravado hiding how hard his heart was actually hammering inside his chest.

Jack stopped the car, pulled the seat forward and released the extra pair of cuffs.

'I suggest you get out of your own accord. I love this car and I don't want to get any blood on the upholstery. *Now*,' Jack spoke quietly, but commandingly. He never had been one for shouting, not really. It didn't work on him, so why would it work on others?

The man edged his way along the seat and stood up

straight, deliberately close to Jack – so close that the stale cigarette smoke filled his nostrils. He was a good half a foot taller and was clearly used to using his height to intimidate.

Jack smiled enthusiastically, he was genuinely amused. His anger had tipped the balance; it wasn't grounded in reality anymore. He felt as though the real Jack had left and now, in his place, was this beast— no, not beast, *demon*. The small part that he had used to fight back, used to swallow down and keep in check now had no master. Jack's shoulders twitched back, his chest broadened, his muscles aligning themselves to be powerful, to hold him so strong that it would take ten large Irishmen to put him down.

Jack chuckled. 'Time for you to stand over here.'

He grabbed the man by the cuffs and led him over to where Tanya had been waiting. 'His phone is on the passenger seat and I'm guessing a laptop will be in his suitcase. First to find where the kid is wins.'

Tanya looked worried. 'Are you sure you want to do this? I'm sure I can hack the GPS on his phone. Shouldn't take me long, just give me ten minutes.'

The detective looked at her, then his captive. 'Yeah, I'm pretty sure. In fact, I think I am going to enjoy it.'

The tall man struggled but Jack kicked the back of his legs, bringing him down to his knees.

'You can't do this, you're a policeman, you'll go down for this and you know what they do to police inside.'

The detective took a deep intake of air through his nose. 'I'm not sure I care. Right, Tan, crack on, I'm going to have some fun.'

The woman's head bowed. It was unlike her to care what happened to someone like this, but then Jack realised it was because she cared what was happening to *him*. He could feel that with each second he was losing himself further into the mania, and with each second he cared less.

The man started to struggle again, only now noticing

the rope hanging from one of the high rafters.

'Don't worry,' Jack said, holding him still and pulling down a large hook on the end of the tether. 'I'm not going to hang you – not from your neck, anyway.'

He caught the hook under the handcuffs behind the man's back and pulled on the other end of the rope, lifting the man to his feet. He now had the child killer in the same position as the priest in Florence had previously had him. The man groaned as Jack pulled it tight, overstretching the shoulder joints and tying it off on a steel pillar.

'Ok, so this is the situation. No one knows you're here; you are in the arse end of nowhere, so no one's going to hear you scream, either. Now, this is what one of your little friends did to me, so I am going to do it to you. And then I am going to ask where the child is. Do you understand?'

The man didn't nod, he just gritted his teeth under the pain and spat at the floor.

'I'm taking that as a yes. Now, I could start asking you where the child is, but I think the full experience would probably be more convincing.' He picked up a screwdriver and hammer that Tanya had supplied from the floor. The man in cuffs couldn't look up so the detective crouched down and showed him the tools.

'Now, in a moment, you're going to tell me exactly where the boy is, where you have buried him and how I get to him. But first, I promise you, this is really going to hurt.'

COME BACK TO ME

Jack had fumbled with the man's feet for a few moments. It was easy enough taking his shoe off, but getting him to stay still long enough for him to get a hammer and chisel and remove the end of his toe like what had happened to him was not going to be possible. He wasn't semi-conscious like Jack had been in Florence. No, this man was putting up a good fight.

Jack's mind changed now; he was looking at his current situation as if it was a DIY job, looking for the most practical way of completing the task. He walked around the back of the tethered man and lifted his leg up behind him, holding it in place between his own legs, like a farrier might with a horse.

'I've had to change my plan a bit, but I think this might convince you to cooperate all the same.' Jack called over his shoulder, his voice as smooth as ice and his heart frozen harder. He gave one big tug on the man's shin to get him in place.

The Irishman was close to screaming as the pain in his shoulders increased.

Jack had picked up a pair of plyers and it only took two attempts to get them locked on to the nail of the big toe.

He released the leg, so the plyers took the entire weight. The man's breathing became fast and panicked – something was hurting, but he wasn't sure what it was – and Jack was loving it. He could see the child's face from the hole, the pain being echoed to where he was now, where he now had become the punisher. He imagined the voice of this kid in his ear, telling him to do it, egging him on like only children can.

'He deserves it, Jack, don't worry, he deserves it.'

The detective ripped the plyers upward, twisting the foot on its ankle joint heavily until the nail gave and tore away from the flesh.

The Irishman screamed just as Jack did too, only his was audible pleasure. Blood spurted over him. He was lost, now, taken by the demon to the dark places and he didn't even want to return, this version of himself was strong and uncaring of consequences.

'Now, I am going to ask you once nicely and after that I will be applying some real pressure,' Jack said softly, trying to control his increasing, excitable heart rate. 'Where have you left the child? Little Freddie Owens?'

The Irishman looked up as far as he could, straining his neck muscles, but then dropped his face back down. 'Go fuck yourself.'

Jack laughed and picked up a hammer. He used the rubber handled end to prise the man's head back up again. His eyes narrowed and he brought his face to within inches of his captive. 'Fuck *me*? In case you hadn't noticed, you are the only one getting fucked here. You see, my friend will find out the location regardless of whether you cooperate or not. So this is just fun for me. So, I guess I should be thanking you.' He allowed the man's head to drop. But Jack paused, an image flashed across his mind, the boy in the hole, his face looking up with dead eyes, and then it turned into his daughter's face. The dead face of the little girl who he had never had the courage to see in person, never been brave enough to say goodbye to her fallen body. Tears formed in his eyes before slowly finding pathways down his cheeks to the corners of his mouth. He gripped the head of the hammer and looked at the man in front of him, rage forming in his heart again.

He gripped the head of the hammer tightly between his fingers, so the handle followed the direction of his forearm.

'How many little boys have you killed? How many sons and daughters have you taken away from their parents? How about I break a bone in your body for each and every one of them?'

And, without warning, Jack brought a right hook down on the man's face, clattering the hammer, his fingers and a jaw bone together with a makeshift knuckle duster effect.

Twice more the detective delivered blows, leaving the man barely awake.

'Well, that's one bone broken, which one next?' the detective asked as he circled his victim. And again, with no announcement, Jack turned the hammer round, held it by the handle and smashed it against the stretched arm. The bone clearly broke just below the wrist. The man's weight now hung on tendons and muscle down his right-hand side. He himself was sobbing, trying desperately to stay on his feet, watching as a pool of blood gathered around his injured toe.

Jack circled some more then decided an ankle would make good target practice next. He swung the tool low and with so much force he followed it through in a large upward arc. It swiped the Irishman's legs out, his screams now tearing at his vocal cords. Jack stood still, watching intently as the man tried desperately to get back upright, his feet slipping in blood and his right arm not giving him any purchase. The detective viewed the scene as if on television – he could have been anywhere in the world seeing this and it would have felt just as real.

'Jack, Jack, I've got it, I think I know where the boy is,' Tanya came running over, her laptop open. 'I've managed to take all the data from his phone and I've got GPS locations.'

Jack didn't look around, he was lost in the gruesome moment. Tanya's voice was there, but it was too far away to hear.

One hand holding the laptop, Tanya used the other to pull his face, forcing him to look away from the stricken captive.

'Jack, come back to me, Jack. I'm here, I've got you, you're ok.'

Tanya's comforting words were enough to bring him to her. His eyes slowly left the broken man and found hers. He didn't feel in control of any part of himself, he felt disconnected, like he was floating along on a current, gently flowing from one side to the next.

'Jack, I've got you. Yes?' Tanya smiled her bright red lipstick at him.

He nodded back, starting to acknowledge the world – the real one.

'I know where the boy is, it's time to leave this. Let's go and get him.'

Jack watched her mouth as she spoke, his mind starting to come on to focus. He took a deep breath and gave her a large reassuring smile in return.

He turned and walked over to where the rope was tied off. He pulled on the slip knot he had tied and the man's body hit the ground with a wet thud on top of the blood.

Jack stood over the fallen man. 'Tell your handler I'm coming for him. I'm coming for all of them.'

FALLEN LEAVES

Tanya didn't press him, she just gave him directions as Jack weaved in and out of traffic as best he could. They had left Bristol and were heading straight up the M5 towards Gloucester.

Jack felt embarrassed, his actions had been so far out of his usual character they had shocked him. He had never seen himself like that before and hated that Tanya had witnessed it at the same time. She had always told him he should be himself, do these things that he repressed and act as he wanted to act, but he didn't think that nearly butchering a man to death was what she meant.

He looked at her as she was zooming in and out of maps on her phone.

'*Or perhaps it* was *what she meant,*' he thought to himself as the memory of the crime scene photos of the killing spree she had gone on years before came back to him. She had done much worse to people and, while they were just as evil, perhaps it was different – the punishment being dealt out by a young woman, by someone who would normally have been a victim in situations like those.

They left the motorway and headed onto A roads, then a B road, finally coming onto a narrow track just outside of the Forest of Dean.

'Are you sure about this? If I drive down there and we get stuck …'

Tanya picked her laptop up off the floor. 'Pretty sure, I can't access the actual text, but he sent a message from here and his GPS data shows that he spent some time here. Hang on, let me research the property.'

Jack didn't hang on, he put his foot down and sent the car fishtailing down the wet dirt track. He could barely keep control of it; the car was not built for this punishment, the suspension slamming up in their housings as they hit bumps.

'Look,' Jack said, pointing at the road ahead. 'Fresh tyre marks. Four-by-four, it looks like. Could just be a farmer, but might not be.'

Tanya closed the laptop. 'No, I don't think it's a farmer. This property was a farm once but got split up into land and dwelling in the sixties. Just been looking on the land registry, and census for the subsequent years.'

Jack took his eyes off the road for a second to look at her, but had to quickly look back at the treacherous road ahead. 'And?'

'Nineteen seventy-one, the property was bought in full, by a local teacher – by one Mr. R. Pearce.'

Jack smiled. 'Knew it. I'm going to call this in. Can you get me the coordinates?' he asked her. He pulled his phone out, unlocked it and dialed, struggling to maintain control of the wheel with one hand. 'This is Detective Jack O'Connor, I need an air ambulance and police support.' Jack paused and waited for the person on the other end to catch up to speed. 'No, I don't have an address, but I have coordinates for the helicopter, they need to get there ASAP.' Again, another brief moment of silence until the person on the phone was able to take this information. 'Yes, it is longitude.' Tanya held a piece of paper up with numbers on. 'Fifty-one point eight one, latitude two point five eight.'

He hung up the phone before the receiver could start asking too many questions. 'Come on, let's save this kid's life.'

The pair came to the front of an old, dilapidated house. It had once been blocked up with chipboard, but only the top windows still had any remaining. The ground floors had remnants of nails and splinters, but the tags written all over them was a clear sign that kids had once used it as a playground.

'Police!' Jack called through the front door. 'Come out quietly.'

But there were no signs of any occupants other than the single pigeon that flew out past them.

'Where do you think he's put him? Buried him?' Tanya asked, following the detective slowly through the front door. They both took out their phones to use as torches. Pieces of the floorboards were missing, rotten through where rain had come directly through the door-less opening.

'I don't know. I can't see him coming here to dig a hole, not if he didn't have to. The cellar, maybe. I had visions of somewhere dark and cold.'

Jack came to a door that was locked; it was directly below the staircase. He rattled the old fashioned doorknob, but it wouldn't budge.

'I'll have to kick it in,' he told Tanya so as not to frighten her with the sudden loud noise.

He planted his foot heavily on it and it sent a shockwave into his bones, a searing pain ending at the tip of his cut toe. He switched feet and kicked again. This time, the frame split, allowing the door to cave halfway in. He shoved it with his shoulder, forcing the frame to come apart.

'I'll keep looking up here,' Tanya said, heading towards the back of the house.

The stairs were still in good condition, they didn't have a handrail anymore but they felt sturdy enough under foot.

Cobwebs hung low, clinging to Jack's short hair and running down his neck. He tried as best he could to ignore it, training his light to the darker patches of the room. The cellar was divided into two, a small squared off section, with a larger open plan around it. The smaller area was pitch black, even with the phone aimed directly at it, the light seemed to be absorbed. Jack realised that it was an old coal bunker, some small black bricks remaining in the corner. He examined the rest of the surroundings. There was evidence that this could be a place to hold someone. There were cast iron loops built into the heavy stonework and a few blankets, all growing a thick, black mold. He poked at the material with his foot.

'I bet forensics would find blood on these,' he thought as he noticed how the mold had grown in odd patterns. A thin mattress stood against the wall. It, too, had a few different types of fungus adorning it, but not enough to hide the plethora of bodily fluid stains.

'Something's not right. The cobwebs are too low, the dust is undisturbed on the floor. Shit, we've got the wrong place.'

He made his way back upstairs, meeting Tanya at the top.

'Anything?' she asked, out of breath from searching the entire house.

Jack looked around, hoping for inspiration in the peeling walls and cracked plaster.

'Old house, old habits, maybe,' he thought.

'Septic tank, there has to be one.'

They rushed to the back garden, all of which was overgrown, brambles covering almost everything. A concrete area was just about visible leading up from the back door.

'If there is, how did he put a body in it without disturbing this lot?' Tanya asked, heading straight into the thorny weeds.

'Freddie!' she began shouting, stepping in and out of the natural barbs blocking her path.

But not Jack, he needed to think. It was not time to rush in now, time was up, it was now or never. The boy would never breathe, never see his parents, never eat another sweet again.

They don't do different, they don't know how. They're taught, they're brainwashed and that's what they know. Shit, I should have asked him more, I should have kept going until he told me everything.'

'Freddie!' Tanya's voice called again, desperation now hitting her, too.

Loud thuds came from the sky and the air ambulance circled them, looking for somewhere to land. Jack looked out at the garden.

'He has to be here, he has to be.'

He covered his face with his hands.

He could feel the young boy, nothing left in him, his eyes open or closed, he didn't know, it was just darkness. Dying wasn't scary, now, it was true and perhaps there was afterlife, maybe he would be free. Yes, that was it, he was going to be released, no more pain, no more torture. Dying was going to be ok.

Jack lowered his arms; they were heavy, just as were his legs, he dropped to his knees, giving up just as the boy had. Maybe he could slip away, too. He fell to his front, twisting onto his side, his head colliding with the hard ground, only broken by some torn ivy. He blinked tears away, no need for them now, all was done, the boy, his wife, his daughter, his friends, colleagues, all dying and he couldn't save even one of them. He looked up at the house and followed the ivy down, between the windows and over the old extension, protruding towards him. His hands gripped some strewn leaves and squeezed them between his fingers, moisture oozed from beneath his knuckles.

'Fallen leaves shouldn't be fresh.'

OIL

Jack held an ivy leaf up to his face. He sat up and noticed more of them around him. A trail of green debris led off around the squared-off house extension. He didn't feel it, but his legs had tucked underneath him and he had stood up. His mind dazed, he walked unthinking along the freshly cut ivy. It was dark down the side of the house but, again with his torch, he was able to make out a shape.

'Another coal bunker? Why would it have two?'

Jack noticed a green copper pipe protruding from the side, leading to the house, telling him it had been an old oil store with a lid completely free of overgrown.

'Hello, police!' a voice called from inside the house. 'Detective O'Connor, are you here?'

Jack didn't reply, his heart was hammering, overpowering his ability to think, he needed to just act.

'We're back here!' he heard Tanya answer for them both. 'Come and help us look. We think the boy is buried out here somewhere.'

Jack walked as quick as he could, but each step was taking an age and he barely had any strength left to carry on. He reached the concrete box, its heavy lid nestled in place. Jack crouched and got the lip of the top on his shoulder then stood up, forcing it open and shoving it back. It fell diagonally from its walls, cracking and splitting as it hit the ground. He lifted his phone, the torch slowly illuminating the impenetrable darkness. He peered over into the oil store.

'He's here, he's here!' Jack shouted, his voice barely a squeak. He reached in, sliding his arms under the child and lifting with all his might. His steps were unsteady and the plastic had some of the old oil on it, making the child difficult to carry, but after a few moments, Jack rounded the corner of the house. He found two police officers and two paramedics, all talking with Tanya. They raced over to him, taking the boy and placing him on the ground, both paramedics getting to work immediately. Jack fell forward onto a large policeman who caught his weight easily and then he, too, was lowered to the ground.

The detective watched as the child was cut from the plastic and an oxygen mask was placed over his mouth. All he could see was the child's long, unkempt, greasy hair flowing over pale-skinned shoulders and neck.

Jack waited until he heard what he needed to hear, what he desperately longed for.

'Yes, we have the child, we have a pulse. Prep for take-off, prepping the casualty on a stretcher now.'

The detective let his eyes close and he fell into a world where he could find peace.

LOVE YOURSELF

Jack felt lips press against his. They weren't warm or wet but they gave the impression that there was something there. His eyes opened to be greeted with emerald discs with large pupils centering them. Freckles dotted the bridge of a small nose, leading down to a full, naturally red smile.

'You saved the child, Jack. That's two, now. Becoming a regular superhero. Maybe a knighthood if you carry on at this rate.'

Jack pinched the bridge of his nose; his sinuses felt thick and heavy with fluid, his head awash with confusion, not that dissimilar to the first few moments when waking with a hangover.

'Please tell me I actually died this time and I'm on my way to heaven?'

Jessica smiled warmly. 'No, not this time, darling; you just needed a timeout with me. I think you want to speak to me. We have a bit of catching up to do, don't we?'

Jack sighed heavily, he didn't have the energy. He would rather have been dead, then maybe he could start to forget this entire mess. He sat up, his limbs not receiving any feedback from his environment.

'Ah, so I'm here to talk with my subconscious version of you. That's not fucking mental at all, is it? Where the hell do I start?'

Jessica sat on the end of what was now apparently a bed. 'How about how Felicity's and my death were my fault and not yours?'

Jack was uncomfortable with this. He had gotten so used to shouldering the blame; he wasn't sure he could shift this particular load onto what was essentially one of his most beautiful memories.

'The story you were writing. The one that was going to change everything, they found out and they came for you.'

Jessica nodded solemnly.

'And Felicity was collateral damage.' He rubbed his eyes. 'I thought it was because of me all this time, tracking down evidence that led nowhere, speaking with informants that had most likely been given false information and all the time I was looking in the wrong direction.'

Jessica reached out a hand and placed it on his, her touch never quite arriving properly. 'I hope you will forgive me one day, darling, but at least now you can finally forgive yourself. I thought I was doing the right thing, I thought I would be able to stop them.'

Jack pulled his hand away; he watched as her face saddened. 'No one can stop them, they're too powerful.' He looked away. 'But I'll try. I'll probably end up dead before I even get close, but I don't have much more to live for now, anyway.'

Jessica walked around the bed to sit by his side. 'I'm sorry, Jack, I got greedy, I wanted to be the one to expose it, to become a great reporter. Will you forgive my weakness?'

'You were a great reporter,' he interrupted, 'and you don't have any weaknesses— I mean, you didn't have any.'

The woman smiled sweetly again. 'Oh, I had plenty, they just weren't as obvious as yours. You were always too kind to spot mine, always putting yourself down, never truly seeing how incredible you were.'

Jack laughed sarcastically. 'I was a mess and now even more so. I have no idea who I am now.'

Jessica stroked the side of his face. 'You're the man who has just saved a child. The man who never forgot his wife and daughter, the man who hurts so that others don't have to.'

Jack turned to look into her green eyes, tears forming in his. 'I don't see her like I see you, Jess, I can't, it hurts too bad. She's not here with us because I'm weak, too weak to bear even the memory of her. I didn't go to see the body, Jess, I'm sorry, I didn't go to say goodbye to our baby girl.' Tears rolled down his cheeks, they hurt, but he deserved it. 'I miss her so much, Jess, I miss our baby, I didn't deserve to have her and I let her go.'

Jessica wiped away a tear but he could still feel its damp presence.

'Hush now, hush. You'll see her again one day, when the time is right, and you'll love her just as much all over again – maybe sooner than you realise. You're so much stronger than you believe, I have faith in you.'

Jack looked beyond his wife; he saw a dark wallpaper embossed with golden, flowing flowers and hummingbirds. He remembered seeing this many years before. He and Jessica had just finished having sex for the first time as a married couple. He had allowed his mind to trace over the patterned wall that day, given it space to turn off and float away to somewhere calm and light.

If I could replicate that, now, wouldn't that be something?'

'Remember these?' he asked, suddenly recollecting the plate that had been beside the bad. It had been covered with liquid chocolate creating the word *congratulations* and dotted with chocolate dipped strawberries. 'Remember how we thought they might have given us a free bottle of champagne or a room upgrade, it being our honeymoon? And all we got were chocolate bloody strawberries.'

Jess laughed. She stood now, looking down at the plate.

'Hey, I loved those strawberries. Just because you're afraid of fruit.'

Jack blinked and the red berries were mostly gone, only their green tips remaining.

'You ate all of them in one sitting, if I recall.'

But Jessica didn't reply, she had left the room and another memory had started to take its place. The en-suite shower was running, hot steam billowing into the room. Jack left the four-poster bed, made his way to the bathroom and sat on the closed toilet.

'I sat here and watched you for like ten minutes; you had no idea.' He was staring at the shower, watching the imperfect image of her as she washed. A second Jessica stood at his side.

Jack gave a small acknowledgement of how strange it *didn't* feel to have two of them in the room with him.

'I knew you were watching, darling. That's why I took twice as long. I loved your eyes on me. My handsome detective, lusting after me, wanting to take my body and make it his. You had no idea what you could do to me with those eyes.' She rubbed his short hair. 'You could get me wet with a smile and I could feel my body longing for you, wanting nothing but for you to be inside of me, to feel you deep inside me as I watched your face, your beautiful face.'

Jack bowed his head. 'This isn't real. That's what I wanted you to feel for me, but you never did, you never looked at me that way.'

His wife now sat on the floor at his feet in a bathrobe.

'I'm sorry, Jack, I should have loved you better, I'm sorry I didn't show you. We never knew how short our time was going to be.' She lay her head on his lap. 'Forgive me one day, Jack, please try.'

Jack stroked her hair. 'I don't blame you. I should have made you love me more. I should have been better. If I had looked after myself, looked better for you, dressed with more care or taken you to nicer restaurants maybe we would have been different.'

She smiled up at him. 'Love yourself, Jack, you deserve more than this.'

And then she was standing in the doorway, dressed in the long flowing black number – the one she had worn to their meal that evening.

'It's time to go, now, darling,' she said, her voice quiet and in Jack's heart, not his ears.

He nodded. 'I'm not going to see you again, am I?' he asked tentatively, not really wanting an answer.

'I hope you don't, my darling, I hope this is the last time I will have to ask for forgiveness. Love yourself, Jack, please, love yourself.'

WATCHING ME NOW

Jack's eyes opened to a stream of fluorescent lights passing overhead. He had been leaning against a window and his neck ached and clicked as he righted himself. He forced his head from one side to the other, trying desperately to free up the cramping muscles.

'Where are we?' he asked the driver.

'Just as you passed out you told me to follow the boy. Some more paramedics came and they wanted to put you in an ambulance, but I convinced them you were safe with me. Told them I was a trained surgeon. Not technically true, but I have done a few castrations in my time,' Tanya replied pulling into a parking space.

'You didn't answer my question,' Jack said, rubbing his aching neck.

'Alright, grumpy, we're at the BRI, it was the nearest place set up to take the boy straight away into ICU. You slept the whole way back, started talking some weird shit back there about strawberries.'

Jack placed a comforting hand on Tanya's leg. 'Sorry, I didn't mean to snap, just had some bad dreams. Did they say if the kid was going to make it or not?'

Tanya shook her head. 'They didn't tell me anything

other than they were bringing him here. I've seen a few dead bodies in my time and that kid didn't look like them. Lots of fight in him left. Shit, he survived the worst of it. Will all be a breeze, now, I'm sure.'

Jack wasn't as convinced. The boy – Cameron – who he had found before only just survived and he hadn't been through nearly as much as this one.

The pair left the car. Jack couldn't be bothered to pay for parking, it would be easier to just get the fine and he knew it wouldn't be towed as there was not enough headroom in the car park.

A young receptionist greeted them at the children's ward. He didn't have his badge on him, but Jack's name had somehow been enough to get them that far. The security was always high on this ward; it made him wonder what had happened in the past to provoke it.

'Can you tell me how the young boy is doing that came in on the helicopter? I'm the officer who found him.'

They watched as the young woman looked on her computer, taking much longer than Jack would have expected.

'I'm sorry, sir, but I don't have a record of a boy coming in on the air ambulance. A young girl has just come in, she's been taken down to the theatre, she needed emergency surgery. Is that the one you mean?'

Jack was getting frustrated. 'No, it was a little boy— well, like a young teenager, his name is Freddie Owens, he's been missing, I've just found him.'

The woman checked her system again. 'I'm sorry, sir, no males have come in on the air ambulance all week.'

Jack slammed a fist down. 'So where have they taken him then? We were told he would be brought here.'

The woman raised her arms cautiously, obviously afraid to answer genuinely.

'Detective O'Connor, how are you, my friend?'

Jack turned to find the doctor who had been caring for Cameron Daley and had also provided him with ten milligrams of diazepam.

'Doctor,' Jack bluffed that he was calling him just doctor out of respect and not because he had forgotten his name.

'Are you here to see young Cameron? He has made a fabulous recovery. He has even been asking when he can meet you.'

Jack turned to look at the receptionist and then at Tanya, torn and not sure what to do.

'Go,' Tanya urged. 'I'll find out what happened to Freddie – they've probably just taken him to another hospital. Go and I'll come find you.'

Jack followed the doctor down a long, straight corridor to a different ward. He could tell the boy had been moved and this was no longer the intensive care unit.

'It always amazes me, the resilience of children. If that were you or I, we most likely would have perished,' the doctor said in his melodic Indian accent. 'Ah, and here we are.' The Indian man knocked on the door of a private room and opened it.

Mr. and Mrs. Daley stood at the sight of Jack. He half expected an assault from the father again but, instead, he approached the detective and threw his arms around him.

Jack patted him gently on the back and relieved himself of the man's grip.

The father grabbed Jack by the crook of his arm and nearly dragged him to the side of the young boy's bed.

Still somewhat pale and weak looking, Cameron managed a smile and offered a hand to shake.

'How about a high five instead?' Jack asked, offering a palm in the air. The boy gratefully slapped it and gave a little laugh.

'Thank you for saving me,' he said, a line clearly rehearsed with his parents.

Jack didn't mind – after all, what are you meant to say to the person who dragged you out of a literal shit hole?

Jack sat on the edge of the bed. 'You're more than welcome. Just glad I managed to find you. I tell you what, if you had been playing hide and seek, you would definitely have won.'

The boy and his parents both gave a little laugh together.

'I don't think I'll be playing that again for a while,' the boy joked.

'How the hell has he still got a sense of humour?'

'So what's next? Get better and in here and then go home to play on a PlayStation?' Jack asked, giving a casual half look at the parents.

'Mum said I could get this game I wanted, she said it was too violent before but now she just wants me to be happy so …'

Jack smiled. 'Is that right? As long as it isn't The Fair Assassin.'

The boy's eyes lit up. 'How did you know? Wait, are you the detective who caught the computer killer?'

Jack rubbed the back of his neck. He hated those moments when kids asked awkward questions in front of their parents.

'No, that was media hype. It's meant to be a good game, though. I knew a boy who enjoyed playing it once. He was a good kid, just like you.'

'Where is he now? Do you think he could teach me how to play it?' the boy asked so eagerly Jack couldn't bear to tell him no.

'I'll have a word with him when I get a chance. Speaking of having a word …' The detective knew a thing or two about segueing a conversation. 'I'm going to need to ask you some questions so I can catch the man who did this to you. You're going to have to be a brave lad, is that ok?'

The boy looked to his father then back to Jack; there was some confusion in his eyes. 'But Dad said you've already got him and that he is locked up in prison. Dad, why did you tell me that if it isn't true?'

Jack waved his hands. 'No, he is in prison, your dad was right. But he had a boss – you know, someone who told him what to do, like on the next level of a computer game. I was wondering if you ever met anyone else? Anyone other than the man who put you in the hole.'

The boy's lip trembled. Jack could see that there were words stuck in his mouth, words that he was too scared to speak. Then Jack thought about McQuade, how she had been in love with her capturer and how it must have started from here, from the same place this boy was at – an immense fear, bearing down out of the air in front of you, all the time, even when you thought you were safe.

He watched as Cameron shook his head. It wasn't an answer to the question, it was replying to the fear playing on his mind.

'Cameron, it's ok, if it's too scary, we can leave it for another day. But if you are feeling brave, if you could just tell me what they looked like, or how many other people you saw,' Jack spoke so softy but, judging by the boy's reaction, he might as well have been screaming it. The young man writhed in the bed as if something was running up his legs, making him uncomfortable.

'It's ok, Cameron, you can tell the detective,' the boy's mum spoke, placing a hand on his shoulder.

The boy edged himself away, her touch clearly unwanted. She reached up to her mouth and turned away, so he didn't see her cry.

'No,' the boy answered bluntly.

There was a knock at the door and someone in a nurse's uniform came through, pushing a trolley ahead of them.

'Sorry, just need to drop off Cameron's food,' she said while pouring him a plastic cup of orange squash. 'You have three courses today, my dear, like being in a posh hotel, here. Here we go.' She placed down the first plate and took the plastic cover off.

She clearly hadn't noticed the tension in the air, but Jack couldn't see how – it was thick enough to insulate an igloo.

'You've got jelly for pudding and then this is for your starter. A nice egg and soldiers.'

The words electrified the boy. He kicked the table over his bed, breaking it and cascading the plates to the floor.

'Get it away!' he screamed, using his legs to drive his body up the bed. 'Get it away, get it away!' His screaming got louder with each word.

Jack saw the boy's hands grip so hard on the frame of the bead above his head that the skin cut on the squared edges. Jack reached up, trying to hold the boy, to stop him from damaging himself more, but his legs became like iron pistons, kicking Jack hard. His feet splayed in the air and his words became nothing but shrieks. The boy jumped from the bed and crouched in the corner of the room. He wasn't resting, he was poised, ready to make another retreat if necessary.

Jack ran around the bed.

'Don't touch me!' the boy shouted at Jack, but his eyes were looking at the food on the floor.

Jack searched the room, desperately trying to see what he was seeing, but there was nothing but a mess of lasagna and vegetables.

Jack showed the palm of his hands to Cameron in an attempt at non-threating gestures like they taught you in the force.

'Wow, Cameron it's ok, I'm a police officer and they are your parents and we are all here to keep you safe.'

The woman who had brought the food in stood at the other corner, the curtain blocking her from view. She would have escaped had it not been for the fact that the boy was closer to the door and she was too frightened to get near him.

'He's here, he's telling me he's here. He said he was always watching and he's watching me now. He sent that.'

Cameron pointed at the food on the floor.

Jack looked at it again, but gleaned nothing new. 'Who, Cameron? Who is watching?'

The boy tore his gaze away from the floor and met Jack's eye. His own were large and round and petrified.

'The man! The man who peels eggs.'

I WAS SO SURE

Jack wasn't surprised. It had been his hunch all along that Agent Charles had been connected in some way to all this – he could smell the pervert on him from the first moment they met.

He walked up through the hospital, somewhat aimlessly, trying to think of a plan, some way to get at the MI5 man, but his mind was thick and clouded with grief, hate and anger.

After twenty minutes or so, he decided to try to make an attempt at finding Tanya, see what was going on with Freddie Owens.

Four staircases and several more corridors later and he started to recognise walls, some with animal murals clearly drawn for the children's entertainment.

Tanya was sitting on a row of blue chairs just inside the ward.

'So?' Jack asked, not meaning to sound quite as blunt as he had, but happy to roll with it.

'How did you get on, first?' Tanya said, standing quickly at his return.

Jack inhaled heavily. 'Well, the kid's pretty messed up.

Won't be eating any boiled eggs for the rest of his life.' Jack received a confused look for a reply.

Tanya's eyes narrowed – she hated not being able to work things out.

'I know who McQuade's handler was and, most likely, Richard Pearce's too. Remember the MI5 agent? The one who wore pinstripe suits too large for him?'

Tanya laughed. 'The one who set you up in Florence and tried to blow us up, you mean? Yeah, I think I remember him. Bit obvious, isn't it?'

Jack nodded in agreement. 'Yes, it is, but that's how it tends to be in the real world – the bad guys look like bad guys and the good guys look like they're getting shat on. The only problem is, how do I get to him? Even if I can, I don't know what to do about it. Can't arrest him, can't inform MI5, don't know who's on the side with him. Not a whole lot of people we can trust right about now.'

Tanya shrugged her shoulders. 'We could kill him.'

It was Jack's turn to laugh. 'We could, but it won't be easy and I don't fancy prison much. Even if he is a paedophile, without a tonne of evidence, MI5 won't take kindly to us killing one of their own.' The detective cupped his hands over his mouth and pinched his nose, his mind trying to work as his subconscious tics took place. 'I think I need a friend with a bit more clout than we have between us. I'll have to ponder this some more. Maybe over a whisky later.' Jack didn't focus his mind immediately; he wanted that idea to float down into place and settle in a little more firmly. 'Anyway, where's Freddie?'

Tanya met his eyes, her mouth in an awkward smile. 'Well, there is a bit of a problem with Freddie.'

Jack shook his head. 'Don't tell me he died, please, Tan, not that.'

Tanya also shook her head, but for a different reason. 'No, not dead, rather that he never existed— well, he did, but you didn't find him.' Tanya wrung her hands.

Jack's eyes narrowed. 'What the hell are you on about?'

'The boy we found wasn't Freddie Owens, it never was,' Tanya replied softly, trying to be gentle with him.

'What? They've identified him already? How? That's impossible. Where is he? Did they take him to another hospital? I need to sort this shit out.' Jack's eyes darted around, looking for someone to blame for the mix-up.

'No, the child was brought here, but they know it wasn't Freddie because it's a girl, Jack.' Tanya reached a hand out to hold his; she knew this wouldn't be easy to take, not when he had been so certain.

Jack smiled. 'It can't be. I saw him; I saw him carve his initials. I felt him get ...' He felt embarrassed to say it, almost as if it had happened to him. 'I felt him get *abused*.' The word rape wouldn't come. 'I saw what he did, I felt it.' Jack sat down on the centre blue seat and rubbed his head, lowering it between his knees. 'I don't understand, Tan, how could I have known if I didn't see it? I was so sure.'

She sat beside him and rubbed his back.

'And if I didn't see it, if it wasn't him, then what does that say about me?'

He didn't want an answer, just in case it confirmed what he was already thinking.

Perhaps this was all just a coincidence, maybe I got lucky with some actual detective work and all these visions were just a sideshow. And if they were nothing but fantasy, how much time had I wasted with these false images when I should have been out there saving a child?' He mulled thoughts over several times, hoping with each turn that they would make slightly more sense.

'So, it was a girl?' he asked her, just to clarify.

'Yeah, early teens, she's in ICU and conscious. They thought her heart had stopped on the flight over, but it hadn't, it had just slowed right down. They're amazed at how well she's doing.' Tanya played up the positive, trying to bring Jack round.

'So she's going to make it then, no problems?' he asked, finally looking Tanya in the face.

She smiled warmly. 'That's what they said. They also

said that another hour or two and the hyperthermia would have shut down her organs. You saved her, Jack, Freddie Owens or not, you saved a life, an innocent child's life.'

Jack smiled, then his face loosened. 'Not so innocent anymore, I fear.'

The pair reached the room where the girl was. The small window in the door was dark but looking through, Jack could see that a lamp had been placed in the corner. He was surprised to see the young girl sitting up and, not only that, she was eating, too. A nurse passed her food and she snatched at it. It was only small pieces of bread, but it was obviously delicious to her regardless.

Jack backed up and allowed a doctor to exit the room.

'Can I help?' she asked, clearly more defensive than in a usual case of a young girl being admitted.

'Yes, I'm detective Jack O'Connor, how is she doing?'

The woman's demeanor softened. 'Ah, you are the one who found her, right?' she asked.

Jack nodded. 'I thought she would be more poorly, she looks like she's doing really well.'

The doctor laughed gently. 'She's a miracle. She's eaten half a loaf of bread and a block of cheese and most of a fruit bowl. Typically, in a case of starvation like this, we would usually slowly introduce food, but it doesn't seem necessary, her appetite is incredible, there's no sign of cramping and nothing has come back up.' The doctor noticed the relief on Jack's face. 'I think she is going to be fine. We are still waiting on a few results and she's by no means in good shape, I mean, she's a very poorly child, but stronger than we could possibly have hoped.'

Jack looked back into the room. 'She's still quite ill, then?'

The female doctor nodded. 'I don't know where to start, to be honest. I certainly have never had a case like it. We've had to use a low wattage lamp as her skin is so delicate the lights were actually burning her. And her eyes, her retinas, would have been permanently damaged if we had left the usual lights on.' She opened some notes. 'Her blood pressure is one of the lowest I've ever seen. Her heart rate is slower than that of a professional marathon runner. She has severe osteoporosis – meaning her bone density is so poor that she has several suspected breaks in major bones that simply won't heal without serious medical attention. I'm waiting on some more blood results; she put up a bit of a fight when we first tried to take them, then we realised that she was fine with female nurses but petrified of men. I think she has several infections, judging by inflammations on her sides and back, and her cough ...' She looked up, away from her notes. 'There is a lot of blood in her cough which could mean a lung infection or damaged airways. Every single vitamin her body needs to function she has been deprived of over a sustained amount of time. She may be sat up and eating, but if we make one false move, she could very well go into cardiac arrest.'

Jack looked back in through the window. 'Has she said anything?'

The doctor shook her head. 'Not a word – unless you include screaming at every man she has come into contact with. There's a psychiatrist in there now; she's just observing, she says she has seen a similar case before, she came very highly recommended. I think this is going to be a very high-profile case – seems social services can't do enough right now.'

Jack laughed. 'Funny, that. Any idea on age, race? Anything so I can start narrowing down who she might be?'

The woman in the white coat shrugged. 'European, could be anywhere between ten and fourteen, possibly older, it's hard to tell due to the emaciation. I'm going to go and chase up the rest of these test results. She's eating well but we need to get the right meds into her to compensate for everything she's been missing.'

Jack smiled and watched her leave. He felt very

relieved, it felt like a lifetime since he had been given any new good news.

'What are you thinking, Jack?' Tanya asked, rubbing his back as he peeked in through the window.

He didn't answer right away, he had to analyse his own thoughts, he wasn't sure where they were at anymore.

'I think she is one tough little girl.' He watched as the slim figure on the bed took the hand of a nurse, so tentatively, as if it might suddenly strike like a poised python.

Jack went to turn when something caught in the peripheral of his vision.

'She's been through a hell of a—' Tanya began to talk, but Jack shot across her.

'Shush!' He cupped the top of his eyes against the glass, desperately trying to get a clearer picture, and stared in hard.

The young girl had turned the nurse's hand palm up and, with her middle finger, flicked it a couple of times.

Jack froze, his heart stopped beating, his lungs were obsolete. He watched as the girl did it three more times again, gently flicking her finger and then recoiling back to a safe distance.

'No, it can't be.' He turned to face Tanya. 'It's … it's Felicity.'

DNA TEST

Jack burst into the room, slamming the door back on its hinges. A woman who had been out of sight through the window stood up in alarm, her notebook and pen scattering across the ground. The nurse who had been previously trying to communicate with the girl stormed towards him, her hands ready to push him out of the room. Jack pushed her aside. He needed to get to her, he needed to get to his daughter and tides couldn't stop him, let alone a short nurse. The woman tripped and crashed into the radiator, splitting her head on the hard metal corner. Jack reached the bedside but the girl had begun screaming the moment he had entered, her voice a visceral scream, punishing the air, its noise alone driving demons away – and that was exactly what Jack was to her, the embodiment of evil.

'Felicity, Felicity, it's me. It's Dad. Felicity, look at me.' He reached out to touch her and she scrambled up the back of the bed, fighting to get away.

Jack took hold of her arms, both hands tight on her wrists. 'It's me, it's me, stop, Felicity, it's me.'

She kicked him in the face, one of his hands relinquishing, but the other tightening, desperately holding onto her.

She screeched and writhed in pain and panic, her entire being becoming the fight.

The nurse had righted herself, blood pouring down her face, but still she showed compassion for the child by grabbing the detective by the shoulders.

'Sir, you have to leave. Sir! You are hurting her,' she said, pulling on him with all her might, trying to see through the blood-stained hair that clung to her face.

'Felicity, it's dad.' Jack tried one more time and then he finally caught a glimpse of her face in the dim lamplight. Just enough to see the freckles decorating cheeks below green eyes.

'You're breaking her arm!' the nurse screamed and finally her words penetrated his ears and reached his consciousness.

Jack looked down at his hands and let go. He didn't want to hurt her, no, but he needed to know.

The girl screamed louder than before. She jumped down from the bed and cowered in the corner – the furthest one from the lamp, the darkest space in the room.

Tanya had now entered and was pulling Jack by his collar, trying to get him away from the mess he had caused. She grappled him through the doorway and closed it behind them.

'It's her, Tan, I promise you it's her,' he said, falling to the floor, a wide, manic smile on his face.

'Jack, what the fuck are you doing?' she said, blowing a strand of hair from her face.

'It's her, Tan, it's her.' Jack's chest heaved heavily, half with exhaustion and the rest with excitement.

Tanya eyed him. 'Jack, Felicity was killed, you know this.'

Jack looked up, his eyes glazed. 'Yes, she was, wasn't she? But, I don't know how, Tan, that is her in that room.'

He stood up and moved towards the door, but Tanya blocked his path.

He held her hand in a tight grip. 'It's ok, I just want to look. Please, Tan.'

But the blind had been closed and he couldn't see anything. The torture forced his body to throw her hand away and pace the hospital corridor.

'You never viewed the body, did you?' Tanya asked, watching him walk and think himself into oblivion.

Jack shook his head. 'No, I couldn't and they told me that the killer had disfigured her face. I was advised not to see her.'

'By who?' his friend asked him.

Jack stopped walking. 'McQuade.'

Tanya walked over to him. 'Do you think she knew?'

Jack screwed up his face, he wanted to say yes as it would make it more likely that his daughter was indeed in that room, but he shook his head. 'No, she told me nearly everything, no reason for her to keep that from me. She thought she could use me because they had both been killed, if she had known she was still alive, it would have made me too much of a liability if I had found out – well, more of a liability than I already am. She had only just started, they must have brought her in to cover up Jessica's work.'

'So how did they confirm it was her?' Tanya asked earnestly.

'DNA test, but then we know how easy that would have been to fake. But if that's her,' he pointed at the emergency room, 'who the hell did I bury? I don't get it, none of it makes sense. I need to know if it's her, Tan, I just need to know, right away,' Jack said. He started to pace again.

'You said the face was disfigured, do you think they did that on purpose? You know, so if you did see the body you wouldn't recognise her?' Tanya asked and to Jack's amazement, she sounded like she believed him. She was clearly on his side.

'Would make some sense, I guess. But why take her

and leave another body?' he asked, nothing rhetorical about his train of thought now.

Tanya started to shrug her shoulders but then stopped. 'In my professional opinion,' she stopped when Jack looked at her, confused. 'I did a year on criminal psychology. I would say that it sounds premeditated. Like revenge, as if it is personal. Assuming that it is Felicity in there, it sounds like what she has been through is far worse than being killed on the spot.'

These words hurt Jack, they found a spot deep inside him that he didn't know existed and burned him like a hot poker. She was right, that little girl in there, Felicity or not, has been through far worse than any murder victim he had come across before.

'So, they killed one of the girls they had and replaced her with Flick, covering it up with DNA results, all to punish Jessica and me?'

Tanya shrugged to him. She was clearly torn between the fanciful and plausible, just as he was.

Jack rubbed at his stubble – it was now closer to being a beard than just a missed couple of shaves.

'Maybe it's not her, maybe I'm losing it again, Tan. I don't know what to think. It's a bit far-fetched, isn't it? My mind is a mess; I can't think straight.'

He leant against the wall and slid his way down to the floor, sitting uncomfortably on the thick plastic floor.

Tanya knelt in front of him. 'It depends on what Jessica had found out and about who. The people you're talking about, Jack, are sadistic, I really wouldn't put—' But Tanya didn't carry on speaking; an idea had come to her.

Jack looked her in the face when she spoke next, 'Why were you so convinced it was Freddie Owens?'

Jack's forehead wrinkled with confusion. 'What do you mean?'

Tanya stood up; she now took her turn to walk and analyse something in her mind. 'I mean, it was only half an hour ago you swore blind it *had* to be a little boy and that his name was Freddie Owens. Why?'

Jack stood slowly, using the wall as much as he could – his body was tired. 'I had … I sort of saw visions of what I thought was a boy, but then I became him, in a way. Then I saw him – well, me – carving his name into a piece of wood, like on a skirting board.'

Tanya turned and faced him. 'His name?'

Jack corrected himself. 'No, it was his initials, it was …' But he couldn't finish.

Tanya nodded. 'An F and an O. Felicity O'Connor.' She took out her phone and dialed a number, but not to speak herself. She handed the phone to Jack.

Jack listened absently minded to it ringing, his thoughts raced elsewhere.

'Bristol Police Station,' a voice answered.

'Er, yes, it's Detective O'Connor.'

Tanya nodded and mouthed Aubrie's name.

'Can I be put through to the pathology lab, please?' Jack had to be diverted a couple of times to locate exactly where Dr. Sellers was working, finally finding her in her office.

'Hi, Aubrie, it's Jack,' again he looked at Tanya for direction, she mouthed three letters clearly. 'How quickly can you get a DNA test done?' he asked.

RUN TO HER

Aubrie arrived at the hospital pulling a small trolley behind her, looking like a tourist at an airport. She was clearly flustered and eager to find out what was going on.

She threw her arms around Jack and squeezed him, whispering in his ear, 'God, I missed you. I'm sorry.'

She eased away, but Jack grabbed her forearms. 'I think it's Felicity, I know it sounds crazy, but it's true.'

Aubrie smiled. 'Well, let's get to work, then.' She turned to the other woman. 'Tanya, glad to see you kept him alive.'

Tanya smiled in response and surprised Jack by not replying with a sarcastic comment.

Aubrie unzipped the trolley she had been towing and removed a small fold-out table, similar to one that Jack had once when he went camping with his parents. She then unzipped a separate compartment and lifted, with some effort, a large machine that looked much like an office printer. Placing it on the table, she looked around.

'All I need is one plug point, the rest is wireless,' she said, looking around the walls.

Tanya pulled some chairs away from the wall. 'Over here, there're two.'

278

Jack picked up the machine as Aubrie moved the table and then placed it back down gently. The pathologist pulled out a tangle of wires and began unlooping them.

'Now, this is the best machine on the market for matching DNA against our database. It isn't, however, the best for matching two people's, but, I have had a thought about a way around it. Normally, it is set for a one hundred per cent match on all stored DNA samples, but as we aren't looking for a sibling, that isn't any good for us, so ...' She plugged in the machine and went to a second bag that had been hanging on the back of the trolley, pulling out her laptop. 'I am going to adjust the settings to get a fifty per cent match. Now, obviously, that won't be conclusive – by which I mean it wouldn't hold up in court – but the chance of this girl not being your daughter with a fifty per cent DNA match, well, let's just say, if it isn't Felicity, you had another child you didn't know about. Your DNA is on the database, yeah?' she asked Jack.

Jack nodded, but then froze. 'It is, but I should imagine it's been tampered with – probably just to make sure there was a paper trail linking that girl's body at the murder scene to me in some way, assuming she wasn't Felicity.'

Aubrie pursed her lips. 'Not to worry, this machine can take seven samples at a time, so we do both simultaneously, load them onto the database at the same time and compare them. May take an extra hour or so but shouldn't be a problem.'

'So how long will it take?' Jack asked, watching as the lights on the gadget began flashing.

Aubrie wired in her laptop to the back. 'It's been done in ninety minutes, but that was a blood sample and got a hit on the database quickly in the States. Our networks are a bit slower and we are doing two samples and then loading them up, so as long as the Wi-Fi on my phone holds out, I would say about three hours. It's the best machine on the market, it's not even meant to leave the lab, we only have it on loan – this costs more than my flat.'

Jack raised his eyebrows, he was very impressed by this little plastic box. Last time he waited for DNA results it had been two days and even then he got a good telling off for clogging up the system.

Aubrie handed Jack a plastic tube with a thin white stick in it. 'We need a saliva sample, you just scrape this on the inside of her cheek – that's where you get the best cells for analysis.'

Jack didn't take it, he was almost too scared to touch it.

'I can't go in there. Every time she sees a man, she turns into a wild animal. She won't let me near her.'

Tanya took it from Aubrie. 'Let me try, if I don't get anywhere, I'm sure one of the nurses has gained her trust enough, leave it with me.'

The redhead took a deep breath and gently pushed the door open and made her way in, watched by Jack closely, trying to get a small glimpse of the child that he hoped was his daughter.

Aubrie opened up her laptop on a chair that she had placed by the DNA machine. It took a few minutes, but she had logged into her phone as a Wi-Fi hotspot and was opening several databases, only one of which Jack recognised.

She felt him watching over his shoulder. 'On the off chance that it isn't Felicity, I'm going to run her sample through European databases, too – on the *very* off chance, Jack, don't worry, I believe you. I had a thought on the way over here. You thought it was Freddie Owens because you thought you saw the initials in a vision, right? But they're the same—'

Jack interrupted, 'Felicity O'Connor, I know.'

Aubrie clicked a few more buttons and stood up. 'I'm not going to deny that it's weird, Jack, I mean, it's more than weird, it's like you're psychic or something.'

Jack laughed. 'Dr. Aubrie Sellers, I didn't think you believed in mumbo jumbo?'

She returned a snigger. 'Yeah, well, I'm still to be

convinced completely, but it's getting harder to deny it the more I hang around with you. You bloody weirdo.'

Jack took a deep breath, the first in a while that felt relaxed. 'Use your scientific mind to come up with an explanation and I will feel much better about it. I promise you, I can't handle all this unexplainable bullshit.'

Aubrie screwed her lips, clearly looking for something that made sense to explain it all. She tipped her head to the side. 'Well, I guess the fact that it's children would make you connect with it all on a deep, subconscious level. And if there was hope of finding a child, of course, emotionally, somewhere deep inside, there would be a draw towards finding Felicity. Maybe that's why you saw her initials and then your focused mind interpreted them as Freddie Owens. I mean, if you were convinced Felicity was dead, you wouldn't ever jump to that conclusion, would you?'

Jack's smile faded. 'I saw her initials and she didn't even cross my mind, what sort of a father am I?'

Aubrie took his hand. 'One who is trying not to torture himself any more than he already has been. Look, let's take your sample and get you your daughter back. She's alive, Jack, I can feel it. Hey, maybe I'm psychic, too,' she joked, raising a slight smile from him.

He took the tube from her spare hand and started unscrewing it.

The swab was hard and had a jagged edge – it didn't hurt, but it was uncomfortable. He had no idea if that petrified girl would let anyone close enough to do the same to her.

He handed it back to the pathologist and watched her start; she flicked the switch on the front of the machine and it started to hum like a loud refrigerator.

'I quickly put in a new buffer and polymer before I left. Strictly speaking, you are meant to do it in situ so it doesn't become damaged, but never mind. Right, ok, I'm going to load just one cartridge.' She lifted a flap on the top and reached for a large, rectangular plastic cartridge, like an old cassette but longer and segmented into long rows.

'Hang on,' she said, quickly grabbing some rubber gloves from her bag. 'Just in case I contaminate the sample – you don't want to find out that we are brother and sister by mistake.' She shot him a smile.

She held out a hand for Jack's sample, took the long swab directly from him and brushed it into one of the segments of the cartridge, of which the top was still visible, sticking out of the machine. She pressed the flat end of the swab, ejecting the sample end down neatly into its correct space.

'Now, let's just hope Tanya gets on ok,' she said, removing the gloves and putting them in a nearby bin.

The pair waited for what Jack sensed was not a long time, but felt that way. Finally, the short woman with the bright red hair emerged, a smile on her face. She had put the sample back in the clear plastic tube and handed it over to Aubrie.

'How is she? Is she ok? Did she let you do it?' Jacked asked rapidly, his voice dry where he didn't take a breath.

Tanya put up calming hands. 'She's fine. It took a few minutes but once I had explained it, she let me do it. She's got these amazing eyes, Jack, they're bright green, just like—'

'Jessica,' Jack said, throwing his arms around his friend.

They both turned and watched pathologist put on a fresh pair of gloves and load the sample. It then surprised Jack when she took out what looked like a supermarket scanner. She plugged it in and scanned the top of the cartridge in two places.

The small LED screen came to life with a touchscreen keypad. She typed in a few details and then closed the top flap, hiding the samples away.

'That just codes the samples, now I've named them they'll go directly into the system and we can compare them against each other,' Aubrie told them, checking her laptop.

'So now we wait, I guess,' Jack said, taking a seat on one of the moved chairs. 'Did she say anything to you, Tan?'

Tanya shook her head. 'No, sorry, she's very frightened, but she's still eating – must get her appetite from her dad.'

Jack laughed. 'At that age, I could eat until I puked and not put on a pound.' He smiled uncontrollably. 'I've got my girl back,' he said delightedly.

The door of the room opened and a short nurse exited. Jack noticed she had a couple of stitches in her forehead. He jumped up and chased her down the corridor.

'Excuse me, excuse me!'

She turned at his voice.

'I am so sorry, I don't know what came over me, I mean, I think it's my daughter, I haven't seen her in years and I thought she was dead,' Jack blurted uncontrollably but stopped at the confusion on the nurse's face. 'I just have to say I am sorry I hurt you, I didn't mean to. Is there anything I can do to make it up to you?'

The nurse smiled. 'It's ok, we see parents get emotional all the time. I was in the right place to get patched up quickly, wasn't I?' she joked, her eyes meeting Jack's, his embarrassment communicating through them. 'So you think she might be your daughter that you thought was dead?' she asked him.

Jack smiled. 'I know it sounds crazy, but yeah, I think so.'

The nurse looked excited. 'That's incredible, I'm so happy for you. Look, she is in the best hands here, we are doing all we can for her, you need to trust us,' she said, nodding at her patient's room.

Jack looked at the door longingly, just as a tall male doctor holding a clipboard entered.

'I know, I just want to see her so bad,' he replied, turning back to the nurse.

She smiled warmly. 'Just give it time, she's suffering

from a lot of trauma. How about when she sleeps I come and get you and you sneak in for a quick look? Don't tell anyone, though – I'll lose my job.' Her warm smile felt like a thousand hugs to Jack, her generosity overwhelmed him.

'Thank you, you don't know what that would mean to me.'

But then something cold ran through his body, anxiety plagued his guts and he wanted to be sick – he had noticed something without realising it at all. His legs couldn't keep up with what his brain was telling them to do and they were saying go, run to his little girl, run to her, Jack.

KNIFE

Jack had barely turned on the spot when he heard the screams start – the sound of fear tearing its way through vocal chords. He couldn't go fast enough, his steps were too slow, he tried desperately to hurry up, but gravity was teasing him.

Tanya and Aubrie watched from the other end of the corridor as he finally made the door and shoved it open.

It gave half way and then stuck – something was jammed behind it.

The screams from the other side became choked, like fluid was in the way of the noise.

Jack took two steps back and came crashing forward, his foot slamming just below the window. Pain shot through him, his missing toe still an agonising, open wound. He tried with the other foot but the door only moved an inch and now the screaming had stopped completely. The detective's mind went into overdrive, running him through what to do without even the slightest of hesitations. He took off his jacket and wrapped it around his fist before plunging it into the glass, smashing it with ease like only a panicked parent could. He flicked the clothing away from his hand and reached in through the open gap. He found what was blocking his entry – it was a chair. He grabbed the back and, with as much power his wrist alone could get, twisted the furniture away. The door relinquished and he fell through.

The male doctor had the little girl around the neck, a garrote in his hands. Her face had gone limp and the thin wire drew blood.

Jack didn't stop to think, he walked directly over to the pair.

The man dropped the girl and pulled out a large knife from his waist belt. This time, some self-preservation kicked in and the detective took a step back. It was a hunting knife, designed for maximum efficiency and the man wielding it looked just as proficient.

Jack took a step away, his back contacting something. It was a drip stand. He grabbed at it, picking it up and aiming the feet at his opponent.

The man laughed and took a step forward, grabbing the metal frame with ease, but Jack held on with one hand, freeing up the other to quickly switch the lights on. The large, tubular bulbs came on instantly, lighting the room with such ferocity that it was actually blinding, but the detective had been expecting it, squinting to shield his pupils just enough to allow him to see where the blade was and grab the arm holding it.

The man was strong and his loss of sight was only fleeting. The pair tripped over the drip stand, the knife being pushed away from Jack's sternum, but the man was strong – even on his back, his one hand slowly pushed the sharp tip up towards the detective's face. Jack gritted his teeth, pushing as hard as he could, but it was no use. He twisted his body under the other man's arm and the knife came down on the floor, but now the detective was wrapped in the man's strong embrace. The hand not on the hilt grabbed Jack's face, digging into his eye sockets.

Jack instinctively let go of the other arm and tried to fight the clawing hand away.

The fake doctor was a good fighter – this had been his plan, he knew the detective's instincts would give him enough time to raise the knife up. It steadied and came down but even a good fighter could not have predicted the sharp teeth of the girl finding his wrist.

She had got up, unseen by either of them, gripped her hands onto the arm wielding the knife and bitten with all her might. Her sharp incisors and canines instantly forced their way through the white coat and broke the skin, then she tore her mouth away, taking a lump of flesh with her, the knife falling away.

The man screamed and jumped to his feet. He kicked the girl in the chest and she fell backwards to the floor, crashing into a bedside table. She had half righted herself again when the man landed a large, black boot on her face, knocking her unconscious.

Jack finally fought his way to his feet. With the other man's back to him, he grabbed at something absent-mindedly and wrapped it around over the fake doctor's head. It was some sort of plastic hospital tubing which he tucked under the man's chin and tightened on his Adam's apple. His arms flailed over his shoulders, trying to grab at Jack's face again. The detective deliberately dropped to his back, wrapping his legs around his adversary's waist, locking him in position as he pulled the improvised weapon tight. He yanked it, all his energy going into cutting off his opponent's air. He could feel his neck collapse slightly where the trachea gave way. The large man's arms reached up at his face one more time before finally falling limp by his side.

Jack tugged again, he wanted to make sure this body had no more fight in it.

Tanya entered the room, followed by Aubrie. The redhead ran to Jack's side while the brunette saw to the girl.

'Jack, let go, Jack, he's dead,' Tanya told him, trying to loosen his hands, but he wouldn't let go. She reached up and stroked his cheek. 'Jack, it's ok, he's gone, you did it, she's safe. Let go, Jack, he's dead.'

The detective's eyes filled with tears, emotion now taking over as he let go and pushed the body off of him. His hands shook as he sat himself upright, staring at the knife that lay on the floor. He breathed hard with exhaustion and he couldn't focus his thoughts – not until he looked to Aubrie and the girl.

'Is she ok?' he asked quickly.

The girl stirred as Aubrie propped her up. She looked dazed, her long hair covering her face, except for her mouth, where blood dripped. She squinted hard and covered her eyes with her hands.

'She's going to be ok, just need to get these lights off and get her back in bed,' Aubrie replied, helping the girl to her feet. She obliged to Aubrie's touch but her legs nearly buckled underneath her, her equilibrium still affected.

Jack looked down at the man he had just killed, a white lab coat, now mostly torn off, had covered a black top and cargo trousers. He crawled over to the body and started going through the pockets, but, just as he expected, they were empty bar a packet of cigarettes, lighter, another knife – this one with a retractable blade – and a handful of money.

Nurses and doctors now rushed into the room, one screaming at the sight of the dead man and the blood on the patient's face.

The young girl started rocking on the bed, her mind coming back to her slowly, anxiety building like a shaken bottle of fizzy drink.

'Take her out, find her another room,' Jack shouted, then he spotted the nurse with the stitches. 'Please, take her somewhere safe, please, do it now.'

The nurse nodded and, with Aubrie's help, they led her from the room, the girl's body going tense, ready to return to attack mode.

A doctor who had been on the phone to the police

knelt down beside the man's body to feel for a pulse, but stopped pretty quickly. He moved over to the detective, who again was leaning back against the wall.

'You ok?' he asked flatly.

Jack nodded. 'Yeah, I think so.'

The doctor looked around at the room, taking in the chaotic mess. 'What should I do with the knife and that?' he pointed at the garrote on the floor.

Jack waved a hand at the room. 'Just leave it, leave everything, help me up and we'll seal off the room. Let the police deal with it then.'

The man helped him to his feet and a pain stabbed in his small toe.

'You don't know a surgeon who could have a look at my toe, do you?' Jack asked the man.

The doctor put an arm under Jack's and helped him hobble from the room. 'Why? What happened?'

'Some bastard cut it off with a screwdriver.'

The doctor nearly dropped him with the shock of the blunt statement.

'Jack, bloody hell, Jack,' Tanya was waiting in the hall.

'Tan, go with Aubrie and the girl, keep them safe, please. You're the only ones I can trust.' The detective stumbled and looked down at his shoe, now leaving bloody footprints behind him.

'Come on, I can get this sorted – if we're lucky, you'll only need a local and we can get you back here pretty quick,' the doctor told him as he led Jack in the opposite direction to where the girl had been taken.

FIRING LINE FOR MURDER

The doctor was young; Jack only now had time to notice. Or was he getting so old that everyone looked young?

'Who stitched this up for you?' he asked.

Jack winced in pain as the needle was inserted to numb the area.

'Just a friend,' he replied through his teeth.

'A doctor?' the other man asked.

Jack shook his head.

'Well, they did a pretty good job, needs some internal stitches, though, the skin alone is a bit thin to hold this. Did they at least let you keep the tip as a memento?'

Jack laughed – he hadn't thought about that, how part of him was probably still lying there on a permanent holiday without him in Florence.

'Can you feel this?' the doctor asked, poking the toe gently with a scalpel.

The detective shrugged and shook his head, it was the first time in days that it hadn't been in pain.

'Right, well, I'm going to open it up, flush it, see how the tendons and muscle look, but it's so small an area I can't imagine there'll be much to look at. I'll stitch from the inside out. They'll be heavy duty – want to make sure they don't come out again until it's completely healed. You'll have to come back in to get them removed or go to your GP. Was going to ask if you can stay off your feet for a few days but I'm guessing that's a stupid question?'

Just at that moment, the door opened and a man in full police uniform, slicked back black hair and his cap under his arm joined the conversation. 'Getting him to stay off his feet for a few *seconds* would be a trick, from what I hear.'

If Jack hadn't recognised him by his appearance, his thick Welsh accent would have told him who he was – he was an assistant chief constable in South Wales.

'Chief, I wish I could say it was a nice surprise to see you,' Jack replied.

The doctor went to stand up. 'Should I leave?'

The uniformed man waved him to carry on. 'No, no, don't stop on my behalf. I only need a brief word with Detective O'Connor. I will watch a professional at work and then we can speak.'

Jack and the doctor met eyes, Jack shrugged, and the needle continued to thread through his skin.

'Will I need a lawyer for this chat, chief?' the detective asked as he watched with fascination at his body being penetrated with steal yet not being able to feel it.

'Not this one, no. Probably the next one and the next few after that,' the man from the other side of the room replied.

The doctor finished up and whispered to Jack, 'Good luck,' before leaving the room.

The Assistant Chief Constable sat on the bed next to Jack and turned in close. Jack had worked with him a few times when their paths had crossed – Bristol was too close to Wales for the ACC's liking and Jack had always admired the way that he had always managed to avoid arguments with his commander, McQuade. Sitting in close, invading that personal space, had always been his style and it meant he could argue with a whisper.

'I'm here, detective, because nobody seems to have a fucking clue what is going on, but reliable sources tell me you know about McQuade's murder and all sorts of other messes. Like, for instance, three dead priests, two dead private security men and a terrorist explosion in Florence. Now, I've been brought into this shit storm from my already busy job across the bridge and I don't know what I am meant to be doing.' The man then clicked his fingers in the air. 'Oh yeah, and now there's a dead body in the hospital at your hand who was trying to kill a child who you found in a hole.' The man spoke quietly and looked directly into the detective's eyes, leaving a long enough pause that it felt as though someone had switched the other man off. Offering nothing, the ACC looked down at Jack's foot. 'And what the bloody hell happened to your toe? Looks like rats have gotten at it.'

Jack was wary of the man. McQuade had been a pretty big player in all of this, who was to say this man wasn't either? He turned up just at the same time as an assassin, which either meant he definitely organised it or was completely oblivious to how guilty it would make him look because he, in fact, had nothing to do with it.

Jack had to take a risk, if he wasn't open and honest, he could very well just be thrown in a cell and never see Felicity again even if she was alive.

He explained about the priest in Florence and how he had got caught up in a paedophile ring business. The finding of the girl in the oil tank at the farm owned by Pearce – he kept that as a personal mission and apologised for going rogue.

'And McQuade? Who killed her?' ACC James asked, his mind reeling from all of the information.

Jack couldn't do it, he couldn't tell this man that she had been a part of it all, even after the hell she had put him through. She had been broken down, used and abused until she had become a slave. She had been treated as bad, if not worse, as the girl he believed to be his daughter.

'She was helping me with the investigation and the stress of the job, the guilt she felt … She took her own life.'

The man nodded slightly. 'Right, well, that's where we do have a problem. You see, the initial report says that she was shot in the head by a third party, with a handgun found at the scene.'

Jack narrowed his eyes. 'No, I was there, she killed herself and that's when more private security stormed in and started shooting up the place. I only just got away.'

The man sighed heavily in response. 'One automatic weapon was found at the scene, which so far seems to match all of the ammunition used there except that of a handgun matching the predicted projection of the wound on Alison. Only two guns needed to make that mess and only two guns found. Now, can you see why I came here myself, detective? They lifted prints from one of the guns – the murder weapon, as it were – can you guess whose they were?'

Jack's eyes rolled. 'Shit.'

The other man stood up and placed his hat neatly on his head. 'Shit indeed, detective. I am here as exactly two hours before, my friend – and, despite what you may think of our relationship, she was a friend – phoned me and left me a voicemail message. Would you like to know what it said?'

Jack looked back blankly, he wasn't actually sure if he was being arrested or not.

'It said, Detective Jack O'Connor is innocent of her murder and that I must buy you time where I can.' He walked over to the door. 'You cannot stay here, you need to go and do whatever it is that needs to be done and then you will be arrested. You murdered a man here today, detective, self-defense or not. And you are also in the firing line for the murder of your commanding officer. Innocent or not, you will have to answer for it.'

WANTING THE PRIEST DEAD

Jack met Tanya outside a room a few hundred metres away from the original one where Jack had managed to just about keep his life.

'Jack, what's going on?'

He ignored her question, it could wait for a few seconds, his were more pressing. 'Where's Aubrie? Is the girl – I mean Felicity – ok?'

Tanya took a moment to compute. 'She's fine, they finally managed to get her to take some sedation and she's asleep. Aubrie moved the DNA machine – she thought it would be best done somewhere more private.'

Jack looked confused. 'Surely that'll mess up the samples?'

'Jack, it's the most sophisticated machine on the market, it has fail safes for someone switching the plug off by mistake, it's fine. I'm more concerned about you, at the moment. Just had two police officers looking for you, they said they were here to arrest you for murder. When I told them, it was self-defense, they said no, not that one.'

The detective grimaced. 'Yeah, they're fitting me up for McQuade's murder, too – pretty good fit as well, by the looks of it. It's ok, it turns out I have a friend pretty high

294

up who actually believes I didn't do it.'

A door opened behind them and Jack turned quickly, his body in flight mode in case it was the arresting officers popping back – or worse, another hitman.

'I can't stay here,' he told Tanya, who opened her mouth to protest. 'The police won't stop coming for me and the Syndicate won't stop coming for her. I've killed one, but more of his puppets will keep coming.'

Tanya looked at him and then at the door to the girl's room. 'You can't leave now, you might have just got your daughter back again.'

Jack closed his eyes, he needed to make her understand quickly. 'We're not even sure if it *is* her, and even if it is, I'll be carried away in cuffs if I hang around and what use would I be to her in a cell? I can't protect her from a police station.' He reached up to Tanya's cheek. 'Please, Tan, I have to ask yet another thing from you. Please, can you keep this little girl – *maybe* my little girl – safe? You are the only person capable.'

She pushed her cheek hard into his caress with affection before speaking, 'So what are you going to do?'

Jack bit his bottom lip, thinking, then shook his head as no full thought would come to fruition, but a small spark went off.

'It's risky, but isn't it always?'

'Have you got our friendly ghost's phone number, still?' he asked his friend.

She smiled. 'You mean Casper Collingwood?' she pulled out her phone and opened the case – the flap contained cards and she pulled one out and handed it to him. 'Don't look at me like that, he gave me his card when he was trying to recruit me, remember?'

'And you kept it?'

She rolled her eyes. 'And you've just needed it, like I knew you would, which is why I kept it.'

He stopped arguing and dialed the number on the phone that Tanya had supplied him with.

Tanya listened in on Jack's side of the conversation.

'Casper, it's Jack, we need to meet. No, now. You can choose where, just make it within walking distance of the BRI. No, I'll tell you when we meet. That's perfect, be there in ten minutes. And you have to come alone.'

The detective hung up the phone but, before tucking it away, he quickly sent a four worded text.

Tanya eyed him suspiciously. 'So, what is it exactly you are planning on doing? You think Casper, that overgrown private school boy, is organising this?'

'Maybe, but I guess to stop the puppets, I'll have to kill the puppeteer.'

Jack liked the spot Casper had chosen to meet, he had been there a few weeks before questioning a man about a motorcycle. It had been one of the only witness testimony's he had against Peters, the serial killer, only it looked like it might be getting thrown out – if it hadn't already. He hadn't heard anything more of the case, he had been trapped in this Syndicate bubble for days now. The top storey of the carpark had some good views – ones that had changed so much over his time in the city. The new Colston Hall, with its gold cladding, shone the street light's glare back at them. In truth, it was lucky there wasn't a show on that night. It seemed to have something new every other day performing there – from comedians to ballet – and the very carpark where he waited for the MI5 agent would be filled to every space. Jack looked over the barrier and saw a few young revelers starting their long night on expensive alcohol. One hundred and fifty pounds he had spent on a night out once – and that was after a twelve-hour shift finishing at eight in the evening.

That'll teach me for being able to handle my drink,' he reminisced.

His breath spiraled into the air in short clouds of mist. It wasn't overly cold, but the hike up the hill and taking the stairs had got his body up above resting temperature.

Car wheels screeched deceptively, making the vehicle sound fast when it was, in fact, moving at nothing more than a crawl. It was Casper's usual – black on black with tinted windows to match. He parked a few meters away, straightened his suit as he got out, and walked with a deliberate heel clop towards the detective.

'Thought the next time I would see you would be across a table and you would be in a grey tracksuit, matching all of the other inmates.'

Jack laughed at the other man's words, spreading his arms wide like a magician who had just stepped out of a previously empty box.

'And yet here I am.'

Agent Collingwood plucked at the sleeves of his shirt, ensuring that they were the correct length beyond the end of his suit sleeves.

'And yet here *we* are.' He joined the detective in looking over the edge of the building. 'Four months,' he said, turning to look at Jack, whose face portrayed confusion at the remark. 'Four months since I have had a night off and lo and behold you call me. I ditched a date to come here, I hope you realise that. Nice little Philippine lass, actually, never had one of those before.' He chuckled a little. 'She's probably still sat there, bless her, not sure she understood when I said I had to leave. She might just think I'm in the bathroom. So, tell me, detective – soon to be *former* detective – O'Connor, what is it I am here for when I could be halfway home, getting my first ride in what is feeling like a monk's lifetime?'

Jack went to turn away but decided that he needed to see his face, see the man's reaction to his question. If he was ever going to use the empathy his BPD empowered him with, it was now. An MI5 agent was taught how to lie – it wouldn't be easy to get to the truth.

'Tell me you didn't know, tell me you're not a part of all this,' Jack said, a sense of finality in his tone.

Casper pursed his lips as he thought before breezily

replying, 'Fine, I didn't know and still don't and probably don't want to. Now, can I get back to my escapades?'

The detective didn't reply, he stared hard at him, not saying a word until the other man spoke.

'Ok, fine, I'm biting. I didn't know what, Jack?'

The detective didn't want to give away too much too soon, but he couldn't help himself, he wanted to drag whatever truth there was out of him.

'Tell me you didn't know about Felicity?' he finally replied.

Casper squinted. 'Of course I know about your daughter, she was murdered a few years ago. It was brutal, I'm not that cold-hearted to forget something like that. It was all over the news. What is this, Jack? Do you think I did it? Do you really think that I killed your wife and daughter?'

Jack shook his head. 'No. I know even you aren't that sadistic. Tell me what you know about the Syndicate.'

'Ah,' Agent Collingwood said, turning away from Jack to take in the view again. 'I know about as much as anyone else who has heard of it. A VIP paedophile ring, operating on the deep web – powerful people, untouchable. But of course, it's all just rumours, no evidence of it actually existing. You'll be chasing shadows if you think that they had anything to do with it. There's been a few investigations done over the years – all resulting in diddly squat.'

He turned back to the detective. 'Is this really why I am here? To answer hypothetical questions about an organisation that probably doesn't exist? When are you going to come terms with it, Jack? She was killed, Jess and Felicity are both gone, even if you found that this bloody Syndicate was real, you don't know that they had anything to do with it.'

Jack smiled in agreement. 'To tell you the truth, I had come to terms with it, I was fine with them being dead and me being alive. You see, Casper, I had nothing left to live for, so I wasn't really alive anyway. Until today. Tell me one more time. You had nothing to do with it?'

'You've lost it, I'm not staying for this, you need to get some help, Jack. I have no idea what you want from me.' The agent went to walk away.

'She's alive,' Jack said, stopping the other man on the spot. 'Felicity. The kid I was trying to track down, I didn't know it at the time, but it's Felicity.'

Casper gave him a suspicious glare. 'What are you playing at, Jack? That's not possible, you know that, right?'

Jack shrugged. 'I know that there is a girl in the hospital who was just nearly assassinated had I not choked a man to death and that she has Jess's eyes and I am currently waiting on a DNA test. That's what I know.'

Casper gave a small exhale, attempting something of a laugh. 'This is a sick joke, right? You really believe that she has been alive all this time?' His face turned stern with anger. 'And you call *me*? You drag me out here because you think I have something to do with it? If this is your daughter, what the fuck would I have to do with it? Why would I take her? Kill your wife, and for what, Jack?' He stepped closer to the detective, his hands turning to fists. 'What, you thought I did it and you would get me out here to what, Jack? To kill me? If this girl is – and, I mean, that's a fucking big *if* – your daughter, and you truly believed it, why have you left her side to come here? Tell me, Jack, what has turned you this crazy to think that I would have done anything to hurt her? What has made you think that I'm a psychotic paedophile?'

Jack leant back against the railings and looked up at the stars, a small break in the clouds exposing a handful.

'Remember Florence? Remember how I was bait for you and your superior?'

Casper shook his head. 'No, you were bait for my superior to catch a murderer and trafficker. I was only there in case you got, and I quote, *out of hand*. I had nothing to do with that case except keeping an eye on you and retrieving that thing from your hotel room.'

Jack grinned. 'You don't know how glad I am to hear that. Because that means even you had the wool pulled over your eyes. While Father Moon may have been a trafficker, and I was used as bait to draw him out, it wasn't for MI5's advantage.'

Casper's hands relaxed and his eyes screwed again. 'What do you mean?'

A disembodied voice spoke from a shadow created by the eaves to the stairwell. 'He means I had my own reasons for wanting that priest dead.'

ANSWERS

Agent Charles stepped from out of the black, his high shoulders giving him the look of someone with half a neck. He wore a hat shading his face but his menacing eyes were just visible beneath its rim.

'Sir?' Casper said quietly, neatly stepping back towards the rail as his superior was aiming a gun towards him and Jack.

'Sorry, Collingwood, you were a good agent – very useful over the last week, actually – but this is where we must part.'

Fire blast left the end of the handgun, hitting Casper square in the chest, smashing his body against the railings. The power gave him enough momentum to topple over the top, but Jack was quick – quicker than the last time he had been in this position. He grabbed Casper by the waist and dragged him to the floor before he could fall over the other side.

'Shame,' the alive MI5 agent said as he advanced on Jack. The detective was trapped under the body of the shot man. He pulled himself free and just had time to get to his feet as the gun reached a few yards from his head.

Jack threw his arms up. 'Why did you let me go to

Florence if it might lead me to Felicity?'

The question seemed to stop the advancing man, who was clearly thinking on the subject. Jack knew he was probably just contemplating how much he should tell him before he shot him in the head.

'I will admit that was a bit naive of me. I had been swayed by McQuade to let you go. I didn't quite know how much trouble you were going to be and I have to respect how difficult you are to kill, detective. I saw the man's face that you battered into soup. Nice work, I must say.'

Jack listened, he couldn't do anything now but try to distract him, try to stay alive for just a few minutes and maybe there was a way out if this not involving a body bag.

'And Father Moon? What was that – just business, I suppose?' Jack asked, keeping his hands raised and still.

The agent smiled. 'What else would it have been? The bastard had started his own racket, bringing kids from Eastern Europe into Italy, France – even the UK, our own backyard! When McQuade told me about that priest who had been killed, I did a little research and it turned out he had been a fly in our ointment before, so it intrigued me. But what I didn't expect was for you to flush out our new competition so quickly. Like a moth to a flame— no, more like a raging bonfire. You should be proud of how much of a threat everyone considers you.'

'So, what? Kill off the competition, then kill off me?' Jack asked.

The man looked at him blankly. 'Yes. I was losing hundreds of thousands of pounds, what else is a businessman to do?'

'And Jessica? And Felicity? Were they just business, too?' Jack spat, lowering his hands now.

The agent took his hat off with one hand, the other one still training the gun on the detective.

He rolled his eyes. 'Now that's McQuade's fault, I knew she was turning, I knew she would try and lead you to her – precisely why I kept her out of the loop.'

'Yeah, well, she's dead now,' Jack responded.

Agent Charles shrugged his shoulders. 'Couldn't care less. Was going to do it myself, anyway, she just saved me the job. No, she was good once, don't get me wrong, but the more ill her father got … Well, you could see she wasn't the same. Never really understood why he kept her around, to be honest.'

'He loved her,' Jack answered, shocking the agent a little.

But he just laughed. 'He *loved* her? Did he tell her that as he watched other men rape her? No, detective, there's no real love in this world – especially the parts that you and I tread in. Speaking of which, I hear your daughter is doing quite well – if it even is her.'

It was Jack's turn to smile. 'I know it's her, why would you have sent a hitman if it wasn't?'

The agent narrowed his eyes.

'Oh, you didn't know? That hitman you sent, he is no longer in your employment. I choked him to death with what may or may not have been a catheter tube.'

Agent Charles laughed heartedly. 'See, detective, this is what I mean, you always manage to scrape through by the skin of your teeth. But I'm sorry to say that after we are done here, I will be attending to that matter.'

Jack shook his head. 'Why? Why make me believe she was dead. Why hurt her at all? It was Jessica writing the piece.'

Agent Charles snarled and replaced his hat. 'Your wife nearly destroyed the entire thing. You have no idea of the information she had on me – on the entire Syndicate. Well, I soon sorted the mole out and then took care of her. I run the entire South West, a lot of people would have been gunning for her anyway, me or not. And if they were exposed, it would have been my head on the block, right next to hers.'

'But Felicity?' Jack shouted. 'She hadn't done anything.'

Agent Charles raised his gun; it shook slightly with anger. 'That was a stroke of genius. We had an accident with one girl, so we just swapped them. Easy enough to cover up – you wouldn't have recognised her even if you did have the balls to see the body, which I know you didn't. And then we just falsified the DNA test. You still don't get it, do you, detective? She was a commodity – a very high priced piece of stock – and I am a businessman.'

Jack sniggered. 'A man? You're not even human. So, these kids are just pieces of meat? What the hell happened to you? How did you get so damaged?'

The gun shook a little more in the man's hand. 'Fuck you, I am the only one with my eyes open. This world is a piece of shit, the good get walked over and the strong rise above.'

Jack shook his head. 'You're not strong, you're the weakest person I have ever met. Loving someone is strength. Giving up on yourself for someone else, that's where the beauty in life is hidden and only the bravest of people ever get to know that.'

The agent laughed mirthlessly. 'Shut up. You think you have all the answers. I said that we switched Felicity's body – that could very well be just another girl in there we wanted to get rid of. Just another swap, like for like. Anyway, that's more than I was going to give you, so you're welcome, detective, now goodbye.' He raised the gun to Jack's head and twitched the finger on the trigger.

A loud clap filled the air and Jack was blinded.

RESULTS

Warm liquid poured down Jack's face and a metallic note reached his lips by his tongue uncontrollably investigating the fluid. He heard a loud thud but didn't feel one. He swayed on the spot and opened his eyes, amazed that he still had a mind capable of sending parts of his body orders. Bright spots danced across his retinas and his field of vision was a blurry one, taking what felt like a lifetime to come back into focus.

Off to his right, a figure hunched over, struggling for breath and at Jack's feet lay another one – one that he thought should be standing.

Agent Charles lay twitching, his face now a gaping, open wound, fresh pink flesh on show with short pumps of artery blood forming a puddle around his head, hat nowhere to be seen. The MI5 agent's body was still alive with spasms not too dissimilar from a seizure. The other man walked over without Jack realising and put two more bullets into the fallen man's back.

It was Agent Casper Collingwood who had fired the deathly shots, but now he dropped his gun and clawed at his shirt, desperately trying to rip it off, his face going pale as he struggled to breathe.

Jack ran the few feet to his side and tore his shirt, popping nearly all of the buttons, exposing a bulletproof vest. He grabbed at the sides and released the Velcro. Casper let in a long, panicked breath and pulled the thick, black material clumsily over his head.

'You ok?' Jack asked as he watched the agent getting his breath back.

Casper put a hand up to indicate he'd talk in a minute, but right now he just needed to breathe.

A few inhalations later, and he spoke, 'Winded and the vest was so tight I couldn't breathe.' He looked down at his chest, where blood started to appear.

Jack looked alarmed, but Casper waved it away.

'It's ok; the rounds just penetrated the panels slightly, I'll live.' He picked up the vest and wrestled one of the plates from its pouch. It was tricky as it was bent out of shape and had a large bullet protruding from it.

'Not designed for a magnum round, only for taking a small pistol, really. Look,' he pointed at the tip of a bullet, still in perfect condition but sticking through a sheet of Kevlar. 'It's all I had in the car.'

'Glad I text you now?' Jack joked as they both sat down and watched the last death throes of the shot man.

'Not really. All you sent me was *wear a bulletproof vest.* You could have given me some sort of warning of what was actually going on,' Casper responded angrily.

Jack smiled. 'I didn't know if I could trust you yet.'

Collingwood looked at him wide-eyed. 'Fucking lucky I trusted *you*, though, wasn't it? And what if he had shot me in the head?'

Jack massaged the back of his own neck, it was hurting with all the tension it had suffered. 'That was a risk I was willing to take,' he joked, his neck cricking.

Casper leant his head back against the wall. 'I bet it was.' He went quiet for a moment in thought. 'Bastard used me. All this time, he kept saying he was working on getting me a promotion and it was all about him making money off of kids. What a cunt.'

Jack laughed. 'Yes, he was. How much did you manage to hear? You looked pretty much dead.'

Casper used his foot to drag his gun up to his side. He picked it up, checked his ammunition and tucked it away. 'I heard enough to know who he was. So, the Syndicate, it *is* real, then?'

Jack wobbled his head up and down in an attempt to answer the question affirmatively.

'And they'll be after both of us now,' Casper exclaimed.

Again, Jack acknowledged this.

'I'll have to report this to someone high up and just hope they aren't involved, too. I don't suppose you have any evidence I could use to back this up?' Casper asked, taking another exhausted breath.

'Only a couple of child witnesses and a mortuary of bones. Oh, and there's a senile old man in a nursing home – McQuade's dad,' Jack answered.

'We are going to need a lot more than that, Jack,' Collingwood replied, taking his phone out.

'Wait, what do you mean *we*?' Jack said, looking at the other man quickly.

Casper now had the phone to his ear. 'Need a clean-up crew, follow this signal, on the top floor of the carpark. Keep this in team, please, there's sensitive material.' He hung the phone up. 'Was that true about Felicity? You might have found her?'

'Yeah, I think it's her – will know for certain once the DNA comes back – but don't change the subject, you said *we* will need more than that. This is on you, now, surely?'

Casper smiled smugly and gingerly made his way to his feet. 'Go back to the hospital, Jack, I'll be in contact. I think we have a lot of work to do.' Casper started to walk over to his car.

Jack shouted after him. 'There's that word we again, you have to stop saying *we*.'

Jack heard the sound of engines entering the lower

levels of the multi-storey. 'Jesus, that was quick.'

He got up and walked to the stairwell. Casper was right, he needed to get back to the hospital, he didn't want to get caught up in all this for hours. He'd just entered the small room that housed the lifts when his phone rang in his pocket.

He pulled it out and nearly dropped it at the sight of Tanya's name on the screen.

'Tan, everything ok?' he asked instinctively.

The line was crackly, but he could just hear her voice, 'Jack, Jack, can you hear me?'

'Yes!' Jack shouted back down the phone. 'What's going on?'

'Jack, Aubrie has the DNA results.'

Jack's heart went heavy and dropped into his gut. '*And?*'

The End

Thank You

As an author it means the world to me that you have taken the time to read my work. If you have enjoyed it please tell your friends, but more importantly please take two minutes out of your day to leave an Amazon review. These reviews mean that writers like me can continue to do what we love and continue to provide you with great story telling. It really can change the career of us behind the keyboard.

ABOUT THE AUTHOR

Cameron is an author who dislikes writing about himself much, but he is going to try anyway. You'll find him in a coffee shop somewhere in Somerset (sometimes Bristol), using the excuse that he is unable to write at home to sit somewhere undisturbed and type a great deal of made up stuff.

With two young children and half a zoo's worth of animals in the house, it keeps him busy and then even busier. He is also one of those lucky men who has a wife who allows him to go off on these ludicrous adventures; like traveling to Florence (all in the name of research, of course) and to whom he will always be indebted. If you see him out writing, please don't hesitate to say hello, ask questions about the book or even about self-publishing. He enjoys meeting new people and if you have read one of his books, he will be very grateful for your support and kindness.